The Dragon Journal

Mike Rimmey

Acknowledgements

Thank you Jesus!

Thank you Deborah for your constant love and encouragement.

Michael Tyler, you may not know this but I was so excited to have you read the manuscript. Thank you for your feedback and encouragement.

<u>CHAPTER 1</u>

Alden Harlock was so excited he almost smiled. Emotions coursed through his veins like ice through the Bering Strait. He didn't know happiness, he only knew domination.

When the word came to his office that the package should be arriving soon, he gave instructions to bring it to him immediately. His subordinates were quite accustomed to following his directions to the letter. Alden said very little; he knew the power of his words.

He swiveled around in his chair and looked out the window. Six stories above the downtown London traffic, he could picture the package sitting on a shelf in a delivery truck, making its way to him. He sat with clenched fists, and cold, steel eyes, anticipating the sensation of success. Though he had several reasons to be apprehensive, he was determined to focus on victory.

He would have felt more at ease if the package had actually been addressed to him. But, unfortunately it was being sent to one of his employees. The only one of his employees he didn't trust. He didn't trust him as far as he could throw him; in fact Alden sat back in his chair and imagined throwing him out the sixth story window.

This employee was difficult. He came highly recommended from several of the board members; before Alden had the board "re-structured" to suit his personal needs. This guy was trouble right off the bat and for years Alden had planned to get rid of him. This guy was too clean though; and even worse, he was a Christian.

Alden Harlock was 56 years old. When looking at a photograph of him, it was hard to tell if it was in color or black-and-white. He always dressed in black. His skin was pale and gray; the pink had left his complexion years ago. His eyes were like wet, battleship steel. His hair was as silver as brushed nickel and it was pulled back into a thin ponytail that fell half way down his back.

The Museum received its regular mail every afternoon at 3:00 precisely; but this was a special delivery and coming by private courier from Prague, he had no idea of the timing.

He had already given two of his most trusted employees the special assignment of keeping an eye on the difficult Christian. They had already begun the surveillance and so far they had nothing to report. The difficult Christian's name was Ian Burbrey. He was always tossing in his views of a Biblical creation. His views did not mix well with Alden's.

Alden sharply poked his finger down on the telephone button that rang his assistant's desk. "Have you seen anything yet?" Alden asked.

"No sir. Ian sure looks nervous though. I mean more than usual; he's a mess," said the assistant.

"He'll be a mess alright, if I don't get that package."

"Sir, if I may ask…what is it? In the package I mean," the assistant timidly asked.

Alden answered the question, "It's a journal; just an old journal…..no big deal. It's not historically significant in any way."

"Then why are we anticipating trouble with Ian?"

"…Because he sees it differently."

The entertainer stood behind the microphone; he lifted the glass in his right hand high in the air. "I think it's time for a toast," he shouted with a smile on his face. "Here's to a long life and a merry one; a quick death and an easy one; a pretty girl and an honest one……"

The crowd roared back right on cue, "A cold beer-- and another one!" The packed house knew the response to every toast. He stood on stage looking out at his audience, tucked a strand of his long blonde hair behind his ear and scanned the room with a confident grin….a typical Tuesday night.

"My name's Ty Hyvek; and it's my pleasure to be playing some music for you tonight." Hoots and hollers from his left, a group of girls on a bachelorette party were just getting started. "Please be sure and take real good care of your waitress", Ty said pointing to a young girl carrying a tray of beers across the dance floor. "And don't forget big Brad behind the bar." A girl from the bachelorette party whistled and then acted embarrassed when everyone looked to see where it came from. And then, Ty noticed a VIP enter the building.

"Oh Yeah!" Ty laughed. "Ladies and gentlemen, it is my great honor to introduce to you….the one and only Frank Hampton." Ty saluted the former Marine Corps Sergeant. Frank Hampton had just walked through the door. He owned the bar and stopped in quite often to check on things. Frank just shook his head and made a waving gesture to Ty as if to say leave me alone and get back to work.

"Alright now you gotta stick around folks, last week we almost got Frank up here to sing a song." Everyone cheered and looked to see if Frank would acknowledge. He stood to the side of the bar still shaking his head, but now emerged the crooked smirk of a smile. Ty set his guitar down in its stand and reached for the microphone, "in case you forgot….you're at Gildersleeves. Stick around, I'm gonna take a short break."

"What break? Its only 9:45" Frank said jokingly.

"Come on Frank, I'm hot tonight. Look at this place, its packed. You're gonna need to expand soon. We were turning people away last Saturday."

"It's true…..nobody can fill this place and get them to keep spending money, and keep coming back, like the great Tyler Hyvek" Frank laughed. "What is this Tuesday? I used to be able to tell what night it was by who was sitting at the bar. Half the time I don't know what day it is anymore. What in the world are you guys watching? How come the ball game ain't on?" Frank pointed to the TV over the bar.

"These college guys like to watch 'keeping up with the Kardashians'", said Brad as he put another case of beer in the cooler under the sink.

"Come on get that game on, the Cards were winning 4-2 in the seventh."

"Hey Frank I'll talk to you later. I gotta make a pit stop and make my rounds," Ty said as he walked toward the bathroom.

"Yeah, I need to talk to you too."

Gildersleeves was the place to go in south St. Louis. It was a place to hang out, a place to meet up with friends, a real neighborhood gathering place. On the weekends you could hear Ty's band, Avalanche. They brought back to life real rock and roll as has survived in very few places. In St. Louis it survived at Gildersleeves. Every now and again, Chuck Berry could be seen at a dark corner table, usually with several very large gentlemen and two or three young ladies. Inside was dark and dingy, almost medieval. The walls were brick, coated with polyurethane, but not covered with sports memorabilia. The floors were wood, and told the story of sixty years of boot scuffs and dropped beer bottles. The stage was front and center, the focal point of the place.

"Hey sounding great tonight", said some guy at the sink in the bathroom.

Ty was just zipping up and pulling away from the urinal, "Hey, thanks a lot buddy" responded Ty. He recognized the guy from hanging around the bar but didn't really know him. As Ty walked back out into the bar he was stopped by one fan, then another, and another. If he didn't know them he asked their names and acted interested in their stories. Everybody wanted to talk to Ty. They wanted to become friends with him, hang out with him, invite him over for barbecues, and just be seen talking to him. They wanted him to know their names. And Ty was one step ahead of all of them. He knew if he played it just right and made every single person that walked through the door feel welcome, and feel like they belonged, then they would keep coming back…..and come back they did. In the four years Ty had been at Gildersleeves, it had gone from a rough little neighborhood tavern to a hopping St. Louis landmark.

Ty Hyvek was the perfect bar room entertainer. He played a mean acoustic guitar and he sang with a smooth whiskey coated confidence. He knew hundreds of songs and he knew how to let people have fun. He looked like a cross between a young Clint Eastwood, and Brad Pitt in "*Legends of the Fall*". His sandy straw colored hair rolled gently to his shoulders and swooped down over his left eye. He was thirty-six years old, and had spent more nights in bars than not since he was eighteen. He was the reason people came to Gildersleeves, and Frank Hampton knew it. His real talent however, was his personality; his ability to make an instant connection with everyone he met. His job was playing guitar and singing, but his business was people.

Ty slowly but surely made his way back to the stage, talking with those he could and promising to catch up later with the rest. He grabbed his guitar and stepped up to the microphone. "I hope everybody has a fresh drink," Ty proclaimed, "Because it's time for a toast". Ty lifted his glass, Cutty Sark on the rocks, but the rocks had melted. "Here's to friends in bars....and pawnshop guitars. I love you guys!" The place erupted and another round of drinks was quickly being dispatched. Ty strummed the intro to "Melissa" an old Allman Brothers song and the Tuesday night party continued. As the night wore on, the toasts continued, as did the music. Four hours and seventy-one cases of beer later, at 1:00 AM the party was over.

As Ty finished a particularly smooth rendition of "Feelin' Alright", he gently sat his Gibson Hummingbird in its stand. "Good night folks; thanks for coming out tonight; thanks for listening; and thanks for being a part of the best neighborhood watering hole in the United States of America". He switched off his amp, and sat back for a few minutes as the people slowly drained out of the bar. When it was finally over, Ty walked off stage to go outside for some fresh air.

Outside the bar the night got suddenly quiet. Ty could actually hear the knocking of his boots against the pavement. It felt good to leave behind the low frequency buzz of a people filled room. He walked over to the rail just in front of his Suburban and leaned up against it. He could see his breath, and the October nightfall had already left a thin layer of frost on the windows of the cars in the parking lot. As he looked up at the stars he took a deep breath. He filled his lungs with cool, crisp air, and for the first time all night he relaxed.

He just stood there and rested a moment. He could hear two cats fighting in the alley behind him. The cars on Chippewa Avenue whizzed by as if they had some where to go at one o'clock on a Wednesday morning; and then the familiar green and white 1956 Chevy Nomad wagon rolled onto the lot. Ty smiled and tilted his head back. He looked up at the stars as the purr of that legendary engine stopped. The door closed with a gentle slam.

"Tyler Hyvek," said a voice still in the dark.

"Hey," Ty answered, although it almost sounded like a question. Matt Hampton was the twenty-five year old nephew of Frank. Ty had known Matt for a couple of years; he hung out at the bar quite a bit. "You know if I were you, I'd be at home with that brown eyed girl in a nice warm bed right now."

"Well," Matt made his way over to the Suburban, "that brown eyed girl moved in with some guy she works with last week."

"Sounds like you're a bachelor again. Come on in, I'll buy you a beer."

It was a rainy day in London. Quite a drama was beginning to unfold at the London Museum of Culture and History. Ian Burbrey stopped at the side door to shake the water from his umbrella and swiped his badge into the reader. He opened the old aluminum framed door, threw his umbrella into the corner and walked down a dimly lit hallway. His footsteps echoed loudly off the marble walls and tin ceiling. He hurried to his desk where he sat and collected his thoughts.

He picked up the phone and began to dial. Then he heard footsteps coming down the same hallway. He hastily returned the phone to its cradle. It was just one of the janitors, who kept walking. He picked up the phone, and dialed again.

"Hello, Peter," Ian said.

"Yes."

"This is Ian. It's been too long, over a year I guess."

"Yes, Ian. How great to hear from you. I was just thinking of giving you a call."

"Well, old friend, I have something here that you have to see. I just got it from the Museum of Ancient History in Prague. In fact I am a bit nervous about keeping it here, among less than hospitable company. You know what I mean."

"Oh, is this a biblical artifact?"

"No, but you're in the ballpark. I don't want to say much on this phone, but I may not get to another phone for awhile. I'm not sure what's going to happen. I'm so glad I got hold of you."

"Ian what's the matter? You sound troubled."

"Peter, this is quite an important piece, and my every thought is on keeping it safe. Can you come to London? There is no one else I trust."

"Ian what's this all about?"

"Peter, I am sorry, I really can't explain now. Trust me; you will want to see this. Please come to London."

"Ian, if it means that much to you, I'll be on the next flight out."

"Oh, thank God. I need your help with this one. Peter, call me as soon as you land."

Ian got up and walked down to the elevator. Before he got there he heard voices from around the corner.

"Where is Burbrey?" It was the Museum Director and Chief Curator Alden Harlock and one of his assistants.

Ian stood statue still holding his breath. He did not want Harlock to see him. He had managed to avoid him now for several days and had hoped to do it again. Ian was one of the Assistant Curators at the museum. He had worked under Alden Harlock for three years but, they had not gotten along very well; it seems they had different world views.

Ian received the ancient book from an old friend at one of Europe's most prestigious museums in Prague. The package came addressed to Ian, but he was worried that Alden had been informed of its arrival from others at the Prague museum. Inside the package Ian found a note from his friend that simply said:

"Dear Ian, I know you will appreciate the priceless truths outlined in this ancient journal. I can assure you it is real. But, I have recently become aware that it is not safe here in Prague. I know you will take care of it. Officially, you can consider it "on loan".

Your brother in Christ,

Alexander Svec."

Just one day after receiving the package, Ian read of Alexander Svec's passing. It seemed that the brakes failed on his car and he sped over a sixty foot cliff. Something deep in Ian's spirit told him it was no accident.

Ian had stored the journal in the ancient writings room, but was considering where he could keep it that would be more out of the way. He didn't even tell Alden Harlock about it, but one of Harlock's flunkies saw Ian storing it and began asking questions. Ian did not want to draw any more attention to the journal; but now Mr. Harlock was demanding his whereabouts.

"I don't know Sir; I have not seen him yet today," offered Harlock's flunkie.

"Well if you see him, you tell him….."

The voices faded out of earshot. Ian ran back down the hall to his desk. He waited a minute to give Harlock time to get back to his office; then he picked up the phone and called him.

"Yes." Harlock barked.

"Hello, Mr. Harlock. I had a message here that you wanted to see me Sir."

"Yes, Ian. We've been looking for that book. What on Earth do you think you're doing?"

"Book Sir?"

"You know that I'm talking about that ridiculous journal. Where is it?"

"Oh yes sir," evidently Harlock found out about the ancient book. "I have it in a locked cabinet in the ancient writings cellar. It is extremely fragile Sir."

"Bring it to my office immediately."

"Your office? I do not think that's a good idea Sir." Now Ian was worried.

"Alright forget it, I'll get it myself. I'm on my way."

"S-Sir, why do you want to have it in your office?"

"Well, not that it's any of your business, but I'm bringing it home this evening."

"Home?" this was absolutely unheard of, and totally unacceptable.....but it was just the type of thing that Ian had feared.

"Yes, I am having a private showing of the piece at my home. I have invited several long-time trusted friends to see what they think of it."

"Sir, that journal is on loan to us through my friends at the Museum in Prague. That journal is my responsibility. If you want to show it, show it here at the Museum. I really do insist that it not be removed."

"Ian, you're over stepping your bounds here. I won't discuss it any further." Harlock slammed the phone down.

At that moment Ian knew what he had to do. He ran down to the elevator only to be met by the sound of footsteps rapidly coming his way. He chose not to wait for the elevator and took the stairs. He flew down the stairs, his heart hammered. He descended the four flights, burst into the ancient writings room, and found the cabinet. The room was dark and he was alone. He scrolled through each of the three sets of numbers on the combination lock, and opened the cabinet. He could hear footsteps in the hall. He grabbed the gray metal box and ran for the far end of the room. As he closed the door behind him he could hear the door at the other end open. One of the voices was Harlock's. Ian could hear him barking orders as he made it to the other set of stairs. He began back up the four flights, not as fast as he came down, but as fast as he could. On the second floor he lost his sixty-three year old legs. They had turned into wet noodles and he crashed to a landing. He had smashed his right shin, but otherwise was alright. He took several deep breaths and started again. In between the third and fourth floor he stopped again to rest for a moment. Just then he heard a voice again; this time on the building wide paging system which was only used in emergencies.

"Ian Burbrey, you are wanted in Mr. Harlock's office...immediately. Repeat; Ian Burbrey, you are wanted in Mr. Harlock's office immediately. Now Ian!"

On that last note Ian got back up and made it to the main level. He ran unimpeded out the side door into the rain. He got in his car and sped away. He had the journal but certainly did not feel safe. He drove through downtown London, his white-knuckled hands held tightly to the wheel. His heart still pounding, he realized what had just happened; and he feared for his life.

"What have we here Ian; another treasure?" said Ian's Brother Malcolm as he propped open the front door and let him in.

"Teddy, I can't go home with this. I need to keep it here; this one may have some heat with it."

"Oh, I can't wait to hear this story."

Over the years Ian had brought an assortment of bones, rocks, tiles, and dirt to store at Malcolm's. It was an hour or so west of London in Marlow. Malcolm had a place in the business district. It was a store front apartment adjoining a coffee shop on one side and a lighting store on the other. Ian stayed with Malcolm quite often, neither of them had ever married.

Ian stepped in the modest foyer and gently set the gray metal box down on the hall table. "Malcolm, don't ask....Have you got anything to eat around here?"

The apartment consisted of a narrow entry foyer, a living room/dining room, a kitchenette, one bedroom, and a musty basement/cellar. The walls were once painted white, but were aged into a hard to define grayish pastel....maybe taupe. The dining room table had a chandelier that hung down from a rusty chain; the fixture had been broken leaving bare forty watt bulbs shining harshly. Ian knew his place was on the sofa, and he plopped down to rest.

"Actually, I was just on my way next door for a cup of coffee. Do you care to join me?" Malcolm grabbed a cap and headed for the door.

"No thanks Malcolm bring me back a sandwich or something will you?" Ian knew that what Malcolm really meant was that he was headed down to the corner for a few pints of beer, but he was glad to have the place to himself. He knew he wouldn't be able to rest until he had done a better job of hiding the journal. He thought about Alden Harlock, and how furious he must be. He also thought about Alexander Svec who had already given his life for it. He picked up the metal box which held the journal and gently carried it to the basement door. He flicked the switch for the basement light but it didn't do much good. "You have got to be kidding." Ian said to himself as he ventured down the creaky wooden steps. A face full of spider webs met him half way down the steps. Ian didn't stop to wipe them away; he didn't want to risk damaging the journal. There was one light, right in the center of the room, another forty watt bulb. Ian found the workbench and set the metal box on the shelf under the bench top. He carefully re-cluttered the area with a few old boxes and buckets that were lying around. "There, that's better." Ian felt like it would be hard to find in this basement. He went back upstairs and turned off the light. As he looked down from the top of the stairs he felt a little relieved.

Ian lay down on the sofa and tried to get comfortable. "What a day!" He thought to himself. Several times he imagined Harlock and some thugs tracking him down. What would he do? And then he thought about his friend Peter Stroudlin. He hoped he would see him tomorrow, and with that he fell asleep.

The bar was now empty except for the help. Big Brad had finished his duties behind the bar, "I'm outa here you guys, see you Tomorrow." He through his backpack over his shoulder; and moped out the front door. This left Frank, Matt and Ty sitting around a table in the middle of the bar. The lights were dim; the air once thick with smoke was starting to clear. The three sat there talking and laughing with a relieved feeling, as if the party was over and the company had finally gone home. For these three friends, this was their living room.

Ty's work for the day was done. He usually slept way past noon anyway, so he enjoyed hanging out to unwind after everyone had gone home, even if it was two o'clock in the morning.

Matt was a bit of an insomniac. He usually showed up at the bar around eleven or twelve if he couldn't sleep, which was about a fifty-fifty shot. He lived alone in a duplex just south of the city, only five minutes from Gildersleeves.

Frank wasn't at the bar as much these days. He had some good people working there that he trusted. He would come in late at night and work on his books, payroll, and inventory; but his involvement was becoming less and less.

So the three would sit and talk, at two o'clock on a Wednesday morning until they had run out of stories to tell; or until one of them would finally admit to being tired and head for home.

"I'm pulling five pound largemouths out of my lake," bragged Frank. "I'm going to be spending a lot more time out there very soon…"

Just then Ty and Matt turned toward the sound of two car doors in the parking lot. Frank didn't seem to notice.

"Let me take a look." Ty got up to go look out the front window. He put his forehead against the glass and squinted to see; then he cupped his hands around his eyes to cut down the glare. "Whoa! You've got to be kidding." Ty ran to the door and started outside. "Frank, call the police!"

Matt flew out of his seat and was right behind Ty before he even got outside. As they ran into the parking lot they saw two men and Toyota pickup truck near Ty's Suburban. The back door of the Suburban was ajar, and one of the men was attempting to carry one of Ty's PA speakers but he dropped it. The other was getting back into the Toyota.

"Hey, get out of here." Ty yelled as they ran toward the assailants. Just then it occurred to Ty, what was he going to do when he got there. He didn't think he just ran, at least he had Matt with him. Ty reached the scene first. He righted the speaker and quickly logged the damage in his mind. Then he noticed his guitar case in the bed of the Toyota and grabbed it. Just then Matt reached the man before he could join his partner in the truck. He crushed his jaw with a right fist that had all of his momentum. The man left his feet from the force of the blow. He fell against the truck and collapsed on the ground. The other guy was grinding the starter of the Toyota to no avail.

"This just ain't your day buddy." Matt said as he stood at the door of the truck. The man behind the wheel looked up at Matt with eyes as wide as silver dollars. He flung open the door in an attempt to knock Matt out of his way as he ran from the truck. Ty stuck a foot out to trip him up. With his escape route blocked, the young man stood straight up and reached into his pocket. Before he could pull it out Matt wrapped him up and fell on top of him on the blacktop. They wrestled back to their feet but Matt held him in a side headlock. In one smooth move Matt swung around in front of him and pulled his head down by his ears into a rising knee. Ty stood behind him in total disbelief. Another knee and the young man stood wobbly in front of them. Instead of one final blow to finish him off, Matt scooped him up over his shoulder and dumped him into the bed of the Toyota pickup. Matt turned and looked at the first one, who was on one knee, but Ty had already grabbed him by the arm and shirt collar and tossed him into the bed of the truck with his partner.

"Should we tie them up are something?" Matt asked struggling to catch his breath.

"The police are on the way. You boys just stand back" Frank said. He was pointing a shotgun at the two in the back of the Toyota. Just then the police arrived.

The two cops sprang out of the cruiser with guns drawn. "Drop that weapon!" One of the cops yelled.

"Hey, I'm the good guy here." Frank tried to explain.

"Drop that gun, now!"

Frank set the shotgun down on the pavement and stood with his arms in the air awaiting the next command. Matt and Ty walked over to Frank. The cops were not quick to holster their guns.

"Alright, you in the middle….. shotgun man…..what is going on here," said the cop still pointing his gun at Frank.

"These two idiots broke into my employee's vehicle, and attempted to steal some valuable equipment. Then that one," Frank pointed to one of the bloody men in the bed of the pickup, "pulled a weapon, and these boys defended themselves."

And who are you?" The cop questioned.

"I'm Frank Hampton. I own this place."

Mike Rimmey

Chapter 2

A black Mercedes SLK-300 screeched to a stop in Ian Burbrey's driveway. Two men got out and stormed up to the front door. They wore suits, and even in the South London gloom, sunglasses. The taller one stopped when they reached the front door and turned to the other man for instructions; he seemed to be in charge.

"There is no need to knock." He said.

With that the tall man propped open the screen door and hiked up his pants a little and got into position. With one thrust of his leg he kicked open the front door. Wood splinters and dust flew in the air, and they marched inside.

"Burbrey!" shouted the one in charge. His eyes were on fire with intensity.

There was no answer. Other than the front door, the place was immaculately clean. The hard wood floors were so shiny the walls mirrored off of them. The living room was obviously used as a library. Mahogany book shelves lined every wall. In the center was a marble fireplace to complete the old world charm.

"Wow, this is a nice place," said large man.

"Not for long. Find that journal; and make its obvious that we've been here."

They searched the bookshelves and did not find what they were looking for. They split up. One went into the bedroom, one into the kitchen. After thoroughly scrutinizing every possible hiding place in the house they began the demolition.

The bookshelves were toppled, the drawers emptied, the furniture overturned. When they were finished the beautiful hard wood floors could not be seen. They stepped outside to go when the silver haired man's smart phone chirped.

"Yes, we just finished looking at Ian's house... Nothing here...Alright you get on it and let me know if you find anything."

The silver haired man was Alden Harlock. His associate had gotten back into the SLK-300, and sat behind the wheel. Harlock was obviously furious. The security cameras caught Ian carrying a metal box out of the museum; Harlock naturally assumed it was the journal. As he got in the back seat he simply said: "Let's get out of here."

Peter Stroudlin arrived from America right on time. It takes a pretty loyal friend to drop everything and come this far at a moment's notice. He made his way in and out of Heathrow airport and hailed a taxi. The black Austin

FX4 was a comfortable back seat for Peter. He gave the driver the address, and off they went.

It was only a 20 minute drive from the airport. Peter struck up a conversation with the driver and got the quick version of his life story. He was born and raised in London and had been driving taxis all of his life. They pulled up to the curb in front of Ian's house. Peter had him wait in case Ian wasn't home. He got out of the car and walked up to the front door. As he approached the steps he could see that there was a problem. The door was ajar, hanging by only the top hinge. What he could see inside the house was a total disaster. Peter, sharp as a tack for his age, did the smartest thing he could have done. He got back in the car told the taxi driver to get out of there and he immediately took out his phone and called Ian.

"Hello."

"Ian, its Peter. Where are you?"

Hello Peter. I am staying with my brother in Marlow. Where are you? Why didn't you call first?"

"Ian, I've just been to your house in London....there is a problem."

"What, at my house?"

"Yes Ian; the door has been kicked in and the place has been ransacked."

Silence on the other end. Peter was beginning to wonder what he had gotten himself into. "Ian?"

"Yes, I'm here. Peter, I am sorry to have gotten you involved in all this, I so need your help."

"Alright, just tell me where you are and I'll come and meet you." Peter leaned up towards the driver, "Head for Marlow," the taxi driver shook his head in acknowledgement.

They headed West on M4 in search of Ian Burbrey. The taxi driver slipped in and out of traffic like a London pro. In no time he had Peter in front of the coffee shop where Ian asked to meet him. It was 4:00 pm …high tea. The place was pretty crowded, probably why Ian wanted to meet there. Peter once again had the taxi driver wait for him, this time he handed him a hundred US dollars for his trouble. He walked in and spotted Ian right away at a table by the window facing the front door.

"Hello there old friend," said Peter as he took a seat at Ian's table.

"Dr. Stroudlin…..Am I glad to see you. Sit down and have some tea while I explain this craziness."

There is nothing as quintessentially English as "tea time". They sat in a café named Rooster's, where the mood was overwhelmingly happy. People of all ages gathered every afternoon for one thing….tea. Over a cup of London's finest black tea, Peter was finally getting the story.

"This is all so sudden, Peter. It started only a week ago. I received a package at my office at the museum. It was addressed to me from an old friend of mine at the Museum of Natural History in Prague. His name was Alexander Svec. We kept in touch through e-mails but I hadn't seen him in years, or heard from him in quite awhile either come to think of it. Anyway, the package came quite unexpectedly, and had only this brief note…." Ian handed Peter a folded piece of paper. Peter unfolded the note and read it:

Dear Ian,

I know you will appreciate the priceless truths outlined in this ancient journal. I can assure you it is real. But, I have recently become aware that it is not safe here in Prague. I know you will take care of it. Officially, you can consider it on loan,

Your brother in Christ,

Alexander Svec

"Ok, tell me about the journal," Peter said patiently.

"Alright then, I should have known there's no beating 'round the bush with you. It is the journal of Sir Richard the Elder of Landolte. He was a tenth century knight in the court of King Alfred of Wessex. He was known for this journal. The journal describes his many battles, but not just against rival armies…but also against dragons…well actually dinosaurs….wait 'till you see it. The journal verifies that dinosaurs were living in Europe at that time."

Peter smiled. Then his eyes began to flit around in his foreground, his focus couldn't catch up to his thoughts. His mouth began to form a word but it didn't materialize. Ian enjoyed watching the moment; he smiled widely and then sipped his tea. Peter still couldn't find a word. This discovery was what Peter had worked his entire life to find.

"This is not fiction Peter. Nor is it just a claim made by a wide-eyed religious archeologist. This is an official government document. It is undisputable."

"Where is it?" Peter finally collected his thoughts.

"Well if you're finished with your tea….it's just next door. Would you like to have a look?"

Peter didn't even answer, he just stood up. After over fifty years of searching and researching, his friend was telling him of the most important historical find imaginable. The idea that dinosaurs and humans lived at the same time was confirmation that the Earth was young; and a young Earth pointed to a biblical creation. The theory of evolution relies on billions of years to accomplish things slowly and randomly….without billions of years there could be no evolution. Evolution taught that dinosaurs and humans were separated by sixty-five million years. The proof that dinosaurs and humans lived concurrently would certainly turn things upside-down. Peter was ready to see this treasure. He motioned for Ian to lead the way.

"I wanted to meet here in case you were followed," said Ian. "You have no idea the danger we may be in. My brother's apartment is next door. There is a back way."

They walked out the back door of Rooster's, past several overflowing trash dumpsters and into the alley. Ian opened the back door of Ted's apartment and they went inside. Ted still wasn't home and Ian didn't expect him any time soon.

"This book, it's dated between the years of 952 and 974; it's so fragile. Most writings of that time…you would expect to see papyrus….but, he used vellum. It's very well preserved."

Peter just followed Ian down the stairs into the basement. Ian bent down at the workbench and pulled out the gray metal box. He opened it. Inside was the journal. The cover was layered tree bark, molded together and inscribed with a circular ivy detail. With a swoop of his arm Ian cleared the top of the workbench and then carefully laid the journal down on it. He slowly opened it and began turning pages, narrating as he went.

"Here are some of Sir Richard's battle notes, he led battles against the Germanic tribes mostly, but there are outlines in here of battles with Wallachia, and the Franks, and Turks….a few others." Ian continued slowly turning the pages. "Now, here….here is where he starts to sketch the dragons. Look at this one."

"Dear Lord……that's an Allosaurus," Peter was astonished.

They looked at the journal for over an hour. Peter was convinced that it was authentic.

"Ian what are your plans for it? You don't want to keep it here for long….it's so damp down here."

"Yes Peter that's why I called you. We have to get it out of here….far away. I hoped you could take it back to the States with you. Alexander gave his life for it; I'm sure of that. Alden Harlock was intending to take it home for a private showing. That's when I knew I had to save it."

"Home…..with a piece like this? That can't be standard practice."

"Of course not. I knew if he'd gotten a hold of it I'd never see it again. I grabbed it just before he did and raced here. I assume it was Harlock that did the work at my house; hate to imagine if I'd been there."

"Ian, I agree. Let's get on the next flight back to the states and the journal with us."

"Thank you Peter, I knew I could count on you. Thank you for everything."

"Ian, this is our crusade….we're working for the Lord now."

Alden Harlock and Adelph, his thug/assistant, sat in the black Mercedes across the street from Rooster's café. Harlock's contacts run very deep in London and it didn't take him long to track down Ian's only living relative. He also had people watching the train stations, and the airport; but he was betting on him running to his brother. They sat in the car silently; he wouldn't allow any small talk. Alden was in the back seat, Adelph in the front. His orders were to shoot to kill if he appeared with the package. If he did not have the package, he was just to swoop in and grab him. Adelph was also an excellent marksman. He had a M40 military 7.62 x 51mm rifle with a 9 power scope. With the heavily tinted windows no one could see them. People walked down the sidewalk, right past their car, without the slightest alert.

Alden's eyes were cold and fixed. He never glanced away, he rarely even blinked. He watched. Adelph was getting fidgety and had considered going out for a stretch, but Harlock wouldn't have it. There was too much on the line; he wanted to put an end to this now. So he watched the front door of that apartment for the moment he knew would come; the moment that Ian appeared with that journal.

Then two men walking up the sidewalk from around the corner drew Harlock's attention. One of them was Ian. They came from the backside of the apartment and were opening the trunk of a taxi. The taxi driver was getting out to help.

"That's him. Right there behind the taxi. He's got the box; drop him."

The passenger window lowered. The blast sent screams. The bystanders scattered. The shooter set down the gun and then grabbed the wheel. The Mercedes swung around and pulled right up to the slain body of Ian Burbrey. The taxi was already gone. Adelph jumped out to grab the box, and tossed it into the back seat with Alden Harlock.

Alden looked at the box, "No! No! This isn't it! Is there anything else? It is bigger. It's a big gray metal box. This isn't it! Get in….get us out of here."

<u>Chapter 3</u>

"First, I would like to thank my Lord and Savior, Jesus Christ; and second, thank you all. I am honored to receive this recognition, and I will always cherish this moment." Kenneth Macklind had accepted several prestigious awards in his life, this one the latest in kudos accentuating his ministry career. As soon as he finished his acceptance speech, he stepped away from the podium and ducked backstage, he was greeted by several colleagues.

"Kenneth, congratulations!" exclaimed a thin gray haired woman, although he couldn't remember her name.

"Thank you so much", Kenneth replied as he kept walking through the dark backstage hallway towards the greenroom. He wasn't the stereotypical "minister." He wore cowboy boots and jeans and a suede sport coat. He was not a cowboy, but he was definitely not a timid man of the cloth either. He was a traveling minister. He spent almost every weekend in a different city, a different church, preaching what he considered to be the foremost of all apologetic messages…..Creation. He spoke of Genesis and six days; and Noah's ark; and an Earth that was thousands, not billions of years old. People were amazed when they heard the story they should have already known. The story clearly told in the Bible. Kenneth told the story as often as he could.

As he made his way through the dark hallway, his thoughts were elsewhere. He had just received the Global Christian Broadcasters outstanding achievement award, and yet he could not wait to get out of the stuffy situation and get back to work.

"Here's the man of the hour!" said an overweight boisterous bald man still 30 feet away. "Kenneth I have someone here that I would like you to meet," he turned to his left pointing his arm at the older gentleman. "Kenneth Macklind, may I introduce you to Dr. Peter Stroudlin."

"Yes, it's great to see you again Dr. Stroudlin," said Kenneth.

"Oh my, you've already met," said the bald man.

"Oh yes, we've known each other for years, how are you Kenneth?"

"Better than I deserve Dr. Stroudlin."

"I am so sick of the titles in this place....please, just call me Peter."

Kenneth didn't really know Peter as well as he'd led on, but they had spent time together at several conferences over the years.

Peter turned to the bald guy and said, "Thank you so much, do keep in touch", as if to say... please leave us alone. The bald man left without saying anything further.

"How have you been?"

"I have had a great year. It has truly been an honor to receive this award but, I can't wait to get out of here. Do you wanna go get a cup of coffee somewhere?"

"Kenneth, that's the best idea I've heard all day."

"I have my rental parked in back, right this way." Kenneth led them through the maze of people milling around in the greenroom and out the back door to the VIP parking lot. They walked down the stairs and found the silver Ford Focus. "It's not much but it's all I've got until tomorrow morning," joked Kenneth as he unlocked the door with the remote leaving Peter to fend for himself on the passenger side.

"Thank you Kenneth, It is nice to get away from the conference for awhile."

Dr. Peter Stroudlin was not just a colleague of Kenneth Macklind's, he was his hero. Now seventy-nine years old, he had been a speaker/author/researcher/champion for Creation Science for over fifty years. He earned his PhD in Biochemistry from Stanford 1956. Stroudlin started as a high school science teacher in 1958 in New York City. Back then God was still allowed in our schools, and Peter Stroudlin taught his students science that lined up with the Word of God. He would often get out the Bible in the classroom. But, by the mid-sixties public school science textbooks were filled with evolution. It happened almost overnight. In 1965 Peter Stroudlin quit his job as a teacher and embarked on a lifelong mission exposing the many lies in the theory of evolution. He started by fighting the school system, demanding truth in textbooks. He got nowhere; the only thing he did get was kicked around and effectively blackballed from the scientific community. There were so few fighting on God's side. Although he often felt alone he never gave up. Through the years, he and his books gained attention, mostly by the far right evangelical church crowd. By the 1980's he was one of the busiest speakers in the country. He had turned his passion into a multi-million dollar business. Kenneth had autographed copies of all of his books. He still remembered how nervous he was the first time they met. Now they were peers, funny how that happens sometimes.

They pulled up to a Krispy Kreme donut shop and went in and found a table. Kenneth drank black coffee, and Dr. Stroudlin had two donuts and a large glass of milk.

"I seem to remember that you have a bit of a sweet tooth," joked Kenneth.

"Ah, I do love my sweets but, look at me; I'm in pretty good shape for my age. You know that I'll be eighty in three weeks."

"Well you're in great shape. What have you been working on lately?"

"That is the reason I came to Virginia. I gave up on these boring conferences years ago. But, I knew you would be here and I have something very important to discuss with you."

"Now this is what I'm talking about….do tell."

"Did I ever tell you about a friend of mine named Ian Burbrey? He was an English fellow; he did some great work all over Europe."

"No, doesn't sound familiar. Did you say *was* an English fellow?" Kenneth asked.

"Yes, unfortunately for me, he went home to be with the Lord last week; a tragic story. Ian left something for me. It is the most incredible piece of history I've ever come across, and that is what I want to talk to you about."

Just then a young man approached the table that had recognized Kenneth. He had long skater hair and wore a tee shirt that said "I ♥ JC. He walked right up to the table. "Hi, excuse me, I know you are Kenneth Macklind, I saw you speaking at the conference earlier tonight. I have your book. We followed you over here and I've been sitting in my car for ten minutes trying to work up the nerve to come and say hi. My girlfriend is still in the car."

"Well my goodness, it's nice to meet you; and I would like to introduce you to one of my heroes….Dr. Peter Stroudlin."

"Oh yeah, It is very nice to meet you sir."

"I would love to sit and talk, but Dr. Stroudlin and I were right in the middle of something very important. Maybe we could catch up at the conference tomorrow."

"Nonsense, Kenneth" Peter said confidently. "It is obvious that God has another time for that discussion."

With a rare warmness and kindness he asked the kid his name and told him to go and get his girlfriend. The young couple joined Peter and Kenneth and enjoyed a long conversation. It turned out that they were both seminary students working on their Divinity degrees. Sharing donuts and coffee and discussing biblical creation with the likes of Kenneth Macklind, and Peter Stroudlin would certainly arm them with ammunition for bragging when they got back on campus. The fact is it would probably be the highlight of their year. Even Kenneth was surprised by the love and patience displayed by Peter towards the young couple. Kenneth was itching to hear the rest of Peter's story but got the definite notion that Peter would not discuss it in front of them.

An hour blew by and then two. The young couple drank coffee recklessly, Kenneth had switched to water. He didn't even notice that the cigarette smoke from the corner was not even bothering him anymore. Peter and Kenneth enjoyed answering questions and explaining their view of Biblical Creation.

"The problem is everybody is afraid to interpret the Bible literally these days," said Peter. "You probably have seminary professors who are teaching Progressive

Creationism. It just doesn't make sense. The 'day-agers' are really doing harm and they don't even realize it." Kenneth concurred; he taught the exact same thing. However, unlike Peter, Kenneth was once an atheist. When he was a Biology major at the University of Oklahoma he studied evolution, and believed it. It wasn't until years later that he had a born again experience and started reading the Bible. So, Kenneth understood both sides of the story. And now, like Peter, he was totally convinced that God created everything in six literal, twenty-four hour days – not vast day-ages like the progressive creationists in many seminaries taught.

"I know many Christians today believe that the six days of creation are day 'ages'; and that each day is billions of years." Peter couldn't help it; he had been preaching this for so long it just came out naturally. "But there are several problems with vast day-ages. First, it rearranges the order of creation. For example, God says He made The Earth before the Sun; no day ager would ever agree to that. But much more importantly is this….to allow for billions and billions of years, is to allow for death before sin."

"Wow, I never thought about that," said the girl.

"The Bible is very clear; there was no death before sin. But, if animals evolved slowly and gradually, then the Garden of Eden was planted on top of billions of years worth of dead bodies. When God finished His creation He saw that it was very good….to God that can only mean perfect. A world that scratches and claws for survival by eating anything that it can hunt and kill seems far from perfect. And it is far from perfect, because of sin it has become imperfect.....a fallen world....not the perfect world God originally created."

"I've never thought of it that way," said the young man. "So would you say that there were dinosaurs aboard Noah's ark?"

Peter smiled. "Oh yes, of this I am sure."

Kenneth Macklind laid in a lumpy queen size bed in a Quality Inn in Arlington, Virginia; trying to find something worthwhile to watch on TV. He settled for a bow hunting show on one of the sports channels. He had two cups of coffee with Peter Stroudlin and the young couple in Krispy Kreme and although it was now midnight, he found his eyes wide open. He couldn't help being giddily anxious about whatever it was that Peter wanted to talk to him about. He knew it was something big, he could tell by the way Peter was acting.

Just then the phone rang. "Hello."

"Hi, I couldn't sleep." It was Kenneth's wife Barbara. "I saw that you called earlier, my cell phone went dead."

"Yeah, I just wanted to check in. I haven't talked to you all day."

"How did it go?"

"Well the conference and the award thing went about like I thought…..pretty boring. But right after I accepted the award….backstage….I met up with Peter Stroudlin."

"Oh, I love Peter, we haven't heard from him in ages. How is he doing?"

"He's doing fine; looks great for being almost eighty years old. I didn't get to talk to him as much as I had hoped. We were joined by a couple of young seminary students."

"Joined where?"

"Oh, we went to Krispy Kreme for a cup of coffee" Peter said hesitantly.

"That sounds like a nice healthy dinner. You probably can't sleep either, drinking coffee that late."

Barbara knew Kenncth better than he knew himself. They had been married for 17 years, and had six children. He travelled quite a bit, but got homesick every time.

"Yeah, but listen to this" said Kenneth, ignoring the comment about his healthy dinner. "Before the seminary students came in, we're sitting there talking and Peter says he's got something to tell me. He said that really, the only reason he came to Virginia was because he knew I would be here and he had something to discuss with me."

"What was it?"

"That's just it, right when he was about to tell me they came over to our table and he wouldn't talk about it in front of them. He said God had another time for that conversation."

"It sounds big."

"Yeah, tell me about it. I can hardly sit still."

"That's probably just the coffee."

"I hope I can catch up with him tomorrow."

"You will. Listen honey, I have to get up early. I'm going to try and get some sleep. I love you."

"I love you too. Tell the kids I'll be home tomorrow evening. Good night."

"Good night."

After hanging up the phone, Kenneth got down on his knees. "Father, I give You thanks and praise. I am so thankful to have a wonderful, loving, caring woman like Barbara. Thank You God. Thank You for this evening and the honor of accepting that award. All glory and honor are Yours Father. Thank You for allowing me to help with Your work. I am Yours Lord. I am here Lord. Direct me, lead me, give me strength, give me vision. Thank You that You will never leave me, nor forsake me. In Jesus' name. Amen."

Kenneth climbed back in the lumpy bed and fell right to sleep.

Frank Hampton raised the three pound hammer and drove the wooden spike into the ground. Eleven good whacks and the job was done. It was a red sign with, 'For Sale by Owner', in white letters and his phone number at the bottom. He put the hammer back in the garage and then sat on the porch to admire his work. Just then Larry the gay mailman came springing up the sidewalk.

"Frank, what's this all about?" Shouted Larry still two houses away.

Frank didn't answer; he didn't want to yell his business all over the block. He just watched as Larry fell over himself trying to rush through the Davidson's delivery next door. Frank couldn't help but smile as Larry walked up the driveway.

"Larry I'm moving. Come on now, you knew this day would come."

"I can't believe this first that good looking young man on the corner and now you Frank, that does it, I'm asking for a different route," Larry pouted.

"You know Mrs. Wurth has a crush on you," Frank said with raised eyebrows as he tilted his head towards his eighty year old neighbor's house, "if you keep this route you might get lucky some day."

"Where in the world are you going?" Larry said, ignoring the comment about Mrs. Wurth.

"Knob Ridge."

"What is Knob Ridge?"

"Knob Ridge Larry; it's in Dolittle County. I've got a one hundred and sixty acre chunk of heaven on earth. This neighborhood is going to crap, and I'm tired of fighting it. Last night some punks broke into Ty's Suburban in Gildersleeve's parking lot, we went out and caught the S.O.B's and all the cops wanted to do was arrest me. As of right now I'm officially retired. I've got a nice little three room cabin on the edge of the woods. The sunsets over my three acre lake, and I'm going to watch that sunset every night and laugh about you poor slobs still fighting the rat race."

"Well, Frank good for you," Larry said. "That's probably the best retirement plan I've ever heard. My folks moved to Coco Beach four years ago, they're miserable in that heat."

"Some time you wanna come down and catch a nice largemouth bass you let me know."

"Oh Frank goodness no, I'm a city boy," Larry struck a city boy pose. "You take care now, you hear." Larry approached Frank for a good bye hug, but he ended up with a handshake.

Just then the green and white Nomad rounded the corner and headed down the street towards Frank's house. Matt tooted the horn and pulled into the drive.

"What's this?" Matt said as he pointed to the for sale sign.

"That's me finally admitting I'm ready to retire." Frank said still sitting on his front steps.

"Where are you going?"

"Matt, I'm ready for a change. I'm gonna slow things down and get out of this city, last night was the capper. Ty should be here soon, you want a beer or anything". Frank stood up and walked over to sidewalk and Matt followed him into the back yard.

"That cabin needs a little work doesn't it?" Matt asked, knowing if the answer was yes he had probably just volunteered himself.

Frank opened a bag of charcoal and dumped a nice pile into the barbecue pit. "I figure I can do a little at a time. I'm retired what else have I got to do."

"Who's gonna be crazy enough to buy this dump?" Ty yelled from the gate.

"Hey Ty, come on back, Frank just said something about a couple of beers." Matt unfolded a couple of lawn chairs.

Ty and Matt sat on the patio, briefly revisited last night's incident with the burglars.

"Man, you were like an animal last night Matty boy." Ty was impressed. "I've been going over it in mind....it happened so fast. When the guy went for something in his jacket pocket, you know he had a gun?"

"I don't know, maybe."

"No, I went to the station today to read the report. They found a .32 caliber revolver in his jacket. I mean the more I think about it...a little different timing, we could both be dead right now."

"Ah, no big deal really, I use to wrestle in high school. Took second in State championships my senior year. I've been in a few scraps." Matt said.

"I've been in a few scraps too," Ty responded. "But, never for a good reason and usually with me getting my butt kicked.

Frank came out of the house, drenched charcoal with lighter fluid and tossed a lit match. As the barbecue pit flared up he said, "I quit".

At first Matt and Ty looked at each other, then back at Frank. "Quit what"? Ty asked.

"Boys, I've had enough. I'm going to retire. Things ain't been the same since Mary died, and that's been over two years now. That crap last night was the last straw. I'm selling the house and moving up to the cabin. As for the bar I have two options; that's why I asked you two over here today, but either way I'm out of the picture. I can sell the bar, or I can turn it over to you Matt, you're the only family I've got left. Ty could help you get started managing it, he's run the place for the last six months anyway. I just haven't had my heart in it."

"Oh Frank, Frank hey c'mon," Ty searched for words.

"No really guys, it's okay; this is what I want, this is what I've always looked forward to, its time."

"Uncle Frank, sell the bar," Matt said.

"Well like I said that's one option. But, I was hoping you'd both be more receptive to the other. I don't need the money. So don't let that even come into the picture. Matt you're looking for work that will put that degree of yours to use, and Ty you already know how to run the place. I love you both like sons, I want you to have it. Now don't say another word about it until after we eat those steaks" Frank slit open the cellophane packages and the red meat sizzled.

Ty leaned back in his lawn chair, "What were you doing with your life when you were my age?" he said as he looked up at Frank.

Frank flipped a steak as he ducked to dodge the smoke, "I was married by twenty-four, Mary was twenty-one, by the time I turned twenty-eight we had pretty much figured out that we couldn't have children. That's about when we bought the bar, we ran it together and put everything we had into it, and we did it together. Thirty years we ran that business together and we never left each other's sides. I've owned that bar now for thirty-three years; I think that's more than enough time to spend in a bar, don't you?"

"I'm thirty-six and I have nothing to show," Ty sighed.

"At least you love what you do for a living, that's key, that's the whole secret," Matt added.

"Sit and relax boys, I'll be right back with a couple of cold ones" Frank headed for the house.

"Hey Frank, you got any iced tea?" Ty asked.

That stopped Frank in his tracks, he turned with raised eyebrows.

"Well I've been hitting it pretty hard lately." Ty provided an explanation.

Frank replied, "Yeah, yeah I've got iced tea."

"Kenneth! Kenneth!" The call echoed through the lobby. It was Peter Stroudlin. He saw Kenneth Macklind walking through the front corridor of the Arlington Convention Center. He was walking as fast as he could, and stopped to catch his breath when he finally reached Kenneth in front of the bathrooms. "Hi Kenneth. Sorry to bark at you; we must talk," said Peter still breathing heavy.

"Okay, I just finished my last speech. I am all yours." Kenneth set down his briefcase and put a hand on Peter's shoulder to settle him.

"There is so much to tell. I planned on spending the day with you and filling you in gradually, but that ship has sailed. I have a plane to catch in three hours. Do you have the time to drive me to the airport and sit with me until I takeoff?"

"I would love to. Actually, I'm catching a plane too. Not until five, but I've got nothing better to do. Why don't you sit here and I'll go get my bags, and then we can go."

"Fine, I need to sit down. I'll be right here."

"Be back down in ten minutes."

Kenneth turned and moved briskly to the elevator. His brown boots slid effortlessly over the red and gold paisley carpet. Mystery still thick in the air, but now Kenneth was relieved that he had found Peter before he left. He stood at the elevator with a small crowd of people awaiting the door to slide open. He glanced back down the hall and could see Peter sitting on the sofa still watching him. He felt the need to hurry. As he got to his room, he was glad he packed his luggage the night before. He picked it up and headed back downstairs. This time alone in the elevator, he took a moment to reflect on the last forty-eight hours.

It started in Houston, Texas. Houston is home. He got up Wednesday morning and addressed the many issues that a wife and six kids can throw at you and still had time to swing by the florist and pick up a dozen roses. He went back home and left Barbara with a dozen long stem roses and a goodbye kiss. He stopped by the post office to mail a package and then headed for the airport, running a little late. He parked, jumped on a shuttle, squeezed through the crowd with one bag and a briefcase; nothing to check. He made it through security, and found the gate where he got to sit and wait for three minutes before the plane began boarding. The minute he got off the plane, he was greeted by a car service that delivered him to the convention center in Arlington, Virginia. He made his 4:30 speaking engagement with seven minutes to spare. That evening, he was given the award, made another speech and ran into Peter Stroudlin backstage. Now he was finally going to find out what Peter was so excited to tell him. Kenneth tried to imagine what it was, but really had no idea.

"Alright, let's go." Kenneth said rolling his luggage down the red and gold carpet.

Peter got up and the two walked side by side out into the parking lot and got into Kenneth's rental car. At last, they were on their way to Ronald Reagan Airport, and they were finally alone.

"I haven't told anyone else about this. I really wanted to, but I didn't. Anyway, I believe God showed me that he wanted me to ask you to help me."

"So, what's up?"

"Kenneth please, let's go through this slowly. Let me start at the beginning. Remember I asked you about Ian?"

"Yes, I didn't know him."

"I met Ian Burbrey in 1986. He was a leading archeologist in England, in the eighties. He logged many great finds. He had just finished uncovering a tremendous Liopleurodon fossil. He took a job as assistant curator in a museum in Southern England where his Liopleurodon was on display. I happened to be in England and wanted to see the new Liopleurodon display and that's when I met Ian. We became lifelong friends after one cup of coffee. You see Ian was a strong Christian. He seemed to keep that somewhat under his hat though, that can make it difficult to remain gainfully employed in a museum run by atheists."

"Yes, I can imagine." Kenneth was on the edge of his seat.

"Several days ago, I got a phone call from Ian. He said that he had something in the museum that I had to see. He said he couldn't describe it over the phone but that I had to see it in person. And that's when I agreed to go and visit him in England."

"What is it?" Kenneth could hardly stand it.

"Kenneth, what is the one thing that would blow evolution out of the water? What is the one thing that would bury it, clearly, once and for all?"

Kenneth took a deep breath as he briefly thought about the question. Then looking Peter straight in the eye he responded. "The age of the Earth." He leaned back in his chair, "Proof that the Earth is not billions of years old, but only six thousand, like every early church leader taught."

"That is exactly what I received from Ian Burbrey, the day he was killed."

<u>Chapter 4</u>

Frank Hampton leaned back in his rocking chair on the creaky wooden floor of his newly repaired front porch. He was soaking up the quiet, and enjoying a few unrushed breathes of fresh air. The lake was still, the air was cool, and the woods were calm. This was a perfect afternoon. For the first time in days, he thought about Matt and Ty and wondered how things were going back in St. Louis. Yet he was glad to be out of the rat race.

"Well hello there," Frank said as a brown and white goat came around the corner of the porch. "Here, I got something for ya," he tossed the goat a hamburger, bun and all. And then Frank laughed as the goat devoured the sandwich. He hadn't laughed much in the last five years, but things were beginning to change. Frank slowly rocked in his porch swing as his goat friend sat by his side. The two of them enjoyed a beautiful sunset.

Then the crunch of tires turning onto Frank's gravel driveway announced a visitor. A red Dodge Caravan stopped, and a smiling man got out waving and heading up the sidewalk. "Hi there!" he said.

Frank wasn't sure what to make of the guy, but he was getting bored with the goat. "Hi." Frank said cautiously.

Still fifteen feet away he already had his hand extended for the handshake. "I am so glad to meet you. My name is Phil Balasky. I am the Pastor of Faith Church, it's in town on Second Street. I just saw you were out and wanted to stop by and say hi."

Frank returned a hearty handshake. "Nice to meet you Phil, have a seat. Would you like a hamburger or anything to drink?"

"Oh, no thank you my wife has supper in the oven, I can't stay too long. She is a great cook; why don't you come by and have dinner with us?"

"Well that is awful nice of you Phil, but I was married for twenty-eight years and I know that it's not cool to surprise your wife with dinner guests."

"You'd be surprised, being pastors it happens all the time, but how about tomorrow night?"

"Yeah sure that would be great. Thank you."

"The address and phone number is on the card, if you need anything call, if not come on over about five."

"Sounds good Phil, see you then." Frank was usually slow to warm up to new people, but he had already heard from several neighbors that Pastor Phil was a good guy. Besides he was thinking about trying to find a nice little country church, maybe this was it.

Frank grabbed his Shimano ultra-light rod and reel and strolled down to the lake. The sky was glowing orange, yellow, red, purple; the colors seemed to be radiating. It was the most spectacular sunset Frank had ever seen; or maybe he had never really taken the time to pay attention to a sunset before. He tied on a white and silver rooster tail and softly cast it towards the sunken tree branch 15 yards off the bank. The lake was a sheet of glass, except for the soft rings from his lure's landing. Frank slowly reeled it in. He could see the silver spinner just beneath the surface. He could feel the slight tension of the tiny spinner bait doing its thing. "Wow, a guy can really do some thinking out here…" Frank thought. He was glad to have met Phil Balasky, and he was actually looking forward to dinner at his house tomorrow evening. He truly was considering going to church.

Frank had never been a spiritual person. He grew up in a home that occasionally went to church, but he really couldn't remember why. Recently he began to feel differently about the subject. Then, after the incident at Gildersleeves he was sure he needed a change. He was not sure exactly what to change or how to change it. But, he wanted to get right with God….or whatever they call it. Frank hoped to talk to Pastor Phil about all of this tomorrow night.

His rooster tail stopped. The water boiled under where the lure had just been. Frank jerked up and set the hook. She went down first. Then Frank watched the line rise as he held it steady. He was careful not to put too much on the 4 pound test. He could see the fish slowly rising toward the surface and then, it jumped a foot out of the water with a loud splash. Frank laughed and held on like an excited little boy catching his first fish. She went back down again, this time taking another ten yards of line with her. Frank had to wrestle the fish clear of the tree branch. It jumped again; it seemed even louder against the silence of the Missouri dusk. Frank reeled and eventually pulled the fish to the shore. He reached down and grabbed it by the bottom lip.

"Oh, you'll go close to five pounds, and healthy!" Frank said as he studied the Largemouth Bass. He looked it over, gave it a quick kiss on the head and gently slid her back into the water. With a flick of her tail she was gone, and once again all was quiet. The sunset was fading quickly and night was falling. Frank stood there and watched the colors drain from the sky. "God, if You're listening…" Frank said out loud. "Thank You….I had a great day." And then he happily headed back to the cabin.

"Do you believe this place? What do you think Frank would say?" Ty yelled into Matt's ear, even though he was standing right next to him.

"He'd say you gotta make hay while the sun shines." Matt yelled back.

They both laughed. Gildersleeves was jam packed. Ty meandered through the crowd and made his way out side for some air. As he stood there watching the cars go by, he wondered what Frank was doing. He thought about how quiet it must be out there, and he wondered if that was good or bad. He missed Frank, who was the closest thing he had to a Father, and thought about driving out to see him. He hoped to remember to ask Matt about riding out with him someday soon. There was a lot to do before that; a lot of people to greet, a lot of songs to sing, and a lot of beer to sell. Business was booming, and Matt was shining in his new role, running the place. Ty was starting to have trouble keeping up. He had the band doing the second set without him to help rest his voice. It was hard to resist though, he was bringing home three thousand a week, no other musician in St. Louis came close to that. Almost every night there were a number of local celebrities on hand. Several of the Cardinals and Rams players, The Channel Twelve news anchors, even the Mayor liked to hang out there. And tonight, in his favorite dark corner.....Chuck Berry sat unmistakably in his white Captain's hat. For Matt, things were going very well; but Ty was looking for something more.

Mike Rimmey

<u>Chapter 5</u>

"What is it?" Kenneth wanted to know. He wanted to know what it was that was so important that Ian Burbrey was killed over it.

"It is the journal of Sir Richard the Elder of Landolte." Peter had finally let the cat out of the bag.

"Okay...?" Traffic was slowing. Kenneth was having trouble concentrating on the road.

Peter explained further, "Sir Richard was the highest knight in the court of King Alfred of Wessex. Long before it was England, it was during the Anglo-Saxon period, 900 - 1000 AD. Sir Richard led many fierce battles in Germania, France, Wallachia, all over Europe. In addition to his bravery battling the Anglo-Saxon enemies, he was well known for battling another kind of enemy.....dragons."

"Dragons?" Kenneth nearly missed the exit for the airport.

"Oh yes, he was known for his bravery in fighting and killing dragons. And here is the best part. He kept a journal. I have been able to find some documentation verifying the journal. It was well known, and well verified.....it is authentic. Sir Richard kept a journal capturing the details of his battles. He told of all his battles against the Germans, the Franks, Turks. It detailed his battle plans and whether or not they were successful. He also drew meticulously detailed pictures of the dragons he fought. He logged every one of them in exacting detail, every feature, every nuance of the creatures."

"And you've seen this?"

"Yes, I saw it at Ian's brother's house. That's where he kept it; he knew they were after him. We got to his brother's house in London, and went down into the basement. He very gently opened the book and began showing me the drawings. There was no question."

"What did they look like?"

"They look like very detailed eyewitness drawings of Allosaurus, Baryonyx, Megalosaurus, various Pterosaurs and Sauropods."

Kenneth's mouth hung wide open.

"You do know what this means…" asked Peter.

"Dear Lord," Kenneth said, still digesting the bomb he'd just been handed. "Dragons *were* Dinosaurs!" Not that the idea was foreign to Kenneth. There were several prominent creation ministries that had been touting the idea for years. But, this seemed like rock solid proof.

"Indeed. There is no way Sir Richard could have drawn the dinosaurs from pictures he'd seen in text books, there were no pictures of dinosaurs. The first fossils weren't discovered until the 1800's. There is no way he could have imagined the dinosaurs to that detail. The only explanation is that he saw them."

"This means a thousand years ago there were still dinosaurs walking around in Europe," said Kenneth thinking out loud. "There's no way for evolution to explain this. And you have this journal?"

"Oh Kenneth, there is much more to the story."

But Kenneth had reached the airport. He dropped Peter off at the main entrance and then went to return the rental. A Pakistani guy with a huge white turban met Kenneth at the Enterprise counter and took his paperwork. Kenneth was a little nervous leaving Peter alone for some reason. The guy with the turban had to ask him twice if he left the keys in the car. Kenneth's mind was full.

It was 10:40. Peter's flight to London began boarding at 12:30, less than two hours to get the rest of the story out of him. Kenneth finished at the rental car counter and pulled his luggage out the curb to catch a shuttle back to the departing flights entrance where he had dropped off Peter. A black Ford van with huge yellow polka dots pulled up and he got in. The shuttle was crowded with people staring down and poking their smart phones. Kenneth found an opening and sat down, but he kept his luggage with him so he could get off faster. The shuttle pulled up to the curb, Kenneth jumped up even before the doors swung open, and he was the first one out. He was practically running through the entry corridor heading towards the security check. Kenneth's mind was racing ahead of him. Why doesn't Peter just go public with it? Why wouldn't every museum in the world want this on display? Was Peter holding out for money? What did Peter need him for? The questions were coming faster than Peter's version of the story.

There he was. Kenneth saw Peter sitting right where he said he would be. "Alright; c'mon. Let's get you through security, and find a place to sit where I can hear the rest of this story."

Peter looked up with weariness in his eyes. "Kenneth, I'll tell you the rest of the story on the plane. I need you to come to London with me."

<u>Chapter 6</u>

The table was set, the candles were lit, and the meatloaf was just coming out of the oven. Lena Balasky was reminiscent of June Cleaver with her flowered dress and apron. She untied the apron when she heard the doorbell. "Phil, he's here," she relayed down the hall to her husband working in his study. Phil jumped up and beat Lena to the door.

"Hello Frank, come on in."

"Hi Phil, thank you so much for having me." Frank and Phil shook hands and smiled. "Mrs. Balasky?" Frank said as he turned toward Phil's wife.

"Please call me Lena."

"Frank have a seat, what can I get you to drink?" Phil said as he started toward the kitchen.

"No, No. You two sit right here and get to know each other. I'll be right back with some lemonade; dinner will be a few more minutes." Lena floated off to the kitchen.

Guests for dinner were a fairly regular occurrence at the Balasky house. Phil believed that inviting someone over to your home to break bread was a pretty special thing; but he also believed there were a lot of pretty special people around him. His church, Faith Church, was the largest church in the county. Officially there were over four hundred members but any given Sunday, Phil would find a hundred and fifty or so filling the seats, seventy-five at each service. Faith Church was listed as non-denominational. Phil had issues with most organized denominations. Knob Ridge had First Baptist, Presbyterian, United Methodist, Church of Christ, Roman Catholic, and four or five others; not bad for a town of twelve hundred people.

Faith Church started in Phil's barn. After about six month's two people got up out of wheel chairs and the Faith Church healing service really took off. After another six month's Phil was able to pay cash for the Disciples of Christ property that closed when their pastor went to jail, and they added on a beautiful new sanctuary. All of this was just three years ago and another expansion was already being considered.

"Are you retired Frank?" Phil asked.

"Yeah, actually I just retired last week. I'm still working on the transition. I own a bar in St. Louis, that's been how I spent my last thirty years; probably not what you wanted to hear." Frank said frankly.

"Hmmm, not what I would have guessed."

"Really…" Frank laughed. "What would you have guessed?"

"I don't know; office manager, sales rep, something like that."

"Well owning a bar is all of that and more…..not to mention janitor, plumber, accountant, security officer…."

"If you want it done right; do it yourself, huh?"

"That's exactly right. But I did have some really good people with me over the years. One lady retired two years ago....put three kids through college waiting tables at Gildersleeves."

"Yeah, Gildersleeves. I saw that place on the news a couple weeks ago. Channel six did that series on St. Louis hotspots. I remember the name....so you own that place?"

"Yeah...like I said, I've owned and ran that place for almost thirty years. But I made the decision to retire and I am going to have my nephew manage it. I am relieved to be out."

"It sounds like there's more to the story." Phil was picking up on something more. Just then Lena was returning from the kitchen with two tall glasses of pink lemonade.

"Oh thank you Lena," Frank said as he took the drink. "I always wondered; how do you make it pink?"

"I don't know; it comes out of the package that way." Lena returned to the kitchen to put the finishing touches on the meal.

"So you're out of the bar business?" Phil said fishing for more.

"As of last Wednesday morning.....this is the first time I've ever been away from the place for more than three days in a row. Hey, look at that deer," Frank exclaimed, looking out the window.

"I guess you don't see many of those in St. Louis," Phil said.

"Actually, even if there were, I probably wouldn't have even noticed. You know it's funny; this last week, I'm really starting to slow down and take a look around. Some guy at Wal-Mart was telling me about these automatic game trail cameras. You mount them on a tree and they have motion sensors that trigger digital photographs. Whenever something walks in front of the motion sensor it takes a picture; and it doesn't use a flash at night it uses infrared technology so it doesn't scare the animals. The good ones are two hundred and fifty bucks, but I bought six of them. I put them all around my property. I am having a blast looking at the pictures of wildlife on my property. Just in the last two days I've seen raccoons, skunks, coyotes, a bobcat, and tons of deer."

"That sounds like a great hobby for you Frank," Phil said. "It's a good idea to get to know what is out there."

"Okay guys....let's eat." Lena called from the dining room.

Meatloaf, mashed potatoes and gravy, peas and carrots, rice pilaf.....Frank couldn't remember the last time he sat down to a family meal like this. Frank and the Balaskys enjoyed a wonderful dinner. Frank told them about his wife Mary; and how she had passed away three years ago. He told them about his nephew Matt; and how he was doing a fine job of running the business. He told them about Ty; and how it was his talent had made the bar a success. They sat and talked for an hour and a half, and the conversation never got difficult. Frank was glad to have new friends in his new home town.

The meatloaf was reduced to a tray of sauce and crumbs. Frank was so full he was laboring to get a good deep breath; he considered loosening his belt a bit. "Lena everything was great; that was the best meal I've had in a very long time."

"Oh Frank," Lena replied. "You are so welcome. I hope we can do it again soon. Why don't you guys go out and sit on the porch, it's a beautiful evening. I'll bring out some coffee."

"Make mine decaf," Phil said as he got up and stretched.

They walked outside. It was a stunningly gorgeous evening. There were two old wooden rocking chairs overlooking the rail with a great view of the valley below. The wraparound porch was squeaky, and the light blue paint was peeling away in a few places. "Have a seat Frank." Phil said. "I'll bring around another chair."

Frank sat and rocked, enjoying the view. He had a similar view at his place. As Phil approached with the other chair Frank said: "Hey Phil, this is really nice. I bet tonight's sunset is going to be just as spectacular as last night."

"You have a thing for sunsets, huh Frank? I do too."

They sat and talked some more. Lena returned with coffee. The crickets were getting louder; and the tree frogs were joining them. Frank was watching a bat zigging and zagging after moths.

"So, now what?" Phil asked. "I mean now that you're retired….things are under control in St. Louis….What are you going to do with your time?"

"You know, we have talked a lot about the past tonight. But, not at all about the future," answered Frank. "I'm not really sure. I haven't given it much thought yet. I do know one thing….I would like to find a nice church around here….do you know of any?"

Phil laughed. "Actually I do." This was the moment Phil had been waiting for all night. "Do you have a Christian background?"

"No, not really. I mean my wife would drag me to church on special occasions; you know Christmas, Easter…" Frank replied. "But I have really been thinking a lot lately about getting straight with God."

Phil smiled and stopped rocking. He leaned forward in his chair towards Frank. "Frank, I am glad to hear you say that. I would love to see you come to our church. But, it's not about going to church; or bake sales; or barbeques; or Christmas; or Easter. It's about having a relationship with the Lord Jesus Christ. I believe once you have that you will want to go to church; but, you should have that first."

Frank just sat and looked he didn't know what to say.

"Let me ask you this Frank; who do you say that Jesus Christ is? In the Gospel of John, the apostle Peter was asked this question. I believe it is a question that everyone has to answer some day..... Jesus Christ is God. God is so awesome and wonderful that for us to even begin to understand who He is, He had to reveal Himself to us in three persons. The three are one ... and they are ...the Father, the Son, and the Holy Spirit. One God – three persons. Think of it this way...water can appear in three phases: liquid, solid, gas; all three are fully water. Jesus is the Son of God. Though His fleshly existence began about 2000 years ago, Jesus has always existed. He is eternal, and all things were created through Him. Jesus is God."

Frank was nodding along. "Okay, he's with me so far..." Phil thought to himself.

"The Bible says that 'All have sinned and fall short of the glory of God'. Because we have broken God's commandments we are not worthy of Him and His kingdom; or what we call Heaven. Have you ever lied? Have you ever stolen? Have you ever taken the Lord's name in vain? Have you ever looked upon a member of the opposite sex with lust?"

"Yeah, all of the above." Frank answered.

"You know what that makes you? Phil questioned.

"Human?" Frank said in his defense.

"What it makes you is a lying, thieving, blasphemous, adulterer at heart. I know I am. The Bible tells us that such people will have no part in the Kingdom of Heaven. God created a place for them. A place called Hell. In Hell, those who die in their sins will spend all eternity apart from God and His goodness and 'there shall be weeping and gnashing of teeth'. If there is one thing I can't stand it's a watered down gospel. Hell exists Frank."

"Hey now Phil, all of a sudden this isn't looking so good for a guy like me."

"But Frank, God made a way for us to be saved from Hell. He sent His only Son to die on the cross for us. Jesus died on the cross for our sins. He was buried and then rose from the dead on the third day just as He predicted. In the Old Testament, God demanded lambs be sacrificed on an alter to pay the price for sin. Jesus became our sacrifice for sin, once and for all. Jesus took our place on that cross; he took your place. He never sinned, but he paid the price for all sin. To be covered…to be saved; you must repent, ask forgiveness, and accept the sacrifice Jesus made on the cross. He died for you Frank."

"Alright now that sounds a little bit better."

Phil smiled widely. He had led people to the Lord many times in his life. He considered it a thrill and an honor. "Frank, if you died tonight…..do you know where you would spend eternity?"

"I'm afraid to think about it."

"Would you like to be saved Frank? Would you like to get to know the Savior?"

"Yes I would."

74

Phil led Frank in a prayer. Right there on the porch, in the presence of that magnificent sunset; Frank and Phil bowed their heads. Lena stepped around behind Frank's rocking chair and gently laid her hand on Frank's shoulder. With Phil's help, Frank said the first real prayer of his life; a prayer that acknowledged his sins and asked Jesus to be his Lord and Savior.

"Frank Hampton, you just got born again. You are a new man."

Mike Rimmey

Chapter 7

"Hi honey," Kenneth hoped this would go well.

"Hi….it's Daddy. They want to go to Chevy's for dinner tonight after you get home," said Barbara surrounded by kids.

"Well…."

"Oh, I haven't heard that tone for awhile. What's up?"

"I have to go to London."

"London! What are you talking about?"

"I am helping Peter with something. I should be back home Monday night."

"Oh, what is it? Did he ever tell you the big secret?"

"Yeah that's what this is. It's very important."

"What?" Barbara was having trouble hearing over the kids.

"I said it's very important."

"What? Go in the other room…..I told you not to…."

"Honey, I have to go… I'll call you as soon as I can."

"Be quiet….I can't hear Daddy…."

"Barbara….I love you; I'll talk to you tonight."

"Okay....I love you....Bye." Barbara was yelling.

Kenneth slipped his phone back into his front pocket. With his thumb and forefinger he pinched the stress at the corners of his eyes. He took a deep breath and looked out the two story tall window at the tarmac. On one hand he wished he was going home; he did miss Barbara and the kids. But, on the other hand, he couldn't wait to get to London and get his hands on the journal. He walked back over to his seat in the waiting area next to Peter and sat down.

"Looks like I picked the wrong week to stop sniffing glue."

"Excuse me," Peter said in a shocked tone.

Kenneth laughed, "I'm sorry.....it's just a bad joke....it's from that old airplane movie...."

"Oh, I'm afraid I don't see many movies."

Just then they began calling for pre-boarding and everyone began putting their things away and getting ready to get on the plane. Kenneth and Peter were in the first boarding group and took their seats. Beyond first class, the British Airways 747 seating arrangements were three, four and three. Peter found his seat at the window and Peter sat next to him. They jammed their bags overhead and buckled up for takeoff. People filed in for fifteen minutes. Just as Kenneth was beginning to think he had an empty seat to his left....there she was; a tall, thin woman with bright red hair. She found space for her bag in overhead storage, and then claimed her seat, right next to Kenneth. She looked like an executive, possibly sales Kenneth thought. She was well dressed with a black business suit that fit like a glove. She simply said "Hello," and then went back to her blackberry. Kenneth hoped this wouldn't stifle Peter again….he still had to uncover the rest of the story behind this journal.

Peter sat quietly with his Bible opened to psalm 23. His lips moved as he read to himself. Kenneth leaned his head back and closed his eyes. The engines revved. The plane moved forward. The nose went up first and then they were air born…..London bound.

After fifteen or twenty minutes, the red haired woman turned. "Hi, I'm Claire." She offered her hand.

"Hello, Kenneth Macklind," Kenneth shook her hand. This is Dr. Peter Stroudlin….he leaned back and offered Peter a chance to shake as well. "Very pleased to meet you ma'am." Peter said.

"Oh, a doctor….what is your expertise?"

"My PhD is in Biochemistry, but my expertise is teaching. How about yourself?"

"Advertising….I'm running an ad campaign for a new client in London…who's getting nervous about their deadline and they insisted I come and meet with them."

The small talk continued for a few minutes….weather, advertising, teaching, London, not much personal stuff. Then she pulled out a magazine from her bag. "I've been reading this fascinating article…..I just can't put it down." It was a National Geographic. "They are learning that the Earth may be six to seven billion years old….It was previously thought to be only four and a half billion."

Kenneth and Peter looked at each other. Peter smiled and Kenneth raised one eyebrow to a 'you must be kidding' level.

"What? Have you read it?"

"No, I'm sorry…..you see it's a little ironic. Peter and I are not only stout Bible believing Christians; but, we both make a living, and have spent most of our lives teaching Young-Earth Creationism. That's pretty much the exact opposite of what you're reading there."

"What do you mean by Young-Earth Creationism?"

"Well….simply that according to God's word, and an abundance of natural evidence…..the Earth is not billions of years old at all…..it's actually only about six thousand years old."

Now she gave the 'you must be kidding' look. "I've never heard anything like that in my life. That just sounds crazy."

"Have you ever read the Bible," Peter asked. "It's all explained rather clearly."

"Okay, the Bible aside; what about this natural evidence?"

"Well let's see," Peter said. "There's the rate at which the moon is moving away from the Earth; the rate of continental decay; the decay of the Earth's magnetic field; the rate at which the sun is shrinking….."

Kenneth picked up where Peter left off….. "The population of the Earth; the lack of helium in the atmosphere; the lack of dust on the moon; the lack of sediment on the ocean floor; the lack of salt in the ocean…."

She cut him off. "Wow I stepped into that one. I feel like you guys are ganging up on me."

"Hey, like I said this is sort of our thing."

"Okay, pick one and explain it."

"Pick one?"

"Yeah, pick one of your little bullet points you just gave me and explain it….I'll give you one shot."

Kenneth smiled. "Alright fair enough…..which one would you like to hear about?"

"Umm, how about the moon moving away from the Earth?"

"Okay. We know the moon's orbit around the Earth is expanding. In other words it is getting further and further away from the Earth. We have good data that says the moon is slipping away about four centimeters per year. That's about this much," Kenneth demonstrated four centimeters with his thumb and forefinger. "Now, even though four centimeters doesn't seem like much…..if you extrapolate that back in time, you don't have to go four and a half billion years to get massively deadly tidal action. Also, in four and a half billion years the moon should be much, much further away."

Peter chimed in, "Look at the population of the Earth. Today it is about seven billion. Evolution teaches that humans came on the scene about one hundred thousand years ago. All of our population models agree that if that were the case, the Earth would be drastically more populated. In fact, most population models agree that it has probably taken just forty-five hundred years for us to get to seven billion. Do you know what happened forty-five hundred years ago? There was a global flood. Every air breathing thing was killed…..except for Noah, his wife, his three sons and their wives; just like the Bible says."

"Okay you guys win…..I don't think I have the energy to argue with you. I'm not saying I agree with you…..I don't want to get religious."

She politely bowed out of the conversation and put on her earplugs to listen to some music. Kenneth looked at Peter and said, "Evolution is religion." They both enjoyed the chance to expose someone to the truth.

Kenneth could hear the music seeping out of her earphones, so he figured it was safe to have a private conversation now. "Alright Peter, I've been waiting forever to hear the rest of this story let's have it."

"Kenneth," Peter was speaking quietly, he leaned closer. "I was with Ian when he was killed."

Kenneth eyes widened.

Peter continued, "They thought he was carrying the journal….I'm sure of that. I had already put it in the trunk of the cab. He was carrying his briefcase. I'm sure they wouldn't have killed him if they thought he didn't have it on him."

"Killed him how?"

"Shot him…..one shot. I was just coming around from the other side of the car; by the time I heard the shot he was already on the ground. I ran back into the car and we got out of there….straight to the police station. That was strange too….almost as if they already knew what was going on. Once they came right out and asked me if I knew the whereabouts of the item Ian was killed over."

"You're kidding….what did you say?"

"I asked how they knew the motive of the murder; and I asked what the item was. Then they very directly asked me again….without addressing my questions."

"Peter, you really have to be careful with this….a man got killed over it."

"Actually there have been two men. Ian got the journal from a man named Alexander Svec from Prague. Shortly after he sent it to Ian, he was in a fatal car accident. His car went over a cliff; Ian was convinced it was not an accident."

"Wow. Who do you think it is…..the museum?"

"I think the museum is involved. The curator, who was Ian's boss, told Ian he was taking the journal home. Ian was sure that if that happened he would never see it again. So, that's when Ian took the journal….he was dead the next day. The museum is definitely involved. But, I think it goes much higher."

It was noon; Ty Hyvek had been awake for half an hour. He sat on the cantilevered deck of his tenth floor downtown loft and enjoyed the warmth of the sun. He laid back in a red, zero gravity, lounge chair and let the bright light soak in. His view could have been on a post card. He could see the Old Courthouse, Union Station, the Arch, and best of all…..the Mississippi River. Watching the river was like watching a campfire; peaceful and hypnotic. He enjoyed it so much more than television. Ty could just sit and watch the river for hours. He had written many a song on that deck; collecting inspiration from the sun and the Midwestern breeze. And at night….the big city lights replaced the stars; and were almost as dazzling.

He had lived there for about five years, most of that time alone. Along the way there were several girlfriends that achieved "move-in" status; but none of them lasted more than a month or two, and right now….there was no one even close. Ty glanced at his watch and logged the time. He still had three or four hours before he really had to think about getting ready. He didn't need to show up at Gildersleeves until about 6:30, but he usually would get ready and run a few errands before the five o'clock businesses close. Today he had to get to the post office, and that was about it. Such is the life of a working musician.

In 1994, Ty fronted a band called "Avalanche". With Ty at the center, they were rockers, with a bluesy, folksy, alt-country groove. They built a huge Midwestern following and were the top bar band from Chicago to Tulsa and everywhere in between. It was during this time that Ty wrote his claim to fame…..a song titled "Every Other Day". It quickly became the song they were known for. For four years the band tried to interest a label in financing a recording; they got really close to striking a deal once but the deal slipped through the cracks. By 1998, Avalanche had broken up. Determined to make something happen, Ty drove to Nashville and recorded the song in the friend of a friend's basement studio. It turned out good….so good that when a well connected producer heard it, he played it for an up and coming band that he was currently working with, and they cut it. It was a rocking country band with major label money behind them. They put it on their début CD which eventually sold over two million copies; and released it as a radio single. Between the mechanical royalties, BMI checks and synchronization licenses, Ty made about a half-million dollars on that song. He took that and paid cash for the downtown loft; and has been coasting on the earnings ever since.

Now thirty-six; Ty had lounged away a decade of his life. Coasting from the success of one song, he took the job at Gildersleeves and collected an easy paycheck. But, he was beginning to wonder if there was more to life; in fact, he was sure that there was…..and he intended to find it.

"Thank you," said Peter Stroudlin, walking past the flight attendant as he and Kenneth were exiting the flight. They turned and headed down the tarmac into the

Heathrow airport. People buzzed in every direction. It was so crowded. Kenneth was having trouble hearing Peter over the noise. They stopped to look at the arrows pointing the direction to the B gates.

"That's where it is...... B-9," remarked Peter. "That's a pretty long walk."

"Alright, let's get this thing and get right back on a plane back to the states," Kenneth said thinking out loud. But, they did not yet have return flight reservations.

They walked briskly for awhile, but Peter was tiring. They caught the speed belt, which helped them make good time, and gave Peter a bit of a rest. They whizzed past people on their way to the locker near gate B-9. They came to the end of the speed belt and Peter stepped off first. He miscalculated the rapid change in velocity, and his upper body kept moving but his right foot stuck solid as a rock. Kenneth had to hop to keep from tripping over him. Peter had taken a nasty spill. He lay face down on the cold gray tile floor. His nose was skinned and bleeding profusely. His right wrist had bent back severely, but it was his left knee that brought the most pain. Kenneth bent down to his side.

"Peter......are you okay?"

He just moaned. "Oh dear Lord.....my knee." Peter was a bloody, twisted mess. Kenneth looked around for help. There were a few women who had stopped to see if they could help.

"Please call for help," Kenneth told them. He tried to get a coherent response from Peter. "Peter would you like to try to sit up? How about just turning over?" Kenneth supported his head and helped him turn over and sit up. His right forearm was clearly broken; the seventy-nine year old bones must have been quite brittle. One of the women brought some paper towels from the restroom and dabbed at his face to clear away some of the blood. Within two minutes help had arrived in the form of an airport emergency car. The medical technicians tended to Peter's wounds and quickly assessed the situation.

"That wrist is broken, and I'm betting that patella is shattered. It looks like this gent's had a change in travel plans," said the medic. They carefully loaded Peter onto the electric powered cart, and hurried off with yellow lights flashing. Kenneth had to trot to keep up, but he managed. At the airport's emergency medical office they made the call for an ambulance.

"Sorry Kenneth," Peter said still wincing in pain. He was beginning to come around though.

"What are you talking about…..just be thankful you're going to be okay."

"No, It was stupid…..I wasn't thinking. How's this for discreet?"

"Don't worry about a thing Peter; I'll make sure you get fixed up."

"No, you have to get the journal and get out of here. Really, go get it now and get it back to the States. Don't worry about me…..You must do it."

"Peter, don't be silly. I'm staying with you. You'll be ready to go in a few days."

Peter grabbed his arm and squeezed. "Now you listen to me.....you go to gate B-9; you get that journal and you take it to a safe place in the United States. I'll look you up when I get out of here.....but, it could be weeks before I'm walking on this knee. I don't need you here with me Kenneth.....this is why I brought you. Now you do it."

Kenneth suddenly felt like a kid in trouble with his dad. He respected Peter too much not to obey his wishes. "Alright, give me the key."

Peter pulled the key out of his shirt pocket and handed it to Kenneth. "This is it. God be with you."

The sun was shining, the birds were singing, the leaves were turning.....it was an amazingly beautiful Missouri October Sunday morning. One after another, smiling people entered the front vestibule at Knob Ridge Faith church. The pipe organ radiated sounds that filled the church with that "Sunday" feeling. The whole congregation joined in singing "How Great Thou Art" with an enthusiasm that was infectious. Some raised their hands, some closed their eyes, some bowed their heads, some looked up to heaven; but everyone was on their feet.

As the twenty-five minute praise and worship session came to an end, Phil Balasky took the pulpit. He delivered a well planned sermon. About half way through, his eyes got caught on a sliver of sunlight shining on the salt and pepper hair of a man in the far back, right corner. He was drawn to that side of the sanctuary; he walked in that direction as he spoke to get a better look. And then he was sure....he smiled and almost lost his train of thought for a moment. It was Frank Hampton.

Frank knew that he had been spotted and his biggest concern now was that Phil would call him up front or make some big embarrassing announcement. He was relieved when it didn't happen. He enjoyed the service, the first one he'd been to in years....and the very first one he'd actually paid attention to. Frank met a few people and mingled a bit in the front vestibule after the service was over.

"Frank, great to see you.....welcome.....what did you think?" Phil said as he walked up from behind.

"Hey Phil," Frank smiled as he shook Phil's hand. "Churches and bars really aren't that different. People come......they enjoy themselves......and then they go back home. At church they just enjoy themselves in a different way."

Phil laughed, "Yeah, but the real difference is what they do when they get back home." His pocket buzzed, and he looked down at the phone to see who it was. "Hey Frank, I have to take this.....please excuse me."

"Yeah, I'll talk to you later."

Phil flipped open the phone. "Hello Kenneth."

"Hi Phil," it was Kenneth Macklind. "I'm glad I caught you.....I was hoping this week would be a good time for that visit we keep talking about. I'm sorry for the short notice."

"This week, sure Kenneth......no problem.....we'd love to see you. We try and stay open to last minute changes....that's the way God works sometimes. Will Barbara and the kids be with you?"

"No, I'll be alone....I hope....It's a very long story. I can fill you in tomorrow. I should be out around noon."

"Okay sure....see you then buddy." Phil closed the phone and slid it back into his pocket. "That was a little odd...." He said to Barbara, who had been standing behind him for just a moment.

"What's that dear?"

"It was Kenneth Macklind......he's coming out this week. He said he'll be here tomorrow."

"Oh, wonderful. I didn't know you had planned on him coming."

"Well, I hadn't really. I mean..... every time I talk to him I beg him to come; this has been going on for two years now. He sounded like he was in a terrible hurry."

"What about Barbara and the kids? Are they all coming?"

"No he said he would be alone.....he hoped.....not sure what he meant by that. I guess we'll find out tomorrow."

The Dragon Journal

Mike Rimmey

Chapter 8

The black Mercedes stopped at the gate to allow it to open. It was gray stone and black wrought iron, and may well have been two hundred years old. That is when the house was built. The house was also gray stone; it was cold, and gothic, and damp looking…..as if it hadn't seen the sun in years. The light posts along the drive were topped by horned gargoyles; and the lights were dim and yellow. It was two hundred yards from the gate to the house and the entire way was lined with perfectly spaced willow trees on both sides of the drive. The willow branches reached down and touched the car as it drove by. The lawn was perfectly manicured; and the driveway circled to the front door. In the middle of the circle was a fountain; twenty feet across and in the center was a strange horned man/goat with water streaming out of his mouth. The base of the fountain was in the shape of a pentagram.

The front door was a single pointed arch that stood 12 feet tall. It was dulled by weather but, was once a dark red, and the shutters matched. The windows were old, single pane, glass rippled with age. In fact, there was only one part of the house that was a recent addition, and it could only be seen from the rear of the house. A large, almost awkward, round, dome topped cylinder reached for the sky. It was a state of the art planetarium and telescope worthy of NASA. It was painted gray to match the stone of the house but, it really didn't quite fit.

The Mercedes paused right in front…..between the fountain and the front door. The car door opened and the man with the long silver ponytail stepped out. Alden Harlock was home.

The house was a seventeen thousand square foot mansion, once owned by his Great-Great-Great-Grandfather, Charles Herod Harlock. Charles was a very successful business man and a thirty-third degree master Mason. Many have suggested that the two go hand in hand. Masonic symbols were still visible on several locations on the house. The southwest cornerstone was engraved with the well known square and compass; and the peep hole in the front door was the center point of a pyramid and the "all seeing eye".

A two hundred year old estate is really not even that old in London. However, through the years many stories have circulated locally about the strange and secret goings on in the Harlock mansion. Alden wasn't born here; he inherited the home from his Uncle in 1990. Since then he had kept things very quiet, and very secretive.

Alden turned his key and went in. The door closed behind him as he kept walking. He sat down in a huge chair near the fireplace in very grand room. He drank a martini which was already prepared and waiting for him. The room had hundreds of candles which were lit and Beethoven soaked up the silence. He pressed the red button on a large remote control and ignited a roaring fire in the fireplace. He pressed the blue button and water began to trickle down a wall sized Japanese waterfall. He sank into his chair and took a deep breath; he had had a rather disappointing day. Now was the time to search for answers.

He began controlling his breathing through stiffly pursed lips. He relaxed and tensed at the same time in a way that must have taken years of training. Alden was thinking. He was thinking and listening. His eyes were open, but he wasn't looking at anything in the room. He went deeper; and deeper; he went inside. Immersed in meditation, his eyes glazed over. He hummed and growled, but he didn't speak. He needed to know what to do. He sat in this state for nearly an hour. He hadn't blinked. His breathing became so shallow it was not even noticeable; and then…..a smile. He blinked and his eyes focused again. He had seen something…..something deep in his mind. He relaxed and finished his martini. Alden Harlock was a man who always got what he wanted. He wanted the journal of Sir Richard the Elder of Landolte.

In his trance Alden had seen the piece of the puzzle that was eluding him. There was another man with Ian when he was killed. Somehow, he now knew that the journal was in the trunk of that taxi; and somehow, he now knew that the other man…..the man that now had the journal, was an American.

The smell of gasoline and freshly mowed grass filled the air; along with the sound of a self propelled 4-cycle lawn mower. Phil Balasky was hoping this would be the last grass cutting Monday of the year. He hadn't gotten to it for several weeks and the wet, extra tall grass was choking up the lawn mower. He had given up on bagging it and was now leaving a trail of softball sized grass clumps. Phil didn't even want to think about trimming…..at least it was cool. In just two weeks the leaves would start falling, and then there would be three or four Mondays of raking.

Monday was Phil's yard work day. He enjoyed physical tasks that were a diversion from his non-stop religious and emotional duties of shepherding his congregation. On Mondays, he didn't look much like a preacher. He wore a Hawaiian shirt and tan cargo pants with flip flops. He felt a little dangerous mowing the lawn in flip flops. Monday's yard work was about as much adventure as Phil Balasky got.

Years ago, in college, Phil had once gone on a caving expedition. He and three other guys had spelunked their way into a cave while on an archeology field study. They crawled in about two hundred yards and camped overnight. He never knew dark until that night. The next day they crawled out; wet, cold, hungry and smelling like their own urine. At the time Phil couldn't believe he was dumb enough to go along with it. Now, he often looked back on that night fondly. The thrill, the uncertainty, the spontaneity; he didn't seem to have much of that in his life nowadays. The answer to that problem was just pulling into his driveway.

It was Kenneth Macklind in his latest rental car. Phil was glad to see his old friend arrive. The sloppy lawn mowing job was put on hold. He killed the lawn mower and left it right in the middle of the yard sitting on top of a huge clump of wet grass.

"Hi Phil!"

"Hey Kenneth, it's so great to see you."

Kenneth looked him over, "How have you been?"

"Oh, I'm doing great…..better than I deserve, I know that."

"Hey, don't let me interrupt…..it looks like your only half done," Kenneth commented on the unfinished yard work.

"Believe me, I don't mind. Come on let's go around back and sit on the patio." They walked around the side of the house into the back yard and found a cozy patio table and padded chairs with a huge white umbrella. "Have a seat. Can I get you anything to drink?"

"Yeah, anything, iced tea, Coke, water….whatever you have will be great."

"Alright, have a seat…..I'll be right back."

The Balasky's back yard had a great view. Kenneth took a moment to take it in. He relaxed in the cushy patio chair and began to feel at ease. He still desperately wanted to get home and see his wife and kids. He was also still very concerned about Peter left alone to heal from his fall in the airport. He still wasn't even sure how extensive the injuries were. But, he was relieved to have the journal and be close to home; yet at the same time, he wasn't sure that he wanted it too close to his family.

"Here we go," Phil walked out of the house with two cans of ice cold Dr. Pepper. "We don't usually have soda. This must be a special occasion."

"Lena remembered. Last time I saw you guys, I was drinking Dr. Pepper like it was going out of style. That must have been what, three years. I have switched to mostly coffee lately but I do still love this stuff. Where is Lena?"

"She's shopping. She and a friend drove into Rolla to hang out and shop and whatever they do. It's a Monday thing. She shops and I do yard work."

"Sounds like a pretty good arrangement. I think I'd rather do yard work. How are things at church?"

"Really good Kenneth. The church is growing; God is using us in a big way around here. We are very busy. I try to set apart Monday as a day off, but it rarely is."

"You mean because of all that yard work?" Kenneth laughed.

"No, I mean usually someone from church calls needing something. Actually, I wouldn't have it any other way. You'll see it this Sunday. Right?" Phil was hinting at the reason for the sudden visit.

"Well…..actually, I don't think so. It's a pretty long story….. I need to tell you about my last five days."

Kenneth and Phil went way back in each other's lives. They met in Oklahoma City in 1986. They were both studying business administration at the University of Oklahoma. Phil was in his third year and Kenneth was a freshman. Kenneth changed majors three times before settling in on Biology, but Phil stayed the course with Business, but in that first year the two really hit it off. Kenneth was along on the infamous night in the cave.

After college Phil rented a house just south of the city. It took six months of working nights at a paint store to realize that he needed more than a Bachelors degree; and he went to graduate school for his Masters in Divinity. That's when

Kenneth moved in with him. They split the bills and somehow managed to make it on no income. They did a lot of walking and ate a lot of Ramen noodles. Eventually, they were each other's best man on wedding days, although eight years apart.

"Okay, what's up?"

"Phil, there are probably only three or four people in the world I would tell this story to…..and your one of them. So please consider, what I need most of all is help knowing what to do next. Prayerful consideration for a clear direction. This is big."

"Wow…..I had a feeling it was."

"Alright, last Thursday, I was speaking at a conference in Virginia….."

Phil cut him off already….. "what was it?"

"It was the Global Christian Broadcasters; I spoke Wednesday and Thursday….I received an award."

"No kidding….what?"

"It was outstanding achievement or something….."

"Hey….look at you….outstanding achiever…."

"Alright, anyway I was at this conference and I ran into one of my heroes….Dr. Peter Stroudlin."

"Hmmm…..doesn't ring a bell."

"Well he's an old timer that's been teaching about Biblical creation for decades. He's the first guy that really stood toe to toe with evolutionists back in the sixties. He fought against the terrible lies in school text books, and confronted the government on the matter. He has written over twenty books and I've got autographed copies of about half of them. I met him four or five years ago at another conference, and we became friends.....I still run into him once or twice a year.....we even had him stay at our house once when he was speaking in Houston."

"What happened to Peter?" Phil was always trying to jump ahead of the story. Kenneth wouldn't have it.

"Whoa, whoa.....slow down; don't get ahead of yourself."

"Alright, alright," Phil was motioning for Kenneth to get to the point.

Kenneth downed the Dr. Pepper. "So, when I finally got to talk with him in private.....he told me that the reason he came to the conference in Virginia was to see me. He was in trouble, and he didn't know where else to turn. He got in the middle of some pretty intense stuff.....and he's almost eighty years old."

"Go on."

"Yeah, so, he starts telling me about this ancient book that documents some really awesome facts about creation; and how this guy in Prague rescued it from being destroyed and sent it to his friend in London. Then his friend in London calls Peter to come and see it.....and just after Peter goes all the way to London his friend gets shot and killed right in front of him. So Peter....remember, he's eighty years old…..gets worried that whoever killed his friend wants to kill him too, so he stashes the book in a locker at the airport."

Phil wasn't saying anything….he just sat on the edge of his seat nodding his head.

"Oh yeah…..the guy in Prague got killed too…..I think I forgot to mention that. Okay, so that's when I ran into Peter in Virginia. He talked me into going to London with him to get the book out of the locker and get it back here to the states."

"What happened to Peter?"

"Alright, we were headed for the book and then to get straight back to the gate to get right back on a plane for the states…..when he fell."

"He fell?" Phil was anxiously trying to picture the scene in his mind.

"Yeah, we got on the speed belt because we were sort of in a hurry but Peter was getting tired. When we got to the end of the belt he just wiped out. I should have been in front of him to help him or catch him….it just happened so fast."

"Man Kenneth…..the guy's eighty years old…..you gotta help him that's why he brought you along." Phil never watered down the truth, but even more so with trusted old friends like Kenneth.

"I know….I know. It was stupid. He's in such great health I just wasn't thinking of him as an old person. I still don't know how bad the injuries are. It looked like a broken arm and maybe crushed his knee cap."

"So, you didn't stay with him?"

"I wanted to…..but, he wouldn't have it. He demanded that I get the book and get it home safely…..and that's what I did. He's in a hospital in London……I came straight here……I haven't seen Barbara and the kids in over a week."

"Okay, so you get the book home safely…..now what. What's in this book anyway?"

Just then they heard a car door slam in the driveway. Frank Hampton marched into the backyard like he belonged there. "Phil, you are a great preacher, but you suck at yard work."

They all spent the next minute laughing. Frank knew how to make a first impression.

"Frank, I want you to meet one of my oldest and best friends. This is Kenneth Macklind. Kenneth, Frank Hampton."

The two shook hands and looked each other in the eye. They smiled and exchanged greetings. Phil told Kenneth that Frank was a Bar owner from St. Louis who had just accepted the Lord and was his newest best friend. Frank sat and joined them in a round of Dr. Peppers.

Kenneth continued his story but kept it impersonal and vague. "So, I was telling Phil about this ancient book that was recently discovered. It turns out to be a journal kept by a knight from the tenth century. He documented his battles, against his king's enemies, and against dragons."

"Dragons?"

"Yeah, he drew wonderful sketches of the dragons he fought. These sketches are extremely detailed. He captured every detail of the creatures; he even colored some of them."

"So, he drew pictures of dragons…..like fantasy drawings or are you saying he actually saw dragons?" Frank cut to the chase.

"I am saying that he actually saw dragons; and here's the best part…..Guess what they called dinosaurs in the tenth century?"

Phil was playing along, "What did they call dinosaurs?"

"They called them dragons."

Lena popped through the back door. "Phil, are you finished with the grass?"

"Hey look who's home," said Kenneth. He got up and went to hug her. "It's good to see you again Lena."

"It's nice to see you too Kenneth. How's Barbara and the kids?"

"They are doing great. I really wish we could all get together sometime soon. I know she would love to see you guys too."

"Well you guys just sit and relax; I'll whip something together for dinner."

"Oh thank you so much Lena, but I really should get going," said Frank.

"Nonsense Frank, you stay," Lena ordered.

"No really you guys have a lot of catching up to do….."

"Don't be silly Frank, besides somebody has got to keep Kenneth company while I finish the lawn. If I don't I'll be hearing about it until next Monday…..give me an hour, okay."

Phil headed back into the battlefield of his front lawn and fired up the mower. The back yard was already done so he was far enough away that it wasn't too unpleasant. Frank decided to stay for dinner and he and Kenneth spent the time getting to know each other. They were both seasoned conversationalists. They found each other fascinating, and were astonished at how much they had learned about each other in such a short time.

An hour and forty minutes later Phil had finally finished the yard work, and Lena had the table set for four. By this time Frank and Kenneth felt like old friends. They enjoyed a wonderful meal, and then headed back outside to the patio to talk some more; the weather was just too nice to stay inside. They talked about fish, and fowl, and deer, and the acorn crop on the oak trees this year; and they talked about the Lord. Frank had been staying up late reading the Bible and much of it he had never heard before. He had many questions…..what was Paul's thorn in the flesh?; what was happening in Acts 2?; Why did God seem more harsh and even cruel in the Old Testament?; Why does Jesus refer to Himself as 'Son of Man'? Phil and Kenneth went back and forth discussing and explaining many things from scripture.

"Here's one for you…" Phil said. "Ninety-nine percent of preachers get this one wrong. It's Ephesians four; twenty six and twenty seven. It says: Be ye angry and sin not; let not the sun go down upon your wrath; neither give place to the devil."

"What do they get wrong about it?" asked Frank.

"Well, what I hear all the time is this idea that it's okay to be mad at someone as long as you make up before bedtime…..it's okay to be mad, just make your peace before the sun goes down. That's not what this means at all. It says: 'Be ye angry and sin not'. That means it is possible to be angry and not sin. It is okay to get mad….at evil. What this says is…..you get mad at evil…..good and mad; and you don't let that anger leave at sundown…..get mad and stay mad."

"Yes, you're exactly right Phil," Kenneth added. "We have to be against evil. I mean it's really easy for me to sit and watch TV and laugh at these sitcoms that make light of immorality in every way. I really have to watch myself on that. Just this last week I came across evil in a form I had never seen before; and sitting here with you guys talking about the Bible and the Lord; I just realized that I am angry."

"What happened?" Frank asked.

Kenneth re-told the whole account. He felt confident bringing Frank in on the story, and he needed help with this.

"So remember that journal I was telling you guys about with the dragon pictures?"

"Yeah," Phil knew what was coming.

"Well it's in the trunk of my car. Want to see it?"

Kenneth brought it inside the house. They all gathered around the journal as Kenneth carefully turned one page, and then another. He narrated as he went the best he could. Phil was smiling from ear to ear; and Frank was serious wanting to know more. Kenneth explained the importance of the book and how much it means to creation science; and how much it destroys the theory of evolution. They all agreed the 'dragons' were clearly dinosaurs.

"What are you going to do with it?" Frank asked.

"I don't know yet. I just know I want to get home to see my family; but I'm not sure I feel safe bringing this book home with me. I need a place for safe keeping that I can trust. I didn't know where else to go."

"Why; of course. Keep it here....or at the church.....or....."

Frank cut in... "I'll keep it."

Kenneth looked at Frank. "Frank I don't know if you know what you're signing up for here.... Peter said his friend Ian was pretty scared of that museum guy. I don't think he'll stop trying to get this back. Two people are already dead because they had this book, and….."

"I'll keep it. I'd be glad to. I have a back room in my house with a gun safe. It's bolted into the studs and set in concrete. It's not totally immovable, but they would have to have some pretty serious equipment to get it out. I'll keep it in there….and you can have it whenever you decide what the next step is. I give you my word…..if someone wants this they will have to walk over my dead body to get it. Now, this is exciting. I feel like I'm on a mission from God."

It was one in the morning. Kenneth turned the key and lifted the handle as he opened the front door and let himself in. He knew how to open the door so it wouldn't squeak. He quietly left his bag in the living room and began his tour of the house. He headed down the hallway. The first bedroom on the left was completely dark. He used his phone as a flashlight. It provided just enough light to see the beds. Mark and Daniel were asleep. The next bedroom had a television on. It was some girl movie….maybe Strawberry Shortcake; he could see three girls fast asleep. Kenneth smiled at Christina and Sarah using Elizabeth's leg for a pillow. "Where's David," he thought. He walked back down the hallway to the couch…..there he was. He fell asleep on the couch watching a movie. Kenneth pulled up his blanket and left him there.

He kicked off his boots and made his way to their bedroom. Barbara heard him coming and got up out of bed. They didn't say anything they just held each other in a long, tight embrace. He kissed her and stroked her hair. "I'm sorry…." He had started to explain but she stopped him with another kiss. "We can talk tomorrow," She said. Her robe was already coming undone. He could see she had nothing on underneath. He kissed her again and lay down with her on the bed. The kissing and touching became more passionate; they made love and then fell asleep in each other's arms.

The next morning came early. By seven-thirty Daniel was practicing his flute, and Christina was asking for pancakes. Kenneth felt great. He was glad to be home. He produced his famous pancakes, and drank two cups of 'not-so-great' home brewed coffee. Over breakfast, he told everyone the story about Sir Richard the Elder of Landolte. They were fascinated, especially the boys, and they ran off from the table to find their box of dinosaurs. Barbara knew there was another aspect to the story that he didn't want to talk about, until the kids were busy elsewhere.

Once alone in the kitchen, the inquisition started. Kenneth was going to try and shield some of his concerns from her, but she was way ahead of him. She began a line of rapid fire questioning that made him dizzy: Who were the men that got killed? Did you know them? Did they know you? What about the police? What happened to Peter? Did they have anything to do with him getting hurt? What if they saw you with Peter? Where is the journal now? Can they find us? How will we be kept safe?

These were some of the very questions bouncing around in Kenneth's head also. He only had answers for some of them; but he fielded each question as it came and did his level headed best to help Barbara feel at ease. However, it didn't really work, she was nervous about the whole situation. Kenneth managed to find a stopping point when two of the boys came running through the kitchen; and then mentioned a trip to the mall to change the subject.

He loaded the whole family into the van and they spent the day at the mall. They needed a family outing; just spending time together was very therapeutic. Every time the girls went in a shop the boys would find a bench to sit and wait for them. They couldn't get enough of Sir Richard. The boys asked a hundred questions, and wanted to know all about the dragons. Kenneth told them of knights in shining armor, and horseback jousting, castles, caves, and dragons. It really was an awesome story. The boys hung on every word.

"What about Peter?" asked Barbara as they held hands walking past the food court.

"I should call the hospital…..what time is it now in London?"

"Well, it's two-thirty here….that makes it eight-thirty there," Barbara was on the ball.

"Yeah I should call. Do you mind?"

"No, are you kidding?"

Kenneth got a piece of paper out of his wallet. On it he had scratched the phone number of the hospital where Peter was taken. One of the medics gave him the number as they were driving away.

He dialed. "Yes hello, I am calling to check on the condition of a patient there…."

A woman with a thick British accent took the call. Kenneth had trouble understanding her and had to repeat himself several times. Finally he asked for Peter Stroudlin and spelled the name.

Barbara asked, "What's the matter?"

"No it's alright. I just couldn't understand her at first. I think she's connecting me to his room." Still on hold Kenneth said, "I think she called me ducky." They were both smiling, "It's ringing. Hello, Peter?"

"Yes, Kenneth…..is that you?"

"Yes, it's Kenneth. How are you doing Peter?"

"I've been better. But more importantly how did things go for you?"

"Peter, I just want you to know everything is fine. I have the…."

"Wait, wait! Don't say anything regarding your location or the precious package."

"Peter, what do you mean?"

"Think about it, you know what I mean. Let's just wait and catch up on that when I get out of here."

"Okay, I see what you mean." This would have seemed overboard to Kenneth, but in light of what had happened he agreed with the extra precaution. "Peter, when do you think that will be?"

"Well I broke my wrist, they were right about that, but that didn't hurt at all compared to my knee. My knee cap was fractured in three pieces and one of the chips slid out of place. They had to do surgery to get it back in the right place. They did that right away yesterday, and I am in recovery. I tried to get up to go to the bathroom this afternoon and I couldn't make it without help. I will probably be here a few more days until they move me to rehab."

"Well Peter, I know you'll be fine in no time. Don't worry about a thing, everything is smooth and calm here. You take it easy and get that knee better; and Peter, call anytime….I mean anytime if you need anything."

"I will Kenneth, thank you so much…..God bless you."

"Okay Peter, good bye." He slipped the phone back into his pocket.

"How did he sound?" Barbara asked.

"He sounded fine. He had surgery on his knee yesterday. He sounded great for an eighty year old man that just had surgery."

"He didn't want you to say anything about the journal, huh?"

"No, I think he is afraid someone could be listening."

"This is pretty scary stuff Kenneth, what do you think we should do?"

Kenneth just pulled her in close with his arm around her back, "Don't worry honey." He didn't have the answer.

The Macklinds made their way around the entire mall….twice. Barbara actually counted a trip to the mall as 'shopping'; and Kenneth just suggested the mall when he couldn't come up with any better ideas. Christina needed new crocs; Elizabeth needed a new dress for her birthday party next week; Barbara needed a new belted cardigan for fall; the boys all needed a haircut…...Kenneth didn't try to know all of this, he was just along for the ride.

When all of the items on Barbara's list had been secured, she declared the trip to the mall a success. Six hours and several hundred dollars later, the Macklinds headed for home. On the drive home, Barbara revealed an idea that she had had while shopping. It seems she has her best ideas while shopping.

"I was thinking…..who is the rightful owner of the journal?" She asked.

"I guess it belongs to Alexander Svec, who is dead; or Ian Burbrey, who is also dead; or the museum in Prague…...I have no idea how it got to Prague. I know nothing of the history of this journal prior to Alexander Svec. Why?"

"Well I think you should have the journal photographed…..you know like professionally photographed and re-created like art galleries do; and then you could keep a copy of it, and then give it back to whoever wants it so bad so they stop killing people over it."

"Actually, that's a great idea."

"Nobody even needs to know you copied it."

"Well at least not right away, until things die down a bit, but this information deserves to be out there. It needs to be brought into the light."

The third floor at Southall Hospital was clear and quiet. There were 40 rooms in the surgical recovery wing and they were only half full. The floor was white, the walls were white and the ceilings were white…..even the nurses wore all white. Peter Stroudlin was in room 316. His nurses loved him, although so far he had been a pretty tough patient. He was complaining quite a lot about their wanting him to get up on his feet so soon after surgery. He would rather have rested a week or two before trying to put any weight on it. But, they had him up four times a day…..just for a few minutes each. His first day of intensive physical therapy was due to begin in the morning. He was resting comfortably now it was 10:30 and he was watching the news on television.

"Now dear, you don't stay up watching the tele all night.....you need your sleep. We have a big day tomorrow, yes?" said his nurse. She had just poked her head in the room as she was walking by. "I'm due to get off at eleven. Your new nurse for overnight is named Elaine. I'll see you tomorrow. Ring if you need anything."

"Oh I will. Thank you so much Jill." Even though he was in tremendous pain, Peter had enjoyed spending the day with his nurse Jill. He was her favorite patient and she spent all of her free time and lunch hour in Peter's room talking and keeping him company. Peter was ready for a good night sleep. He was not in much pain at the moment and he was getting sleepy. He hadn't had much sleep at all for two nights in a row, and he finally felt relaxed enough to rest.

Jill was at the nurse's station checking her e-mail and changing her shoes. She was getting ready to go home after a twelve hour shift when Elaine walked in. "Am I glad to see you," Jill said.

"What, it looks pretty slow around here," Elaine responded.

"I know it's just been one of those days. I'm ready for a nice hot bath." Their small talk continued for five or ten minutes; they had managed to make it to eleven o'clock. "I'm off then; see you tomorrow night," Jill said as she slung her purse over her shoulder and turned to go.

Elaine followed right behind, "Oh Jill, one more thing....what's the story with the man in 316? Isn't it a little late for visitors?"

"Visitors?" Jill seemed surprised. "I was just in there half an hour ago and there weren't any visitors. Besides he doesn't know anyone here…..he's visiting from America. The poor dear is all alone. That's why I spent so much time with him today. He reminds me of my Father."

"Well, a man came out of his room…..just when I was walking in a few minutes ago," said Elaine.

I'm walking down that way on my way out anyway….come on, I'll introduce you. He is such a sweetheart. I meant to check in on him one more time before I left anyway," said Jill. They walked down the hall together. The door to room 316 was ajar. "That's funny, I'm sure I closed that half an hour ago." Jill slowly peeked in the room; she walked over to Peter's bed, Elaine accompanied her. "Oh what a dear….he's finally fallen asleep," Jill said as she softly patted his arm. "Oh Dear God," Jill shouted as she reached up and pushed the emergency button. She fingered his wrist in search of a pulse as she bent over and put her face close to his mouth. He wasn't breathing.

Within seconds more nurses arrived on the scene. They began CPR and rescue breathing. Several doctors from the fourth floor rushed in. The medical equipment they carted in filled the room. The doctor ripped open Peter's hospital gown to expose his chest. He prepared two metallic paddles with gel and then yelled "Clear". The manual external defibrillator snapped and buzzed. Peter's chest rose and his body stiffly lifted off the bed, and then it came back down limp again. He did it again….. "Clear!" The doctor continued….. "Come on man….come on." He tried pounding, to no avail. Ten minutes went by quickly; then twenty; then thirty.

The other doctor put his hand on the first doctor's shoulder, "I think that's all we can do….."

Jill was crying. She couldn't imagine what could have happened. He seemed so full of life. At eleven thirty-eight PM, in room 316 of Southall Hospital in West London……Peter Stroudlin was gone.

It was almost noon, and the sun couldn't make up its mind. It was in and out behind thick dark clouds. There was a chance of rain and it was beginning to look promising.

Just behind the lake on the downhill side of the dam, three deer were nibbling on clover. They never even heard the shutter of Frank's game trail camera that was strapped to an oak tree just fifteen feet away.

Frank sat on his porch watching a grill full of burgers brown over the flames. Matt and Ty were due anytime. They had called the night before and left a message on the machine that they were coming to visit. So far it was a pretty nice day; Frank was hoping the rain would hold off so they could eat lunch outside on the porch.

Frank's place was actually a fairly nice home. Although he called it a cabin, that was only part true. It was originally built as a one room log cabin. It was a hunting cabin erected back in 1969. But, through the years each of its owners added on to it. The front section of the house that encompasses the porch and the front door was actually the only portion of the house that displays log construction. The rest of the L-shaped home was covered with tan vinyl siding. Frank had no plans to add on any more, it was plenty big enough for him.

Just then the Nomad cruised into the driveway. Frank laughed at Ty leaning way back in the passenger seat; he appeared to be sleeping. "What do you get in that thing, about twelve miles to the gallon?" Frank asked Matt as he got out and slammed the driver's side door.

"I don't even add it up…..I don't want to know," said Matt.

"Oh sleeping beauty is with you…."

"Just resting my eyes…..there wasn't anything to look at past Wentzville," Ty joked. "Man, your way out in the flipping sticks." Ty was a city boy; and he would just as soon stay in the city near the comforts of his high rise condo.

Ty and Matt advanced up the driveway and onto the front porch. Ty sat down on the porch swing. Matt hugged Frank and said, "Man, do you even know how to cook anything besides hamburgers?"

"Oh listen to you complaining…..you know my burgers are the best you've ever tasted, don't even deny it."

"Yeah, I guess you're right," Laughed Matt. "Are they done, I'm starving."

They had a nice lunch, which consisted of Frank's secret recipe cheeseburgers and iced tea. Matt complained about Frank not having beer on hand. While they were eating they gave Frank an update on how things were going at Gildersleeves.

"I'll tell you Frank, I had no idea how much work it is to run a bar," Matt admitted.

Frank replied, "Only successful bars…..it ain't that much work to run an empty one. I know; I've seen it both ways. That tells me you're doing something right."

Ty spoke up…. "It's only been one week without you Frank, nothing's changed. But let me tell you something… young Matty here has really stepped up to the plate. He hasn't beat the crap out of anybody since you left yet either."

"Oh, don't even remind me of that," said Frank.

"Did we tell you about the channel six news feature? They are doing this series on St. Louis hot spots and they want to do an episode about Gildersleeves."

"Hey, that is great. Not that you need the exposure, but free advertisement never hurts. When are they doing it?"

Ty said, "I don't know, next week or the week after. Matt's waiting on a call from Sharon Shaefer."

"Hey, Sharon Shaefer? I love Sharon Shaefer. She's been the channel six news anchor for fifteen years. I never watched another channel, all because of her," said Frank.

"Well she was in the bar twice last week. I guess she's scoping the place out."

Matt continued, "Yeah, and Chuck Berry too. I think he likes her."

"Hey, it's always a good thing to have Chuck in the place. A legend like that; it's just good for business."

Frank was happy that things were going so good for them, although he was certain he didn't miss it at all. After just one week of peace and quiet, he wanted nothing to do with that old life anymore.

After lunch Frank said, "hey you guys gotta see this. Come on over here to the computer."

In corner of the living room, Frank had his office. It didn't seem like the right place for it but he wanted to keep the spare bedrooms for guests; and the only other room that would work was the small room in the back with the gun safe. So he used the living room. They pulled up chairs around Franks desktop PC to see what he had to show them.

"What is it that a raccoon?" asked Matt.

"Yeah, he's just a baby isn't he cute?" Frank was proud of his wildlife.

"What are you going around the woods stalking animals so you can get their pictures?" It didn't make sense to Ty.

"No, I'm not going around stalking animals; are you kidding me? I put trail cameras around the whole property. I've got one behind the dam….so far that's the best one. Then there's one to the west of the driveway; one down by the cedar field…..I did see a nice buck on that one. There's one over by the creek; one straight back by the fence; and one behind the cabin."

"Wow, do you sit and think of ways to waste time….." Ty said. He couldn't think of anything more boring than looking at pictures of pesky little animals.

"I think it's cool. Let's see the deer." Matt showed some interest.

Frank went through a stack of SD cards with hundreds of pictures. Ty seemed a little more interested when he saw the bobcat. Matt appreciated Frank's new hobby. After an hour or so of oohs and aahs, Frank let them off the hook and shut down the computer.

"You guys want to grab a pole and go down to the lake and catch a nice largemouth bass?"

"Actually, we really should start heading back to St. Louis." said Matt.

"Yeah, it ain't the 'city that never sleeps' but it's a little livelier than Knob Ridge." Ty said as he got up and headed for the door.

"Alright," Frank said. "There was one more thing I wanted to tell you too before you go. Get ready for this one…..I don't know how either one of you will take this. I got saved last Saturday night."

"Saved, saved from what," Ty asked.

"I mean I got born again. I found Jesus."

Matt just stood there in silence and Ty almost fell over laughing.

"Well I must say that's not how I pictured you'd respond," Frank said.

"No, no Frank I understand, I think that's great," Matt said. "I dated a girl that was Methodist for about six months. Her whole family was born again and they were pretty cool to hang around."

Ty collected himself. "Frank, now I've heard everything. A born again bar owner."

"Well, I ain't a bar owner anymore. The old Frank is dead. I am a new creature."

"Alright Frank," Ty said. That's cool…..you're entitled to your religious preference or whatever, this Jesus stuff…..it's just not for me, that's all. Come on Matt we better get going."

"Hey Frank, I do think it's great. Good for you. You take care and we'll talk soon. We'll let you know how the channel six thing goes." Matt gave his uncle a hug and turned to go.

Ty said, "Frank it's great to see you. We miss you in the bar that's all." Ty also gave a hug and then jumped in the Nomad.

The sun shined through the south facing kitchen window of the Macklind home. Kenneth and Barbara sat at the corner breakfast table talking. Kenneth could see the kids in the backyard; and he could see the dog chasing them. They were all laughing and running; even the dog.

He was relieved to get home and see that everything was okay. However, now that he had verified his family's safety, his thoughts had turned back to Peter and the journal. He was eager to get the journal photographed and catalogued. It turned out that Frank had a friend in St. Louis who knew a guy who owned his own photography studio. Frank said the guy would do the work for free and wouldn't ask any questions.

Kenneth figured even if something happened to the book, he would still have the photographs to teach from. It had to be done; in fact he had an appointment with this photo-journalist the following morning.

"Kenneth, are you listening to me?" Barbara asked.

"Oh, yeah, what? Sorry Barb….my mind just drifted there for a second." Kenneth just realized she had been talking for at least ten minutes and he hadn't heard a word.

Just then the phone in his pocket began to vibrate. "Saved by the bell…" Kenneth thought to himself. "Oh, it's an

English area code….It must be Peter." He said as he answered the phone.

"Hello, is this Mr. Kenneth Macklind?" said the British voice on the phone.

"Yes, this is Kenneth."

"Hello sir. This is Diana Wellington. I am the chief patient liaison at Southhall Hospital in London, England."

"Yes, hello. My good friend Peter Stroudlin is with you there. How is he?"

"Yes, Mr. Macklind that is why I am calling. Mr. Stroudlin listed you as his primary contact. I got your name and telephone number from his emergency contact list."

Kenneth knew this wasn't good. He closed his eyes and grabbed Barbara's hand as he braced himself for the news.

"Sir, I'm afraid I have some very bad news. Mr. Peter Stroudlin died last night. He passed away of an apparent heart attack. He was pronounced dead at eleven-thirty eight PM; after a team of our best doctors were unsuccessful in their attempt to revive him. I am sorry."

Kenneth squeezed Barbara's hand. He didn't know what to say. He had to concentrate just to remember to breath.

"Sir; I know how shocking this terrible news must be."

"Yes, it certainly is……"

"Mr. Macklind…..we do need to notify his next of kin. The U.S. State department has already been notified…..this being an international issue. If you could help us with further contact information…..do you know any close relatives of Mr. Stroudlin's?"

Kenneth took a deep breath, as he exhaled he looked up and tried to be calm. Barbara moved in closer. "No, his wife passed away years ago; and they never had any kids. I don't know about brothers or sisters…..he never spoke of any. I do know the President of his foundation…..James Boswell; I'll get you his number. All of his assets are run through the foundation. Mr. Boswell should be the one you contact."

Kenneth pulled up the number on his laptop. He gave the information to the patient liaison and that was it; a courteous but quick telephone call in a very business-like manner. With nothing else to say he hung up the phone.

He looked at Barbara in amazement, "I don't know what to say."

"Honey, he was eighty years old."

"Seventy-nine; and he was in great shape."

"Sometimes a fall like that is all it takes. Remember Grandma, after her fall she went downhill fast."

Kenneth just sat there looking out the kitchen window for awhile. So much had happened so fast.

The next morning Kenneth flew to St. Louis. He rented a car and punched the address of the studio into the GPS. Now behind the wheel of a shiny blue Mazda 3, he made his way out of Lambert Field and headed downtown.

Still miles away, he could see the arch in the distance. "The kids would like that," he thought to himself. "We should come back and go up in that someday." He drove past downtown on highway 70, and headed south on 44. The studio was ahead, just off the highway on Gravois Avenue. Kenneth pulled up in front of the studio. His car was the only one in the lot.

Now he was a little nervous. He trusted Phil and Frank to bring the journal and meet him here at the photographer's studio; but he would rather have done it himself. He checked his watch…..he was fifteen minutes early.

A new navy blue Chevy Suburban pulled up next to Kenneth. A bouncy long-haired guy got out and came over to the window of his rental car. "Hey, you Kenneth?" He said.

"Yes, Kenneth Macklind," he extended his hand for a greeting.

The long-haired guy shook his hand firmly, "Hi Kenneth, I'm Ty. I'm a friend of Frank's. They should be here any minute."

Just another car entered the lot. "Hey here's Dave," Ty shouted, as if to say…..see, I told you they'd be here any minute. Dave was the photographer. He was a friend of Ty's from the bar. He had shot Ty several times. It was his photograph of Ty that made the cover of the Riverfront Times.

Right behind Dave as if on cue, was Phil and Frank. "Alright, Let's get this inside…..precious cargo here." Frank was carrying the gray metal box which contained the journal.

Dave unlocked the front door and let them in. "It's nice to meet everyone. I am Dave….and it is my pleasure to be helping you with this project today. I have us all set up in here." He led them into the back room where there was a large expensive looking camera on a boom stand and a well lit table.

"Oh this will be great," said Kenneth. He was very impressed. It was a very professional studio the lighting and equipment looked like it was very high end.

Dave continued, "Let's set the book up here…..how delicate is it?"

"Very," said Kenneth.

"Okay, the book will sit here." Dave focused the camera and took a few test shots. He checked the light meter and then changed some settings on his computer. "Alright, because it's so delicate I would like for you, Kenneth, to do the page turning. We'll just go slow and steady, one page at a time."

"Sounds great," said Kenneth. "Let's get going." Just then Kenneth's phone rang. He checked the incoming number and saw that it was from England. "I'm sorry guys, I have to take this….Phil can you turn the pages. Just be very careful with them."

"No problem, I've turned a few pages in my day," said Phil.

"Thanks Phil." Kenneth stepped outside. "Hello."

"Yes, hello…..is this Kenneth Macklind?"

"Yes it is…"

"Hi, you don't know me…...my name is Jill Wright. I hope you don't mind….I just felt like there is something you should know about Mr. Stroudlin."

"What? How did you know Peter?" Kenneth asked.

"I was his nurse at the hospital. I spent several days with him; and since I knew he was all alone I spent extra time with him….we sort of hit it off. We talked a lot in the two days I spent with him. He told me about you, and how you were with him when he fell, and how he sent you back to the States with some important work."

"Yeah, what a mistake….I knew I shouldn't have left him," lamented Kenneth.

"Well sir, I had to do some snooping to find your phone number. I had to talk to you….Mr. Stroudlin mentioned you were all he had left, and the only person he knew he could trust. Actually, I would most likely get in a lot of trouble if my boss found out I called you about this."

"What is it Ms. Wright?"

"Well.....Let me try to explain. I was with him the night he died; I was with him up until about thirty minutes before it happened. It was shift change time.....about eleven o'clock. The overnight nurse.....Elaine was just coming in and we sat and talked a few minutes before it was time for me to leave. I was just telling her what a wonderful man Mr. Stroudlin was and she said something that alarmed me. She said that it was strange for him to have a visitor so late."

Following along Kenneth said, "Hmmm, a visitor?"

"Yeah, so I said I was just in there thirty minutes ago and he didn't have any visitors....and I explained that he was an American visiting England all alone."

"So, do you think it was just a doctor that she didn't recognize?"

"No. Elaine is a Supervising RN. She has been there for like twenty years. There are no doctors that she doesn't recognize. It was strange though.....after all the commotion of trying to revive Mr. Stroudlin.....Elaine and I sat and talked for awhile. I just didn't want to go home. As she replayed the scene in her mind she became very frightened. She said the man that she saw coming out of Mr. Stroudlin's room was kind of creepy."

"How so..."

"He was smiling…..she said he was smiling at her in a very creepy way. He didn't say anything to her he just smiled and as he continued down the hall, Elaine said she heard him laughing."

"Oughh, that is creepy. Was this information given to the police?" asked Kenneth.

"Oh yeah, that's another thing….Elaine did report this to the Hospital administrator, and to the police. She got nowhere….they wouldn't even acknowledge the possibility of foul play of any kind. And this morning she and I were both called separately into the Administrator's office and we were told that it would be best if we didn't make anything out of this. Elaine had been pressing the issue a bit….she was told to drop it immediately."

"So this Elaine, she sees a creepy guy coming out of Peter's room at eleven o'clock at night and the hospital administrator tells her to drop it?"

"Yes, we were both told to drop it. Actually, to finish the story…..She saw the creepy guy coming out of the room at about ten forty-five PM. We both went to check on him as I was leaving about five after eleven. That's when I found him…..with no pulse and not breathing."

"Will there be an autopsy done?"

"No. At that age….the doctor on the scene pronounced the cause of death to be natural…..a heart attack."

"He comes out of Peter's room at ten forty-five; and Peter's found dead twenty minutes later. This is crazy. Who do I call to demand some action over there?"

"Well if you do that you will get me in a lot of trouble. But you know that....so what, I don't really care. This is outrageous. I don't really know who to tell you to call though. I will look into it for you though."

"Well Ms. Wright...."

"Please call me Jill."

Okay, Jill. I am so shocked by this I really don't know what to say. I am grateful for your help. I hope I can call you again when I've had time to process this, or if I have any more questions."

"Absolutely. Mr. Stroudlin was a special man. It didn't take me long to see that. I would love to help you in any way that I can. Oh! One more thing; the creepy man that came out of his room.....he had a long silver ponytail."

"Ponytail?"

"That's what Elaine said.....his hair was about half way down his back.....a long silvery-white ponytail."

Kenneth sighed and said, "Okay Jill, I appreciate the call. Thank you."

Kenneth walked back inside the studio and sat down on staring at a point in space somewhere near the floor. The photo shoot was going well they were about halfway done already. Phil and the photographer were busy working; Ty and Phil noticed that something was wrong with Kenneth.

"Hey there Kenneth, what's wrong buddy?" Ty Asked.

"Well, last night I found out that Peter died…..now I just got a call from his nurse at the hospital that is implying that he was murdered."

They stood in silence for a moment…..nobody knew quite what to say. Then Frank tackled the eight hundred pound gorilla in the room. "Do you mean to tell me that somebody out there wants this book so badly that their killing everyone in their way until they find it?"

Kenneth stood up and looked Frank right in the eye, "Yeah, that's exactly what I mean."

"Who?" Frank asked.

"I don't know…..the museum; the BBC; the NSA; area fifty-one; Satan; Illuminati….I don't know!," admitted Kenneth.

Frank Hampton fired right back, "Well boys…..I think it's high time we found out."

The Macklind home was on the sunny side of the street. It was a three thousand square foot, straight across ranch from the early 1960's. They don't build houses like it anymore; they take up two much land. Nowadays, they can cram twice as much house on a lot half the size. But, this quiet Houston suburb was picture perfect.

Kenneth's landscaping was very nicely done. He enjoyed the yard work, but unlike Pastor Phil, he really did take it quite seriously. Barbara was the designer. Kenneth just organized the troops to make the designs come to life. With six kids that needed a way to earn their allowance, landscaping was the perfect family activity. The Macklinds had been recipients of best the landscaping award on the block for three years running.

Kenneth pulled into the driveway and got out of the car. He stopped to look at the latest addition to the front yard; a beautiful pacific yew; he even took the extra step of lighting it. Kenneth adjusted the electrical wiring on the lighting unit. He thought it was showing just a bit too much.

As Kenneth was fiddling with the new tree light, Mark and Daniel noticed Dad was home and came out to see him. "Dad," they yelled.

"Hey guys; told you I wouldn't be gone long this time. How is everything going?"

"Okay. Did Elizabeth break the light? She ran over it on her bike," Mark said proudly.

"Mark, no….it's not broken....I was just adjusting the wire," said Kenneth. "Let's go inside and have a family meeting."

Kenneth had already planned his speech. He was going to insist that Barbara and the kids go and stay with her Mom and Dad in San Diego for a week or so. He didn't want to scare them, but he just felt that until this issue was resolved, they would be better off away from him.

The boys ran into the house alarming everyone….. "family meeting, family meeting……"

Barbara came out into the living room, "What's going on?"

"Well, I mentioned to the boys that I thought we should have a short family meeting and they ran off screaming like crazy," Kenneth was past the point of no return now. "Sit down, sit down everyone."

He knew he should have talked to Barbara first privately, but here they were…..family meeting. Kenneth kept it vague and positive, and the kids all unanimously agreed that trip to California was a fantastic idea. Barbara reluctantly agreed, and Kenneth immediately began helping them pack for the trip.

It was a big job. Six kids; clean clothes; bathroom stuff; school books and laptop computers…..and then there was Barbara. She had four bags just for herself. By the end of the afternoon, they were packed and ready to go.

Kenneth was sure it was a good idea. The kids were excited, and Barbara was looking forward to seeing her parents. Kenneth knew her dad had a shotgun, somehow he was glad about that.

"Okay, so what are you going to be doing? We never covered that," Barbara wanted to know.

"The truth is, I don't know yet. As soon as you and the kids leave, I'm going to Phil's to figure this out," Kenneth explained.

Goodbyes were said; everybody got a hug and a kiss from daddy and off they went. "What an awesome woman," he thought to himself. "Taking six kids on a twenty hour drive in an SUV; not many women would attempt that." He knew they would be fine.

Chapter 9

Alden Harlock sat in the den of his dark English mansion. He filled his glass from an old green glass bottle. The cork was dark with age, and the label was scratched and peeling away at the corners. It simply said "Mun Schweiz" bitters….1857. The strongly fragrant, highly alcoholic drink was a favorite of his. Like everything else in his life; if he liked it, he owned it. Harlock was so fond of these rare vintage bitters he bought the entire stock from a private cellar in Venezuela. He now owned every bottle on the planet.

He hadn't been to the museum in days; and he hadn't planned on going back until he recovered that journal. The only reason he ever pursued the curator position was to increase his access to artifacts. He ran an interesting museum; but his private collection was the real treasure.

The lower level of the Harlock mansion was a secret stockpile of ancient religious artifacts. No one had ever seen it, except a handful of close friends and the contractors that were hired to install the displays. However, fame was not what Harlock wanted.

The collection included….. Many Babylonian inscriptions from the period of Nebuchadnezzar; several Mesopotamian amulets; several Egyptian canopic jars; and the fully mummified body of an Egyptian Pharaoh. There was much gold, much grandeur, and much magnificence; but Alden did not collect these things for their worldly value. His ancestor Charles Herod Harlock had started the collection and passed it along with the house; with the stipulation that the recipient be "like-minded".

Alden's father was not "like-minded" and after a long legal battle and several years of courtroom proceedings; it was determined that the estate could be withheld from his inheritance. It was after his father's death that Alden stepped up and claimed the estate from his Uncle. His father's brother had held the position of executor of the estate; and Alden met the stipulation that his father could not. Alden Harlock held a cross upside-down, he slammed it down on a stone table breaking the arms of the cross as he renounced Christ and glorified Satan. With this display he proved himself a worthy inheritor of the property.

His interest in the journal was not because of its monetary value, nor was it because of its historical significance. His interest in the journal of Sir Richard the Elder of Landolte was purely personal. It contained truth that he did not want to see the light of day. It damaged the validity and the believability of Satan's greatest lie, evolution.

"Hello," Alden said quietly as he picked up the ringing phone. It was his assistant/bodyguard/driver Adelph.

"Yes, Mr. Harlock…..it's me. Shall I come by and pick you up this evening?" said Adelph.

"No, I will need you in the morning. Be ready to accompany me on a trip to the United States. I have your passport and paperwork in order."

"Yes Sir, where are we going?"

"Houston. That idiot that was with Stroudlin at the airport…..we need to pay him a visit. Be here at seven. We will go straight to the airport. Oh, and Adelph….this will most certainly be an aggressive mission."

"Yes Sir, I'll see you then Sir."

Adelph was Alden's thug. He was six feet six and one half inches of rock solid muscle. He would do anything Harlock demanded. He wasn't the slightest bit moved by shooting Ian Burbrey and at the time....he didn't even really know the reason.

Alden held up his glass and tilted his head back. He studied the color of his bitters as the light from the fireplace shone through them. He finished the glass and threw it into the fire. The glass shattered and the fire boiled to a new height. He spent the rest of the evening studying maps of Houston, and anticipating the next move after that. It was a chess game, and he expected to win.

Mike Rimmey

<u>Chapter 10</u>

Frank Hampton had been retired for well over a week now. He hadn't even gotten the chance to get boring. He was on a mission. He had been on the phone all morning, calling in favors from his many friends in the St. Louis Police Department. He also knew a guy in the St. Louis FBI office, and had a message in with him as well.

So far they were all telling him the same thing….. it's pretty hard to get an international investigation started. But, he had an hour before Phil and Kenneth were due to be there so he figured he could make a few more calls. He also wanted to make his rounds and check his cameras before they got there.

Sitting at his desk in the living room, he dialed the phone… "Hey Bob, this is Frank Hampton……; Oh fine, how have you been?.....; Yeah, I'm retired now, I have Matt running the place…..; Yeah he's doing a great job, you know Matt…..; Yeah Ty's still there….; Well listen the reason I'm calling is; I need a little advice….; I know this guy who died in the hospital in England; and I am quite certain he was murdered…..; No, I'm totally serious….."

Phil Balasky was knocking at the door. Frank grabbed his cup of coffee and let him in. "Hi Phil have a seat, you want a cup of coffee?"

"Yeah sure," Phil sat on the couch. "What do you think about all of this Frank?"

Frank brought Phil's coffee, "Well I'll tell you I have a lot of contacts in St. Louis, you know I met a lot of cops over the years. I know a couple of lawyers, and a judge too. They all think I'm nuts."

"What do you mean?"

"I've been on the phone all morning, you know explaining the situation. It's like if you get killed in another country nobody wants to touch it. The judge just hung up on me."

"Yeah, it's a touchy situation, I really don't know what we can do but, I just want to help any way I can."

"I just don't like people messing with friends of mine. I like Kenneth, I mean he's not really a friend of mine, but he's a friend of yours and that's close enough."

"Well Frank, I'm sure glad to hear that; and I know Kenneth would be too."

"Tell me something Phil, what am I missing here? I mean what is so important about this book that we're all ready to stick our necks out for it? Yeah, it's a cool old book, I mean the pictures of dragons are great and I can see how the connection can be made between dragons and dinosaurs, but so what?"

"Frank, it all goes back to the authority of scripture. Kenneth can explain this much better....that is what he does for a living, but it's all about Genesis. You see if you're not Christian then you probably believe in evolution, that's a given. But, today there are millions of Christian believers who try to incorporate evolution into their theology. They say that God created the world in the beginning, and then He used evolution to bring about the changes over time to get to where we are today."

"Yeah, I've heard that argument, what's wrong with that?"

"Well, for one thing it casts doubt on God's word. Look, in the book of Genesis, God tells us that He created Adam on the sixth day. He said that He created him from the dust of the earth, and then He breathed life into him. Now, if evolution is true, then Adam was conceived in the womb of his mother, who must have been a transitional hominid species, and Adam contained the genetic information because of a mutation or something that made him human.

Many Christians today talk about the book of Genesis being a beautifully written book of poetic metaphors and wonderful allegories. But, there is no metaphoric connection between the two. In evolution Adam had to have a non-human mother and father….he was the first human. But in creation God made him from the dust of the ground. He just made him…..on the sixth day.

By the way….the Hebrew word for day used in Genesis 1 and 2 is yom. Yom can mean periods of time other than a day, but in this case it indicates an evening and a morning…..it can only mean a literal twenty-four hour day.

The problem is when Christians slide on this….people say hey, no big deal what's the harm. Well, the harm is when you slide on creation then maybe there will be doubts about the flood, and Noah's ark; or the Ten Commandments; or the prophecies about Jesus. Well, we know it said this but, what did that really mean. And then the next thing you know you're in the New Testament, with doubts about Jesus dying on the cross, or His resurrection. We can't slide on scripture Frank, not even a little bit. The authority of scripture is everything.

Creation is not just an apologetic issue Frank, it is the apologetic issue. How you view your origin, will determine how you live your life. For example, if you see yourself as a product of an accident, without a purpose, without any direction, without any design, with no God, then after you die you're worm food. You push up daisies and it's over. So why do the right thing, why live with any standards at all? Why not just get what you can, can what you get and sit on the can?

But, if you see yourself as a creation of the one and only true and almighty God; now that's a different story. Your life has a purpose; your life has a design. God planned you with a wonderful purpose in mind. He knew you before you were even in your mother's womb. He made a way for you to be with Him for all eternity. Yeah, now that's a different story."

"That is a different story. That's for sure," Frank was glad he finally saw the light.

"Knock, knock, anybody home?" It was Kenneth. He had just arrived, in yet another rental car, and stood at the open window looking in.

"Hey Kenneth, come on in," said Frank.

"We were just going over greatest battle between good and evil the world has ever seen; the battle for creation."

"Yeah we're right in the middle of that one all right," Kenneth said. "So what do you think we should do next?"

"I think we should find out who killed these friends of yours and bring them down," Frank said.

"That might not be so easy."

Frank said, "Tell me about it. I've been on the phone all morning talking to friends of mine who are cops, FBI agents, lawyers, judges....I got nowhere."

"Yeah the judge hung up on him," Phil added.

"Oh before I forget again.....there's something important I forgot to tell you guys. I was so upset by the phone call from Jill, Peter's nurse that I totally forgot the most interesting thing. She said the head nurse was coming in for her shift and she saw a guy come out of Peter's room. This was like eleven o'clock at night.....way past visiting hours. She said the guy was smiling and laughing. Peter was found dead like twenty minutes later. Anyway this guy had a long silvery-gray ponytail."

"Ponytail....?"

Yeah, you know that can be a distinguishing characteristic. There aren't too many guys walking around with a long silvery-gray ponytail."

"Yeah thank God for that. I hate ponytails on guys. Frank said. "I mean Ty has pretty long hair and I give him trouble about that sometimes but he knows I better not ever see him with a ponytail."

Phil and Kenneth laughed. If nothing else, Frank was good for that.

They had all pictured the man with the silver ponytail. And each one was thinking the same thing. Who was it? Could

Peter really have been murdered over this journal? What if he came after them?

Frank was the only one who wasn't even a little scared. He came from a different background. Some English fellow with a ponytail didn't scare him. But Kenneth and Phil were a different story. Kenneth worried for his family, and Phil was somehow excited by the thrill of the unknown. For this unlikely team the future was uncertain and the anticipation was so thick you could almost see it.

"Well I've decided that I'm going to publish the finding of the journal," said Kenneth. "I've got the pictures as a back-up, so if it gets taken away from me.....so what. I'm going to put it all over my website, write a book about it, and speak about it every chance I get."

Phil perked up, "Kenneth that is exactly right. That is exactly what you must do. Satan would love to keep this journal secret forever. You can't let that happen."

"Thank you guys....for everything. Phil, Frank, I really mean it....thank you. I couldn't have done this without you both; and I'm not finished with you yet.....I'm going to need your help."

Kenneth's heart skipped a beat as his phone rang. Somehow he knew it wouldn't be good news. It was the Houston Police Department "Hello, Mr. Macklind? This is Detective Brogan. We are here at your home....there has been a break-in."

"What!" Kenneth didn't know what else to say.

"Yes sir….I'm here with your neighbor Bill Reyes. He tells me you are out of town."

"Yes, I'm in Missouri."

"Okay sir what about the rest of your family?"

"My family is out of town also…..how bad is the damage?"

"Well sir the interior has been tossed around quite a bit. It looks like they were looking for something."

"Who was….did you catch them?"

"Sir that will all be in the official report….I can't discuss any more with you now."

"Wait a minute….what do you mean you can't discuss it? That's my house you're standing in, now you tell me what's going on."

There was a pause. Detective Brogan walked out to his car and made sure nobody was listening. "Alright, here's the deal. Your neighbor called 9-1-1, and Houston PD arrived and caught two perpetrators hot in the act."

"Okay, now that's what I wanted to hear," Kenneth said.

"Wait a minute Mr. Macklind. The story has a bit of a twist to it. HPD brought in the two suspects for questioning, and before they could be arrested, they produced some pretty impressive State Department paperwork."

"Paperwork! What was it a get out of jail free card?"

"Actually, yeah.....even better than that. They have the highest form of diplomatic immunity. We can't even write them a traffic ticket. These guys are completely untouchable. The Chief says in thirty years he's never seen anything like this. My point in telling you all of this is.....I don't know what you have...but they want it. You better be careful."

Kenneth was shocked, "Are you saying that these people have a license to hunt me down and steal whatever they want?"

"Yeah Mr. Macklind, that's pretty much what I'm saying."

"Well, that didn't go as smoothly as I had hoped," said Alden as Adelph was driving away from the Houston Police headquarters.

"What do you mean? We broke into someone's house in broad daylight, got caught red-handed by the local police, and less than an hour later we are driving away free as a bird," Adelph had a different view of the situation.

"I would rather remain under the radar. They may be trying to follow us now."

"I'll keep an eye on the rearview mirror. The thing is…..there was no sign of the journal at Macklind's house. What makes you so sure he's got it?"

"The journal wasn't at Macklind's house, but neither was Macklind. When we track him down we'll get it."

Alden was sure of that. He knew it was Kenneth Macklind that was in London with Peter Stroudlin from the accident report filed at the airport. He also knew that the only phone call that Peter Stroudlin received throughout his stay at London's Southhall Hospital was from Kenneth Macklind. It didn't take much to figure out the connection. A Google search turned up hundreds of hits on Kenneth Macklind and his "Crusade for Creation". Once Alden saw that Macklind was a Christian colleague of Stroudlin's; he knew he had the journal…..he just knew it.

How Alden Harlock knew all these things was simply a matter of asking the right people. That is, asking people that fell under his dark authority. People that included top officials in the U.S. State Department and CIA; the British Prime Minister; a dozen head officers of the United Nations, and leaders in just about every Nation in the world. All he had to do was ask, and they went out of their way to comply.

There is one connection that ties all of these people together. It's not a government or political body; it's a secret society, and Alden Harlock was the Chairman of the Board. Alden Harlock was the Supreme Grand Master of the European Brotherhood of Freemasons; and that was just the beginning. His power ran even deeper and stronger than that. He was also a member of another secret society.

He was elite, and his society was so secret, many believed it did not even exist.

Adelph was driving. "Where to now?" He asked.

"A place called Knob Ridge, Missouri. I think he's staying there with his clergyman friend."

"I bet that's a fun place, sounds like quite a metropolis," Adelph quipped but Alden didn't laugh.

They flew north on highway 59 towards Nacogdoches. Adelph wasn't worried about a speeding ticket. He figured they would make the ten hour drive in a little over seven. As the cow fields and fence posts blurred by, Alden was going over every possible scenario in his mind, and how he would respond.

They passed Shreveport, and then made their way into Arkansas. Then they passed Springfield and caught highway forty-four towards Knob Ridge. Alden was wishing he'd brought a bottle of his bitters from home. He was beginning to get tense.

It was well past dark, the highway lights led the way. Adelph saw the sign for the Knob Ridge exit. "Six more miles."

"Alright let me take a look," Alden tapped his GPS. "Get off at the Knob Ridge exit and make a right onto highway T."

Adelph couldn't resist, "You must be kidding…..This is how they name the roads over here? T?" He often tried humor but very seldom got a response from Alden. This time was no different.

"Five point three miles on T and then left turn onto Highway B. It's less than a mile from there."

They reached the exit. Adelph barely slowed down, he squeeled around the corner onto Highway T. The speed limit dropped to thirty-five mile per hour inside the Knob Ridge City limits, Adelph slowed to sixty. The town looked vacant. They hadn't passed another car since they got off the interstate. They passed Knob Ridge City Hall, the Police Station, and several restaurants…..all of which were deserted.

"Here….stop….pull in here," Alden directed.

Adelph whipped into the parking lot. It was a church and unlike the rest of Knob Ridge, there were a dozen or so cars in the lot. He didn't bother maneuvering inside the white lines of a parking space; he just pulled up to the front door and stopped the car. They both got out.

"Alright, just follow me, stay calm and do what I say," Alden gave Adelph his orders.

They walked into the front door and immediately saw several women sitting at a table under a large wall sign that read, "Welcome to Knob Ridge Faith Church." The bright orange letters almost made Alden's eyes water. He approached the table.

"Well Hello there….welcome to Faith Church," said one woman.

"Hallelujah," said another.

The first woman continued, "Are you here for the Bible study? I think they are almost done but feel free to go on in and join them."

"No thank you," said Alden. "This isn't my….. denomination."

She could tell immediately from his British accent that he was not from Knob Ridge. Exotic visitors were always big news, and she couldn't wait to get this guys story. "Well then, how can I help you?"

"I would like to see your Pastor. I believe his name is Phil Balasky."

"Oh my, he's not here tonight. He usually is but he had some other important mission work going on. Have you come for healing? We have a healing room just down the hall."

"Healing?" Alden wasn't prepared for that. "No…..what about a man named Kenneth Macklind. Is he here?"

"Oh I just love Kenneth Macklind," the woman proclaimed. "Praise Jesus, he is a delight. And what a wonderful family; do you know he and his wife have six children?"

Another lady came over to see the stranger and overheard them. "I heard they are trying to adopt another one. They might go to Kazakhstan to get the baby."

Yet another woman joined the growing crowd at the greeting table. "Oh yes, I do wish we would have him come and speak again soon. It has been so long since he's been here."

"No, he is here," said the first woman, offering more information than she had been asked. "Darla saw Kenneth and Pastor Phil eating lunch today at the diner."

Alden turned and looked at Adelph as if to say "now we're getting somewhere."

The ladies took turns spewing out all of the information they had on Kenneth Macklind. Alden really didn't even have to ask many questions.

"Last time he was here he spoke on the age of the Earth. I just learned so much. You'd be surprised, so many believe in that evolution."

Alden patience was being tried, "Yes, I've heard that. So, I really need to find them do you know where they might be?"

"Who Kenneth, I'm sure he's with Pastor Phil. I think that's got something to do with the mission work he's been doing," said the first woman.

Again, another woman cut in, "I'm sure they are over at Frank Hampton's. You know that Frank Hampton is new here…..he's such a nice man. Praise Jesus he came out of that tavern and got saved. He got baptized here last week."

The Jesus talk was too much for Alden. "Okay, Frank Hampton's, where is that?"

"Why Frank's place is the nice little cabin by the pond on Lost Creek Road," said one of the ladies.

With that Alden and Adelph were off. They turned down an evening of Bible study and coffee cake to continue on their mission. They sped out of the parking lot with Lost Creek Road up on the GPS. The ladies thought it was odd, but they had no idea what they had just done.

They rounded the corner, turning onto Highway T. In a matter of minutes they found Lost Creek Road; and there it was…..Hampton on the mailbox. They rolled onto Frank's property. They didn't knock. The door was unlocked. Frank was in the living room organizing his tackle box when they walked in.

Frank was calm, "What do you want?" he said as he stood up.

Alden didn't answer he took one step to the left leaving Adelph a clear shot. Frank never even saw it coming. The bullet struck Frank an inch below his right collar bone. He fell back against the blood splattered wall and collapsed to the floor.

Adelph returned his 9mm to his pocket and began a quick sweep of the house. "Here it is…" he called.

Alden came to him standing in front of a 3 x 5 metal gun safe. "Yeah, it's gotta be in there."

Adelph had an idea, "I'll go check in that shed for a chainsaw or something of the like."

"Wait a minute; just check the guy's pockets for the key. Use your head Adelph."

They rolled Frank over and found his keys. They were quite a pocketful. On an old Budweiser key chain, there must have been thirty keys. Adelph tossed them to Alden.

Alden commented, "Budweiser, how refined… he was a connoisseur of fine beers."

"Did you think he might be a Mun Schweiz bitters drinker?" Again Adelph tossed some humor.

Alden walked up to the safe and began trying likely keys. After five or six failures he was feeling a surge of frustration, and then he saw the orange key. "This must be it." It was the same color as the trim around the top and bottom of the safe. Alden inserted the key and turned. They both smiled as they heard the snap of success. The door opened and they immediately saw the metal box that held the journal.

Adelph was impressed by the gun collection, "Oh yeah….check out the old Browning Sweet Sixteen….very nice," but Alden wanted only the journal.

Alden grabbed the gray metal box. He brought it to the dining room table and opened it to verify the contents. There it was; the journal of Sir Richard the Elder of Landolte. "Okay Adelph old boy…..Let's get out of here."

By out of here, Alden meant out of the United States and back home to England. His diplomatic immunity had worked wonderfully in Houston, but he didn't want to push it. He knew the State Department would be watching him closely, and though there was no sign that they were being followed......he could feel an uninvited presence.

Alden placed the journal in the backseat, secured in its gray metal box. Adelph started the car. "I'll be right back," said Alden. He walked off to the end of the house and found a row of bushes. He walked down to end of the row and unzipped his fly. He hadn't used a restroom since Houston. He found a nice patch of goldenrod and marked his territory.

"Alright, all set?" said Alden as he got in the passenger side.

Adelph knew the plane was waiting for them in Houston so he started back, just the way they had came.

At the George Bush Intercontinental Airport awaited the third member of Alden's team, Benton Atwater. Benton was Alden's pilot. A white and blue, fairly nondescript Learjet 55 was in the commercial hub, full of fuel and ready to go.

Benton's phone rang, it was Alden. "Hello, Mr. Harlock."

"Success Benton. We have the journal. How fast can you get to St. Louis?" Alden didn't like the idea of another seven or eight hour drive all the way back to Houston.

"That's a little over an hour and a half sir."

"Perfect, that's about how far we are from the airport. Meet us there and call me when you land. Let me know if you have any trouble."

Benton shared in Harlock's preferred political status, "Oh there won't be any trouble sir. I'll see you at Lambert Field St. Louis."

Adelph turned around and headed east on forty-four. They passed a sign......'St. Louis – 119 miles'.

They barely spoke at all in the ninety minutes it took to get to the airport. Alden leaned his head on window and closed his eyes. Adelph didn't know if he was sleeping or not but he didn't want to risk waking him.

The silence broke with the phone call. "Hello, Mr. Harlock," it was Benton. "I am ready and waiting for you at Lambert Field's East Terminal. We already have clearance for takeoff. We can depart as soon as you get here."

"Excellent! Well done Benton. We'll be there in......about ten minutes."

Adelph took the Lambert Field exit and found the East Terminal. They left the car at the curb and went inside......Alden, Adelph and gray metal box. They flashed their VIP credentials and didn't even have to go through security. They walked directly out onto the runway where Benton was waiting. They boarded the plane, and locked the door. The airport employees just stepped aside and stayed out of the way; they figured they were rock stars or something. With no questions asked, the Learjet was on its way to London, England.

Knob Ridge Faith Church was beginning to clear out. The services had just ended. The good folks of Knob Ridge were heading for home; except for a group of five or six ladies that were responsible for clean-up. They had already begun picking up empty cups and plates, and putting away what was left of the cinnamon streusel coffee cake.

"Well hello there," Pastor Phil had just come through the door. He had Kenneth with him. The ladies all stopped what they were doing and came to get recognition from their Pastor.

"Well hi Pastor, we're just about finished cleaning up here…..we had a great service tonight."

"Praise God. What did I miss, anything exciting?"

"Oh yes," one of the ladies said. "June Crump got healed of that migraine. She had that headache for three days, and tonight it just lifted right off her."

"That's wonderful. That's why we're here isn't it," said Phil.

As they were chit chatting, another lady rushed over to the group. She had been in the bathroom when Phil arrived and was disappointed that she had already missed some of the conversation. "Did you tell him about the visitor?" she asked.

Phil responded, "No, Clara, what visitor?"

"Oh my, he was so mysterious. He came in about seven-thirty…..he was actually looking for you Kenneth."

Kenneth got hit with a bad feeling. Very few people knew he was there. "Looking for me?"

"Yes, he seemed like it was somewhat important, oh, and he had a big guy with him that didn't say anything. We asked them to stay but he said it wasn't his denomination. You know who he sounded like? He sounded like Hugh Grant with that English accent."

Another lady jumped in…. "Oh I loved that movie 'Notting Hill', did you see him in that?"

Kenneth and Phil looked at each other with a puzzled urgency. "Did he leave his name or any contact information?" Kenneth asked.

"No, they left in a pretty big hurry to go find you. Shirley told them you were at Frank Hampton's".

"Dear Lord, Frank!" Phil gasped. The two of them ran out to Phil's van, by the time Phil jumped and slid across the hood to the driver's side Kenneth was already in the passenger seat. Phil peeled out leaving the parking lot.

They arrived at the scene a few minutes later. On the drive they were careful not to jump to any conclusions, or to speak anything negative. These two seasoned men of faith knew that fear was the opposite of faith, and they knew that God's word says in Proverbs 18:21 that "death and life are in the power of the tongue." At the same time they both knew there was a good chance that the visitors were after the journal.

They pulled onto Frank's property slowly. As they got out of the truck they both looked around for any sign of anything out of the ordinary. They walked up to the front door, Kenneth knocked. "Frank?" Kenneth called. Phil pushed the door open, it was unlocked. The living room lights weren't on; the light was on in the back bedroom but the house was completely quiet. "Frank, anybody home?" Kenneth called again. There was no answer.

Then they saw him. To their left in the dimly lit corner of the living room Frank Hampton lay slumped over on the floor. There was a good deal of blood on the wall. Without hesitation, Phil walked directly over to Frank, "He's okay, he's going to be just fine...." it was Phil's faith talking. Kenneth stood his ground and just watched. "He's been shot, but these aren't fatal wounds. Frank, you're going to be fine," Phil said, this time a little louder. "Frank, can you hear me?" Phil got down on both knees and grabbed Franks hand, "In the name of Jesus Christ of Nazareth.....Frank, wake up."

Frank coughed. "It's Okay Frank, we're here. Kenneth and I are here." Frank moaned and struggled to get a good breath. "Kenneth call 9-1-1," Phil shouted.

Knob Ridge, Missouri has one ambulance but no hospital. They take emergency patients thirty-six miles to Rolla, the nearest somewhat large city. In cases like this they just call Rolla for a helicopter. The local paramedics tended to Frank the best they could for about half an hour. Frank was stable, but still losing blood. Just when they were starting to worry they heard the distant chop of the helicopter.

Kenneth and Phil put every light they could find on the driveway. There was a spot near the road that was flat and clear from trees; it would be tight but it was the only close place the helicopter could land. The spotlight of the helicopter zeroed in on the make-shift landing pad. The pilot announced his plans over a loudspeaker…. "This is emergency aircraft…..I will land in the driveway…..I see the lights, looks like plenty of room…..please stand clear, I'm coming in for a landing."

The EMT's jumped out of the helicopter and ran with their heads ducked to verify Frank's condition. They were satisfied that his vital signs were stable enough to attempt the flight.

"Where will you take him?" asked Phil.

"We are going to BJC hospital in St. Louis. They have one of the best trauma centers in the world. He'll be fine, but we gotta get going. Even for us….it's about forty-five minutes away."

"Can we come with him?" Kenneth asked.

"How are you related?" asked the pilot.

Phil spoke up, "I'm his Pastor, and this is a dear friend. He doesn't have any family in town. We're all he's got. Please let us come with you."

The pilot responded, "Alright, sure…..I know I'd want my Pastor with me at a time like this. Let's roll."

They loaded Frank in the helicopter, he wasn't conscious. Phil and Kenneth got in and buckled up, and off they went.

It all happened so fast. Kenneth and Phil left Frank's house earlier in the afternoon to go and get something to eat at the Tin Roof Diner. Frank didn't want to go; he said he felt like taking a nap so they went without him. At the diner they prayed and talked and prayed some more. Finally, over a grilled turkey melt, Kenneth felt peace about having reached a decision.

He had made up his mind that he was going to go public with the finding of the journal. In the end they both strongly agreed that the truth was more important than the fear of what might happen. Kenneth had planned to call a press conference in the next day or so and make known to the world the latest finding which strongly supported a biblical young earth creation.

He was willing to offer the book to the museum in Prague, since that's where it came from, but only if they would agree to erect a proper display and draw attention to it. But from what he gleaned from the story as Peter told it; the Prague museum probably didn't even know they had it. Alexander Svec stumbled across it in an old archive room that hadn't been seen in decades. Kenneth was starting to think maybe he was the book's rightful owner, and he knew of three or four creation based ministries that would gladly put it on display at their museums.

"He's going to be okay," Phil said loudly to be heard over the noise of the helicopter.

"Yeah, I just can't believe how fast they tracked us down," Kenneth admitted.

"Oh, in all the chaos I forgot about the journal….did you check Frank's gun safe?"

"Yeah, when we were waiting for the helicopter to arrive, I walked back to check on the safe. It was open…..the journal was gone."

"ughhww no!," Phil yelled. "I guess you don't think it could have been just a random break in?"

"Frank had some cash and a bunch of guns in that safe. They didn't touch anything but the journal. Those ladies at your church…..remember the visitor with the English accent?"

"Oh yeah, God love them…..they're just so kind and trusting…..too trusting. I guess they just told them everything they wanted to know," said Phil.

"It's not their fault. Frank's a tough old Marine….I'm not worried about him. When we get to the hospital we should call Matt and Ty."

"Yeah, they should know right away. I have to call Lena too; she probably doesn't even know what happened yet."

They could see the lights of downtown St. Louis ahead in the distance. The pilot landed on the roof of the Hospital where there was a large group of hospital staff waiting. They wasted no time in getting Frank off of the stretcher and onto a hospital bed. One nurse changed the IV bag, while another was busy getting vital signs. Another nurse was there to escort Phil and Kenneth to the waiting room. St. Louis's BJC was operating like a well oiled machine.

Before they knew it Phil and Kenneth were in the waiting area; each on the phone with his wife. For Phil it was a relatively calm call, Lena handled the news like a champ and just asked what she could do to help. For Kenneth it was a different story. Kenneth tried to explain what had happened in a non-alarming way, but it was impossible. Barbara was alarmed. After thirty minutes of talking it out she seemed content with the notion that at least it was over. Kenneth gave her his love and hung up the phone knowing it was just getting started.

The flight was a long one; the drive home seemed even longer. Adelph pulled past the gate at Harlock Manor, Alden was finally home with his prize. He had invited Benton and Adelph in for a celebratory cocktail. They also were expecting their paychecks.

Alden was never more relieved to be home. The incident in Houston was actually much closer than he had realized at the time. Even with diplomatic immunity he should have been held for questioning; at least until the British Ambassador arrived to meet with U.S officials over the matter. Alden definitely got away with one this time. The worst part was how happy that made him.

He led Benton and Adelph into the dimly lit parlor. The carpet was a thick, two inch shag and the color of barbecue sauce. The walls were the same color. Alden walked behind the bar and uncorked a bottle of Dom Perignon 1959.

"Gentlemen….. I thank you. Your efforts and your commitment have been truly been an asset to me. Here is to our success," Alden said as he lifted his glass.

Benton and Adelph met his glass with a crystal clear ring. They did not spend any time revisiting the trip to America; that was over. To Benton, it was just another private jet mission; to Adelph it was a little boring; and to Alden, it wasn't pretty but he got what he wanted. That was all that mattered, now to the celebration.

Alden continued, "I am having a celebration, I would like to invite you both to attend. My circle of friends will enjoy meeting you, and perhaps you'll tell the story of how we recovered the journal."

Benton responded, "Thank you Alden, I would love to attend." He was actually thinking of the potential clients he could meet. "But is this actually a party to celebrate the recovery of the journal; it's such an unknown piece."

"Oh yes, this is indeed an event worthy of celebrating. I've had many celebrations similar to this in the past; we are all so looking forward to it."

Alden Harlock had quite an unusual 'circle of friends'. They would be coming from all over the world for the celebration. Not to celebrate the discovery of an exciting historic document; but the destruction of one. At this party, Alden planned to burn the journal of Sir Richard in the presence of a cheering crowd of fellow God haters.

The guest list would be a small, hand-picked sample which included Alden's peers from museums around the world, professors from some of the world's finest Universities, famous movie stars and television personalities, some of his "brothers" from the highest echelon of Freemasonry, and basically anyone Alden had met over the years who genuinely enjoyed and shared his love for Satan, and his hatred for Almighty God. Alden was infamous for his "theme" parties. Really, they were nothing short of ritualistic religious ceremonies disguised as intellectualism.

It all started in 1999, when an interesting piece came through his museum. It was a stone carving from China which was dated to approximately 2700 B.C. The carving had a picture which depicted huge masses of people at the tower of Babel, all working together. It also had text that described the confusing of the languages, and how they migrated to what is now China. The piece was three feet high and one foot wide and solid stone. It weighed over four hundred pounds, but Alden had it delivered to his home and had a party where guests took turns jack hammering the stone until it was reduced to a pile of gravel. As party favors each guest received a chunk of the stone as a souvenir.

The China stone provided strong biblical support and actually reinforced the Genesis account of the tower of Babel. The minute he saw it, Alden knew it would become a huge news story, and glorifying to God. He wouldn't have that. Since then Alden had scoured the globe for every biblical artifact he could get his hands on. About once a year something would come along that would merit a party.

Once, in 2005, after a long dry spell on biblical artifacts, Alden had to settle for choosing a first century Roman writing about Pontius Pilate. It was previously unknown, and it did validate scripture, but there were others like it.

Alden had a party and burned it, but many feared his parties were losing steam.

The journal of Sir Richard not only told a version of history which authenticated scripture, it brought with it a new twist. Alden feared that if it got out into the world, the equation would be drawn between dragons and dinosaurs, and every dragon legend would now be seen in a different light. It was a light that eliminated billions of years of mystery, and illuminated Genesis as a historically accurate document. Alden couldn't wait to burn that journal.

Adelph and Benton finished their champagne, collected their hefty paychecks and went home to catch up on some much needed rest. Alden began writing out his guest list. The invitations would be in the mail first thing in the morning.

"Olga!" Alden called. Obviously she wasn't in earshot. He walked over to the intercom on the wall and pressed the "talk" button. "Olga," he said calmly.

"Yes, Mr. Harlock," she responded.

"Olga, I'm planning another one of our parties. Let's get together and make out a list of things that will need to be done."

"Shall I reserve the grand ballroom at the Bilderberg?" She asked.

"No, We'll be staying in London for this......let's talk about it first thing in the morning," he said.

"Yes sir, I'll see you then."

Alden had never married. Olga was the closest thing he had to a spouse. She was his housekeeper of twelve years. She had her own suite within the estate, and was excellent at doing her job and staying out of the way. Actually, Alden very seldom even saw her. But in twelve years he never had one complaint. Olga got nice living quarters and was paid very well. In return she performed all of the cooking, cleaning, laundry, maintenance, and just about anything he asked of her.

Alden sat in his favorite chair in the great room sipping a glass of his favorite bitters and looking at the journal. He had it on display under a glass dome in the center of the room. A single beam of light from a recessed can shined down from above, illuminating the journal and reflecting off the glass. After a thousand years, the journal's days were numbered.

<u>Chapter 11</u>

It was midnight at Gildersleeves. Ty was leading the band through a fiery rendition of an old St. Louis favorite….. "Can I Call You a Cab" by Mama's Pride. The band was right on. Ty was trading licks with Marc, the lead guitar player; and Matt was behind the bar just watching and enjoying the music. The loyal crowd had seen this many times before but, as always…..they were out in full force enjoying another round.

Matt felt his pocket buzz, as the song continued. He looked at the phone and didn't recognize the number. He knew he wouldn't be able to hear in the bar so he took a step outside. "This is Matt," he said with the best bluesy rock in Midwest blaring in the background.

"Hi Matt, this is Phil Balaski. From Knob Ridge……I met you when you came to visit your Uncle Frank."

"Yeah, I remember. What can I do for you Phil?"

"Well its bad news I'm afraid. There has been an accident. Kenneth and I are here at the hospital…...we thought you should know right away."

Matt reached for the rail and leaned back against it. Then he braced himself for the worst. "Is he alright?"

"Well, he's been shot…..in the chest. They have him in surgery as we speak."

"Where is he?"

"Barnes-Jewish Hospital on Kingshighway…."

"Yeah, I know where it is. We'll be right there."

The Emergency room was full of people. There were the usual accident victims; broken legs, twisted ankles, lacerations, concussions…...and there were sick people there too; flu, sore throats, fevers, etc. The place was packed.

Matt and Ty stormed right up to the counter. "We need to see Frank Hampton," Matt said.

"Yes, could you spell that please?" The woman behind the counter was pleasant and as helpful as could be expected. "Okay let's see……," she pecked away at the computer keyboard. "Yes, here he is……He was brought in earlier this evening; he's already been admitted, but he doesn't have a room yet. That usually means the patient is still in surgery. The waiting area for him would be on the third floor."

Matt and Ty proceeded to the nearest elevator and went up to the third floor. They got off and followed the signs towards emergency surgery. They were almost running when they flew past the doorway to the waiting room. Ty caught a passing glimpse inside and noticed Phil kneeling on the floor with his head bowed. "Hey….," Ty yelled as he reached back for the doorway. Matt skidded to a halt and retreated to the waiting room with Ty.

"Hi guys, Frank is in surgery right now. We should be hearing something pretty soon."

"What happened?" demanded Matt.

"Two guys with English accents came into our church tonight asking about me and Kenneth. Some of the ladies on our greeting team told him we were at Frank's. We weren't there. They came in shot Frank and stole the journal," Phil gave a quick, condensed version.

"Frank got shot protecting your journal?" Ty was obviously angry. "I'm sick of hearing about this journal…..I can't believe this…..where were you guys?"

Kenneth stepped in, "Matt, Ty, I'm so sorry. This is all my fault. I feel so bad about what has happened."

"Alright, alright…..let's not lose our heads here," Matt wanted to find out what had been done about it. "Who were these guys?"

"I don't know. It all happened so fast. All we know so far is that they had British accents, and no one at the church had ever seen them before," said Kenneth. "We gave brief statements to the local police before we got in the helicopter…..they said they would be in touch."

Just then the Doctor walked into the room. Everyone turned towards him to listen. "Hello, I'm Doctor Towerman, I have an update on Frank Hampton. Is there a member of the family here?"

Matt spoke up, "I'm his nephew, these are all friends, we're all together."

"Alright do you mind if we all have a seat?..... thanks. Now, I do have some encouraging news. The bullet struck just between the first and second rib; that's a big deal. The bullet didn't hit any bone as it entered Frank's chest cavity.

If it had, the rib bone would have fractured into many tiny splinters that would cause a lot more damage."

"Rib? I thought you said he got hit high on the chest?" Ty questioned.

Dr. Towerman responded, "The ribs actually start up at the collarbone so the first and second ribs are about here…." He pointed to the spot on his chest. "It was well clear of the heart and any major blood vessels. He does have a partially collapsed lung; and the bullet shattered the shoulder blade as it exited. That's what we are working on right now; and it's going very well. The lung is showing signs of being very repairable, and the scapula….shoulder blade….will heal nicely with time. The surgeons working with Frank right now are the best chest surgeons in the world. He is in good hands. The most critical thing right now is the lung…..but as I said all signs are pointing to a successful operation. In fact, they should be closing him up shortly and then we'll be monitoring that lung very closely for the next week or so."

"When will he wake up?" Matt asked.

"He may sleep a while after the surgery; he has had a very strong dose of anesthesia. You should be able to see him in the morning, but he'll probably sleep most of the day. He was awake just before he went in to surgery."

"Oh, you didn't tell us that….was he alert?" asked Phil.

"Yes, he was in a great deal of pain, as you might imagine, but he managed to get off a nice long string of cuss words and then he said 'fix me up Doc….I gotta get back out there.' He was only awake for a few minutes."

All four broke smiles at the thought of Frank's tenacity. "You got an old marine in there Doc, he's as tough as they come," said Ty proudly.

"You can't be tougher than a chunk of lead moving eight hundred feet per second," the doctor lectured as he walked out of the room and back into surgery.

"He's going to be okay…." Ty said as he leaned back in his seat. Ty continued, "How much help do you think the police are going to be? They probably get gunshot victims all the time out there in the woods duck hunting and running meth labs and what not. We are going to have to get involved here if we want to get the people responsible for this."

"Look guys, right now we just need to be here for Frank. Let's just try and relax and maybe get a little rest and hopefully we'll get to see him in the morning," Phil said optimistically.

"I ain't going nowhere…..and I doubt if I can sleep in this chair," complained Matt.

The four of them sat quietly for awhile watching a Seinfeld re-run on the waiting room television. They were the only ones there. Phil tried to stretch out into two seats but couldn't quite get horizontal. Ty got a Mountain Dew from the vending machine and settled in for the long night.

Seinfeld led to Frasier; and then to TMZ, and then to a re-broadcast of the local news. Phil stood up and stretched, "I'm going to take a walk. My back hurts from these chairs."

"Yeah, I'll go with you," Kenneth said.

Matt looked over at Ty to see if he was awake. "I'll tell you one thing," he said. "As soon as Frank pulls through this, I say we get on a plane to England and find these jerks who did this and beat them senseless and bring this journal back."

Ty responded without looking Matt's direction, "I'm so freaking sick of hearing about this stupid journal. I don't give a crap about the journal, but I'm with you on finding the guys that did this."

"Hey look, it's obviously important to Frank. He stuck it in his gun safe and was proud to be keeping it for him. Frank is really getting in to this church stuff."

"Yeah, I know….this is just a really weird situation. I mean…..I just can't believe somebody just walks up to you front door and shoots you and steals things out of your gun safe. I mean in St. Louis, in a big city….. maybe. But way out there….I just can't believe it. I mean there's like sixteen churches for every bar. I don't even know if there is a bar in Knob Ridge."

"There isn't. Dolittle is a dry county."

"Dry county? You see what I mean. I mean you see what we're up against here. It's a different world. I just don't understand it; and Frank, he just moved in lock, stock and barrel….and he loves it. He just sits around looking at his pictures from all of his wildlife cameras……"

He stopped. Matt sat up on the edge of his chair. Ty's mouth was open as the light bulb lit up in his head. "The cameras."

"Yeah, Frank's got those things all over the property. They have to show the guys who did this. They have time and date stamps and everything."

Phil and Kenneth were coming back from their walk.

"Did we miss anything?" Phil asked.

"Not really, except the sun's coming up," Ty said looking at Phil. "Hey, did you guys check Frank's game cameras? I bet they caught some of this."

"We just thought of the exact same thing," said Kenneth. Its only two hours away, let's go check it out this afternoon."

"Wow, I haven't pulled an all-nighter in years. Would you look at that sunrise…..glorious. Anybody want to pray with me. Wherever two or more are gathered…."

"Yeah, that's about the only thing we can do,' Kenneth said.

To everyone's surprise Matt stood up, "yeah, I'm in."

They looked at Ty but he didn't look back. Nothing further was said as the three of them bowed their heads and closed their eyes. Phil raised his palms, "Dear Father, we come to You today in Jesus' name. We bow our heads and humbly ask forgiveness for falling short of Your perfect will.

Father, we thank You that You will never leave us, nor forsake us. Thank You that You are with Frank right now. Thank You Father for Your mercy, Your strength, and Your grace. We come together right now Lord to ask for fast healing for Frank, and for an easy and pain free recovery.....in Jesus' name. Amen."

Matt felt a little better. Everyone was seated again; now they were joined by an old couple awaiting the news of the results on their son's surgery. Matt wasn't concerned about the additional company, he wanted some answers. "Hey, Kenneth. What's the deal with this journal, I mean why would anyone want to kill people over it?"

"Well, you see it's a solid historical document that clearly refutes the theory of evolution. Evolution is a world view. If evolution goes down.....that world goes with it. Apparently, they like their world just the way it is."

"What view, what do you mean?" asked Matt.

"How you see your origins will determine how you live your life. You see, if you believe this universe is the product of a random accidental explosion....a big bang; and if you believe that you are the product of another random accident; and that through billions of years of time and chance we have arrived where we are today......then you are the most important thing in the world. And, your moral standards are based on what *you* believe to be 'right'. There is no reason, no design, no purpose for life; it just happened. And, when this life is over....that's it; so you better get all you can, can all you get and sit on the can....you know what I mean?

But, if you believe that you were created by the all-knowing, all-powerful, Almighty God and that He knew you, and loved you even before you were born, and that He knows every hair on your head, and is here to help you……well, that's a very different story. Our moral standards are based on His Word, the creator of all things has given us His commandments and He has told us how He wants us to live.

The people in the first part of that example…..the evolutionists…...the atheists...….the guys who shot your Uncle Frank and stole the journal…..they don't like being told how to live."

"Yeah but who thinks about it that way, I mean evolution is in Science class, it's not part of most people's everyday lives," said Ty.

"Tell that to the six million Jews who died in the holocaust."

"What do you mean?"

"I mean Hitler's vision for an Aryan utopia was based on his evolutionary worldview. He saw Germans as a form of Humans that had evolved higher up the ladder than other races. He felt completely justified in trying to wipe out lesser races. In Mein Kampf, Hitler used the word evolution many times. He strongly believed that he needed to preserve the stronger German race; and not let it become mingled with the weaker Jewish race. It sounds crazy now, but he did have many supporters. "

"So who do you think this guy is?"

Kenneth sat back in his chair and looked up at the ceiling as he took a deep breath. "I don't know….."

Phil finished the thought for him, "But I have a feeling, one way or another, we're going to find out."

"Come on," Ty said. "You must have some idea…..a starting point, something."

"Well," Answered Kenneth. "I'll never be convinced that Peter Stroudlin wasn't murdered. Remember, his nurse on the floor that night saw a strange man coming out of his room…."

Ty cut him off, "Yeah, the guy with the silver ponytail?"

"Yeah….. the guy with the silver ponytail. I don't know who he is, but if he killed Peter, then he's probably the same guy who killed Ian Burbrey, and Alexander Svec."

"And tried to kill Frank…." said Matt.

Ty continued the questioning, "Yeah, what about the ladies at your church…..did they notice a silver ponytail on the guy with the English accent?"

"Yeah, I already thought of that. They didn't notice…...they don't remember enough to be useful. The only thing they mentioned that was interesting was how big one of them was. The guy that did all the talking was normal height, but the other guy was huge apparently. He didn't talk but he sure didn't go unnoticed," said Phil.

"Look, this guy with the silver ponytail obviously has an English accent….he's from England. Now just who do you think he is? A museum guy? A British commando? A hit man? What?"

"We don't know for sure if he's from England or not. Remember, this all started in Prague. Ian Burbrey's museum in London would be a good place to start though."

They could see Dr. Towerman coming down the hallway. He had changed from his scrubs and was now wearing Dockers and a shirt and tie. "Hey guys, you were right about him being tough," Dr. Towerman said as he entered the room. He walked over to the four of them and crouched down in front of them and smiled. "The surgery went even better than we had hoped. His lung is already showing signs of recovery. It's amazing; he is doing great. The nurse should be here soon to get some information from you and go over the visiting times but if you make it brief…..I think you could go and see him now. I want him to get a lot of sleep today…..but he's awake right now, and he's been asking for you guys." He stood up and all four practically jumped out of their chairs. "Follow me."

They walked down a sterile looking white hallway behind Dr. Towerman. All was quiet except for the sound of five men's footsteps. They came to his room and slowly nudged the door open. He peaked inside and saw Frank lying in his hospital bed with his eyes open. "Alright," Dr. Towerman whispered. "Make it quick and I'll stand guard and keep a lookout for Bea."

They filed in slowly. Ty asked, "Who's Bea?" as he passed the doctor.

"His nurse," he answered with a grin.

"Hey Frank," Phil was the first to get to him.

"Look at you," Matt said. "It takes more than one bullet to keep you down, huh?"

Frank labored over a breath and mustered up an answer, "Ain't the first time I been shot, this was nothing."

They all laughed. Phil said, "Frank we are so glad to see you're doing fine. The doctor said surgery went great."

Kenneth stepped up to the bed with a tear in his eye, "Frank, I'm so sorry. This is all my fault. I never should have risked your safety like that....."

"Hey, hey...." Frank stopped him with a raspy whisper. "He caught me off guard that's all. Let's get that journal back and I'll keep it again and this time...."

"Alright, alright what's going on here? I knew something was up with Dr. Towerman standing at the door like that. Let's go, I'll meet you at the nurse's station I need to get contact info and all that fun stuff but you're not staying in here.....maybe visitors tomorrow but not today. Now let's go." It was Bea. She marched them out of Frank's room like a drill sergeant.

Dr. Towerman had a slightly guilty look on his face, "I warned you guys about Bea."

She responded, "Yeah, yeah, I'm sure you did. Now let's move."

"Get some rest Frank," Ty said as he left the room. "We'll see you soon."

They assembled at the nurse's station and took care of business with Bea. She assembled a list of everyone's phone numbers and addresses. Matt stepped up as the primary contact, being the only family he had left. When Bea had no more use for them they made their way to the front lobby and discussed their plans for the day.

"Hey," Phil said. "It just dawned on me that we came here last night in a helicopter."

"I don't think they offer a round trip," said Ty. "Come on, I have plenty of room in the Suburban. Actually, I have plenty of room at my place too, why don't you guys stay with me?"

"That would be awesome Ty, thank you. We are going to need a car though eventually. How about if we rent a car and meet you at your place?" responded Kenneth.

"Man you just love to rent cars don't you?" Ty joked.

Kenneth laughed, "I should get special treatment, this is like the sixth car I've rented this month."

"Alright, there's a couple of car rental lots on the way." They all walked out to Ty's Suburban, and headed for the highway. A few miles down the road Phil and Kenneth got out at the car rental lot. It wasn't a great neighborhood but it looked like they had plenty of cars. "You want me to wait so you can follow me?"

"No go on ahead, I've got GPS."

Okay, I'll be there, I just gotta drop off Matt, and then I'm heading home." Ty gave Kenneth a card with his address on it.

"Thanks Ty, I really appreciate it."

Ty arrived home and sunk into his red lounge chair on the patio. The sun was reflecting off the arch as Ty sat high above the morning rush hour traffic. He thought about putting on a pot of coffee, but really he just wanted to get some sleep.

He left instructions with the concierge in the front lobby regarding his out of town guests in case he dozed off. Ty knew they would be in good hands, so he relaxed in the morning sunshine. The street noise ten stories down provided a perfect background for sleeping. He was out when Kenneth and Phil showed up thirty minutes later. Understanding the situation perfectly they didn't wake him. They each found a comfy spot to get horizontal, Phil in the guest bedroom and Kenneth on the living room sofa. Before they knew it they were fast asleep.

Phil was in the kitchen when Ty finally woke up and came looking for something to drink. "Hey, you found it, I never even heard you guys come in," said Ty.

"Yeah, we didn't want to wake you…..we just crashed too. Kenneth must have gotten up just before me, he's not here… he might have taken a walk or something."

"I can't believe how late it is. Six and a half hours in a lounge chair and I'm a new man."

"Wow this place is awesome. Ty, I love this 1960's modern space thing you have going here. This is the coolest place I've ever seen."

"Thank you. And I want to make this clear, you and Kenneth both; I want you to stay as long as you want. There's plenty of room and I'm glad to have you."

Ty looked in the fridge. It was pretty scarce. There was a bottle of lemonade, and a big chunk of Gouda cheese, still in the red wax shell. He grabbed it and some glasses, a knife and headed back out to the deck. They were sitting there talking as Kenneth came in.

"Hey you're up. Wow look at this view."

"Hi Kenneth, have a seat and join us for lunch….cheese and lemonade. Man, I have got to get to the grocery store."

Phil said, "Ty was just telling about his success in the music business."

"Yeah and I want to tell you just like I told Phil, you're both welcome to stay as long as you want. I'm glad to have you. And I promise to get some groceries."

Kenneth sat down and poured himself a glass of lemonade. "Thank you Ty, That's awfully kind of you. I wish I could stay but I just decided that I need to round up my family and get home. This has been a crazy couple of weeks for me, but I just took a walk and did some thinking…..it must be even worse for my wife and kids. I haven't seen them for more than a day in the last three weeks. I just need to get home and let things get normalized again. I don't have peace about any other option. I'm sorry you guys."

Ty agreed, "You're right, family comes first. I'm with you man, go get 'em."

Phil shook his head in agreement, "What can I do to help?"

"Well, you may need another car," he laughed. "I'm taking this rental to the airport and heading out to California this afternoon."

"No problem, I just might hang out here with Ty a few more days."

"What time is your flight?"

Kenneth looked at his watch, "it's in a little less than an hour, do you think I can make it?"

"If you hit the road right now, if traffic isn't bad you should be okay."

"I'll keep in touch…..Tell Frank I'll be checking in with him in a day or so. Maybe Phil will invite me out to speak at his church, I've cancelled half a dozen or so speaking engagements already so, I'm pretty sure I'm available."

"You bet, we'll see you soon, and we'll tell Frank you said hi. Now get going and take care of that beautiful family of yours."

As soon as Kenneth left Ty said, "Man you ministers got it made. Work, don't work…..Life's one big vacation."

Phil replied with a smile, "Not for me, I haven't had a vacation since we started the church in our barn three years ago. But, Kenneth….. he has done very well for himself. He's a lot like a musician. You know, residual income from book sales, DVD's and he is a highly sought after speaker."

"Yeah," Ty said. I guess we're not so different after all."

Mike Rimmey

<u>Chapter 12</u>

"William – Stop everything and see me at once! – Ted." This was the message scribbled on a sticky note and stuck to the computer screen in William Wellshire's office. When William arrived it was the first thing he saw. It was also the first thing he ignored.

Instead William casually walked down the hall to the coffee pot and poured the steamy, black beverage, into a white Styrofoam cup. He was in no hurry to hear what his boss wanted; in fact, he already knew. He gingerly sipped his coffee and then started back to his desk, this time he was noticed.

"Well, well, if it isn't the man of the hour."

"Yes, I heard you're a wanted man…"

The comments came one after another like dominoes as William walked through the cubicles. The chatter lingered long after he was past. He reached his desk, and sat down to enjoy his morning cup of coffee, quite calmly.

"William, you better get in there. Ted wants to see you right away," said a young woman from the next cubicle.

"Yes, and how did you know that?"

"Alright, I read the note on your desk, everyone did. Better get it over with."

"Yeah, I think you're right; just as soon as I've finished this cup of coffee."

He powered up his computer and checked his e-mail. Then he read some news and checked his Facebook page. He slurped the last of his coffee; the time had come….. time to see Ted.

Ted was the boss, and William was an investigative reporter for London's BHQ Channel six television newscast.

"Hey Ted," William said as he barged through the closed door of Ted's office. "You wanted to see me?"

"Yes, have a seat Bill," Ted knew he didn't like to be called Bill. "I just want to make one thing clear. If you push forward on that Mason story, you're going to find yourself in the unemployment line faster than you can say 'Shriner'. We've talked about this William. You are way out of line here."

"Ted, do you remember what happened last May? The Great Britain journalism awards, do you remember that? Yeah? And out of your ace reporting staff of overpaid, under ethical journalists…..Who was it that brought home the award for good old channel six?"

"This isn't about awards William."

No, it's about journalism. And you know what Ted? There's only one person at this station who's doing it, journalism that is, and that's me."

"Alright, Mr. Journalist, let's hear it then. What earth-shattering Freemason scandal have you uncovered this time?"

"First of all, you are implying that I am exceedingly focused on Freemasonry. That could not be further from the truth. In fact I haven't mentioned Freemasonry on my segment for at least six months. I have however, done controversial stories on the Catholic Church; Mormons; and the Church of England. And secondly, I already know you don't support the story so you will be the last one I tell my latest and hottest secrets to. Suffice it to say, I have a number of sources that would never speak to me again if this gets screwed up. Also I must say…..this is huge."

"Alright William, let me take another approach. You are a fine investigative reporter…..no question. In my thirty-four years in this business, I'd say you are right up there with the best I've ever worked with. For a young man, you are an old fashioned, hard- nosed reporter, and an asset to this company. So…..it would be a shame to lose you. But, I'll say this again…..if you push forward with that story you are out. William, there are political forces involved here that you don't want to mess with."

"Are you kidding me? I stare into the eyes of those political forces everyday and tell them they're going down. I bring one thing to this station Ted, reality. The millions of people that watch this newscast every night can see that. But, if you'd rather they see that on a different channel that's fine with me," with that William stepped out of Ted's office and closed the door behind him with a slam.

His phone was ringing as he got back to his desk. It was Rory, William picked it up. "Hey Rory, what's up?"

"Another party, that's what's up."

"What?" He almost dropped the phone.

Mike Rimmey

"Meet me at the Manhattan Arms in an hour."

"I'll be there."

Rory was one of William's most trustworthy informants.
He was not a homeless, ex-junkie, street-wise vagabond
like most of William's other informants. Rory was a janitor
at Oxford University. He had befriended many of the
professors, and faculty members there, and was very well
liked and trusted. There was very little that came through
the halls of that grand old University that Rory didn't hear
about.

William met Rory one night at a pub near the campus. He
was investigating one of the professors, and just happened
to strike up a conversation with Rory that paid off nicely.
William called Rory the next day to thank him and offered
him a "job". What he actually offered him was cash for
juicy information on corrupt university scandals.

William had not heard from Rory in several months; so he
assumed this one must be something good. He was glad he
got to the Manhattan Arms first. It was a good crowd for
mid-morning, but William managed to get his favorite
booth. He sat down and ordered a beer, hoping to change
the direction the day was going. Though he acted cool in
Ted's office, the argument had upset him. He loved his job
at Channel six and just wanted to stay on there as long as
possible. But, the truth was more important.

The previous winter, William had broken a story on
corruption in the Church of England, and took a great deal
of heat for it. The story upset everyone from Ted to the
Queen. It was tremendous investigative work, and was the
piece that landed him the award. Ted was torn between

being happy about the recognition it brought the station and firing William for the pressure he received. In the end William got orders to keep his stories less controversial, and to get prior approval before running every piece.

Things had gone smoothly for about six months or so but then he got an unbelievable tip on some very illegal corruption within England's Masonic Temple. He got the tip from Rory and had just started following up on several of the leads when Ted squashed the whole story. At least Ted though he had squashed it. William knew if he could nail down the proof, the story would be so hot he could run with it at channel six…..or somewhere else.

Now, he could hardly wait to hear what Rory had to say. They knew about the parties of an elite group of academia; parties where priceless artifacts were destroyed as the world's utmost intellectuals watched and enjoyed. The last one of these parties was over a year ago. Rory alerted William to it, but he couldn't get anywhere near it. This time he knew he had to get invited somehow.

"Hey Rory," William sounded legitimately glad to see him. "Have a seat, how is everything going?"

"Not too bad, I just married off my youngest daughter. The wife and me are empty nesters we are."

"Oh that's great; congratulations."

"Hang on there," Rory said with a scowl. "I can't stand the bum she married. I'm praying she comes to her senses."

"Oh, wow. That would make things difficult."

"Anyway, you won't believe what I heard. There is another one of those special parties coming next week."

"How did you hear?"

"I was talking to Dr. Cranepool. He loves to tell me about his famous friends. Every week I'll see him in the hall and he'll come up and be like…..Hey Rory, guess who I ran into this weekend. And it will be Elton John, or one of the Royals, or some famous businessman. So, yesterday I see him in the hall and I asked him who he saw this weekend. And he says…..nobody, but wait until next week…..and he starts telling me about this party that will have tons of rich and powerful people. So I kept asking him about the party, you know where, when, who…..and he clammed up fast."

"Okay, so what else?"

"Well I could tell he was excited about this so I knew he would be on the phone sooner or later talking about it so I slithered into a nice comfy spot in the crawl space above his office and waited."

"Holy smoke, are you kidding me? You're like James Bond or something."

"Yeah, I hung in there for an hour and a half, and…..nothing. I was starting to think it was a dead end when his phone rang. Bingo."

"What? Who was it?"

"I don't know who it was, remember I could only hear half of the conversation. But, he got practically giddy right away. He says….. 'oh yeah, I'll be there…..I wouldn't miss it for the world.' Then he says….. 'Yes, I got my invitation today. It's an ancient journal written by some knight who claims to have fought dragons."

"Dragons? What is that all about?"

"I haven't got a clue but that's what he said. Then he responds to the person on the other end and says….. 'Of course there will be brothers from the Lodge, you should be there. Oh yeah…that's the whole point."

"The whole point? What did he mean by that?"

"I don't know, but that's what he said."

"What else did you hear?"

"`Oh yeah, I think I found out the location."

"You're kidding…..where?"

"Well, he says to the other guy... 'I was kicking myself for not going last year'……and then he says…. 'Okay then, I will see you at the Grand Olympian."

"Grand Olympian, I thought they were going to tear that old place down."

"I don't know….but that's what he said."

"Okay, what else?" William was getting himself worked up.

"Well, I did hear one other thing of interest. I saved the best for last."

"What, what is it?"

"I heard a name…..sounds like the man of the hour……Alden Harlock."

"Alden Harlock, now we're getting somewhere. I've been closing in on him for years. Phenomenal work Rory…..hear anything else?"

"No that's it."

"Wow Rory, I think you're really on to something here," said William, as he took a small notebook out of his coat pocket. "Alright now let me get this down before I forget. Let's see…..ancient journal….dragons…..Grand Olympian……and best of all one of my favorite three hundred people…..Alden Harlock."

"That's it for now…..I'll let you know when I find out more."

William went back into his coat pocket, this time for the cash. He pulled out a thick roll that was a little over two hundred pounds. "Here you go Rory, keep your ears open in that place. Please try to find out more. Now, you'll have to excuse me, I can't wait to get to work on this."

Benton Atwater was awake for the first time in nearly fourteen hours. He sat up with a powerful thirst and an extremely full bladder. First he went and relieved himself and then grabbed a beer from the fridge.

He lived in a small apartment so close to the airport that he could walk home; which he always did since he didn't own a car. Stumbled, would be more accurate. He was a regular at the Downy Duck, an airport pub in the East terminal at Heathrow. It was a hangout for off duty airport workers and old pilots who were looking for stewardesses. Night after night, Benton would sit at the Downy Duck and tell the same old stories; which didn't always have the same endings....depending on how easily the rum was going down.

Benton had been married three times. All three were flight attendants that he met at the Downy Duck. And, all three ended the same way.....when he met another flight attendant at the Downy Duck. One of them was a beautiful German woman who didn't speak the slightest bit of English. That marriage only lasted two months, and out of that time they had only spent a couple of days together; which is why it lasted that long.

Benton's women troubles were only the beginning of his problems. There were no children involved with any of them, nor were there any hefty settlements or alimonies. For Benton, his luck at the poker tables was far worse than his luck with the ladies. When he wasn't at the Downy Duck, he was at the Fremont Club hiding behind a bad hand.

Through it all, he managed to maintain his pilot's license and wedge his way into the private chartered jet industry.

He was chartering just three or four flights per month and making ends meet. However, Alden Harlock paid much more. He really wanted to impress Alden and win over some high end business at the party.

Benton sat at his kitchen table. He swigged the beer to rinse the rotten taste out of his mouth. He thought about going back to bed but knew a good hot shower would be better. But, before he got up from the table a woman with short brown hair walked into the kitchen and threw a plate in the sink.

"Oh you're alive," she said.

Benton didn't respond. He looked at her and desperately tried to remember who she was and why she was there. He looked around at the mess in the kitchen and the huge stack of dirty dishes in the sink. "If you're my new housekeeper, you're fired."

"Lovely…..I didn't think you'd remember. You were pretty lit," she said. "I'll just bring you up to speed….. we had a fantastic evening together, you said you had plenty of room for me to move in here, and you said you were rich. I knew the rich part was just the rum talking, but I'm ready to move in anyway."

Benton leaned forward at the kitchen table and buried his face in his cupped hands. Then he tried to rub off the pounding headache in his temples. Then he looked up at the woman again, this time scoping for potential, and finding very little in her less than beautiful face. "Listen sweetie…..I don't think so," he said.

She unleashed a tongue lashing that would have made Dennis Leary blush. Then just as quickly as she had appeared, she was gone. He could hear her cussing and screaming half way down the block.

He dialed the phone…. "David, its Benton. What in the world did I do?"

It took a few moments for the laughter to stop. "Oh my friend, is that cat just now out of the bag?" David was the barkeep at the Downy Duck.

"Just tell me…..was she from the Downy Duck?"

"Yeah, but don't worry; she's not a flight attendant. You don't have to marry her. And, you'll probably never see her again either."

"Thanks. Bye."

Benton went back to bed, but he couldn't sleep. He was too worried about the women that were in his life and the money that wasn't.

Mike Rimmey

Chapter 13

"Here we go, let's see what we have here...." said Phil. He plugged the SD card into the slot in Frank's computer. "Alright here we go."

"Okay, cool, these things are stamped with a time and date. What was the date yesterday?"

"You're too young to start forgetting what day it is Ty." Phil looked at his watch; yesterday was the twenty-third, October twenty-third."

"Okay, keep going. Here is the seventeenth, eighteenth. How come most of these pictures are at night? Don't deer and skunks come out in the daytime?"

"Well they do, but they are just as active at night. These cameras have infra-red technology, and take great pictures in the dark."

"More deer....hey that's a nice one. Okay, the nineteenth.....deer, deer, what is that ugly thing?"

"That's an opossum."

"Nasty. Okay we should be getting close."

Phil Balasky and Ty Hyvek sat in Frank's living room looking at the pictures from his trail cameras. It was a last minute decision to drive out and check. Ty was missing a performance with the band at Gildersleeves, and Phil hadn't even told his wife he was back in Knob Ridge yet. At the same time they were excited and terrified to see what the pictures would show.

Then the picture popped up on the screen. Phil's mouth fell open. Ty studied Phil's reaction, not knowing exactly what this meant. For several moments neither one could speak. They were looking at a picture of two men walking past the camera. Their backs were toward the lens as the camera captured in crystal clear detail the man with the silver ponytail.

"I gotta call Kenneth," Phil said.

Ty kept advancing through the photos. Then they looked at the SD card from the other cameras as well. In all there were six clear shots of the silver ponytail. There were several shots of a very large man and even a shady glimpse of his face. But, the man with the silver ponytail.....his face eluded the camera. Ty pulled out a CD and saved the pictures to it. Phil was on the phone.

"Kenneth, how is everything?"

"Okay, I guess. I'm stuck the airport here in Denver. I've been waiting here for an hour and a half already and they just announced another delay. I feel like running to San Diego. What's up....is something wrong?"

"Uh, no, no, there's nothing wrong. Uh, I just thought I'd check and see if you made it home yet. I'll be praying for you," said Phil.

"Thanks buddy. I'll call you tomorrow."

Phil just couldn't do it. He could tell Kenneth needed to get back to his family. He just didn't want to add more worries to his trip.

Ty was looking out the window at the lake. He was entertaining an impulsive thought. Ty had suddenly an overwhelming desire to go to London and hunt down the man who shot Frank. He knew Matt should stay behind and Kenneth was already gone home; and he knew Phil was about to become his unlikely partner on this journey.

"Phil, let's you and me get on a plane first thing in the morning; and let's track down this dude with the ponytail and let's get Kenneth's book back."

"No Way."

"Come on Phil. Let's go," pleaded Ty. You and me; come on…..Kenneth has gone back home to collect his family and make peace with the wife….Matt can stay here and look after Frank….he has to stay and run the bar anyway. But, you and me…..we can do this. I'm free; you can get your assistants to run things at the church until we get back. Call it a sabbatical. Come on….a week….let's give it a week."

"Ty, these people are killers. We don't even know who they are except that one of them wears a ponytail; that's not much to go on."

"Yeah, but I bet we could figure it out. And this ain't just any guy with a ponytail; this is a guy with a silver ponytail who has an overwhelming interest in old journals. We could find him. Trust me, we could find him. If you don't want to go…..I'll go by myself."

Ty and Phil got in the Suburban and drove over to Phil's house, still discussing whether going to London was a good idea. Phil wanted to stop by and see Lena, but she wasn't there. She was at church; he forgot it was Bible study night.

"Ty do you mind dropping me off at the church? I really need to see Lena, and get a good night sleep before we go."

"Go? Do you mean you're ready to go to England?" Ty asked.

"Yeah, I've been thinking about it…..I guess you talked me into it. I mean Kenneth and I were talking about going. He needs our help on this one. I owe him that."

"Well Alright. Let's roll."

"I'll check on flights when I get home later. Just meet me at the airport in the morning."

"Hey don't forget you're two hours away."

"I'll be there. See you then."

Ty pulled up to the front door of the church. Lena ran out to meet him in the lobby. They waved as Ty pulled out of the parking lot on his way back to St. Louis.

Ty was already sitting in the uncomfortable chair for twenty minutes when he got the text. "I'm running late….meet you at the gate." He was already at the gate, and there was only forty minutes until takeoff.

An elderly black woman was escorted by her nephew into the gate 7b waiting area. She took the only vacant seat while her nephew went to get her a cup of coffee.

"Excuse me young man," she said. "They put the printing on this so small….is this the right gate?"

Ty looked at her itinerary, "Yes ma'am, you're in the right place."

"Oh are you going to London too?" She said as she parked her walker and took a seat next to Ty.

"Yes, my first time," Ty said.

"Oh, I think you'll love it. My husband, God rest his soul, took me three years ago. I have a grand-daughter that lives there now; she'd due to have her first baby any day now. At my age I hope it will be a smooth flight."

"Are you traveling by yourself?"

"Oh no my nephew Nathan is with me. He went to get us something to drink."

Ty liked the old woman; and though he wasn't the type that usually started up conversations with strangers, he felt like talking. She seemed kind and gentle and experienced all at the same time.

"What about you now, are you traveling by yourself?" she asked.

"No, a friend is meeting me....really a friend of a friend."

"Boyfriend or girlfriend honey?"

"It's a man," Ty had a feeling he knew where this line of questioning was headed, and he didn't want to go there, so he tried to change the subject. "He's a Pastor."

"Oh honey I've known many Pastors in my time.....some good some bad, she said, and then went directly back to her previous thought. "Now what about a girlfriend? Do you have one or not?"

"No ma'am. I'm single.....and happy that way."

"Oh my, a good looking young man like you.....you need to find that *one*. You know what I mean? There is *one* person on this Earth that God made just for you. You need to find her."

"Yeah, if I could find *her*, I guess that would be alright. The problem is I've given it a shot a couple of dozen times and haven't even come close."

"Oh honey, you need to follow the Holy Ghost. Do you have Holy Ghost power? Do you know what I mean be that?"

"No, I don't think so."

"Well, once you receive Jesus Christ as your Lord and Savior you're saved….that's the first step. And then you receive the baptism of the Holy Ghost…..that's the next step. When the Holy Ghost come upon you, you get mighty spiritual power, and He will be your helper and bring all things to your remembrance, and reveal things to you that you would have no way you could ever know. And then you'll be a real man honey, and you'll find that *one*, the *one* that God has for you."

"Yeah well, I guess we could all use that kind of power. I'm just not likely to walk into a church to find it."

Oh honey, you don't need to be in a church…..with the baptism of the Holy Ghost, the church will be in you; praise God, the Holy Spirit will be in you."

Ty didn't understand, and she could tell. The announcement had just been given for preboarding to begin. She knew she didn't have much time left with Ty.

"Now listen honey, I believe the Lord has brought me here to help you. Would you pray with me….take my hands."

Ty reached out and held her fragile hands. He could feel the loose fitting skin wrinkle around the back of her hand. She looked into his eyes and said, "I believe the Lord just gave me a word for you honey. I am going to prophesy a blessing into your life."

Ty felt ridiculous. He could tell people were watching. He no longer wanted any part of this, but he didn't want to offend the sweet old lady either, so he just closed his eyes and hoped it would go quickly.

"You are going to be a mighty man of God. And you are going to meet the woman that God made for you….I believe you are going to meet her on this trip. Jesus is going to save you and lift you up to be a mighty minister of His word, and give you the woman of your dreams….if you'll just turn to Him."

"Come on Auntie Dot," said her nephew who had just returned with the coffees. "We need to get you on that plane."

She let go of Ty's hands and looked at him with a smile that lit up the room. "Now honey," she said. "You pay attention, you look and listen for the Lord, and He'll be with you. God bless you now…..it sure was nice talking to you."

Her nephew helped her up, and guided her and the walker through the line and onto the plane; and just as soon as she had appeared….she was gone.

"Wow," Ty thought to himself. "That doesn't happen every day." He glanced around to find that nobody had paid the slightest bit of attention to him. He once again found himself sitting alone.

"Hey," it was Phil…..finally. "They start boarding yet?"

"Yeah, I was starting to wonder if you were going to make it."

"I'm here….it wasn't easy, but I'm here. How about you, everything okay?"

"Oh yeah, I'm just sitting here receiving prophesies, you know same ol', same ol'…."

Phil looked confused, "What?"

"I'll tell you later….that's us. Let's go."

The trip to London was underway. They boarded the plane; slowly, they single-filed their way to their seats. As they passed Dot and her nephew she reached out and held Ty's hand. "I know that girl is going to be so beautiful. I am so excited for you honey." Then she looked at Phil. "Oh hello Pastor, God bless you on your trip. You keep an eye on this one."

"Thank you ma'am, I will," Phil said, still very confused.

They kept pushing through the plane and ended up three rows from the rear. They threw their bags overhead and sat down. "Who's the old lady?" Phil asked.

"Just some nice old lady I was talking to while I was waiting for you."

"Must have been some conversation…..."

"Yeah, I think it was."

Ribbons of sunlight streamed through the vertical blinds in Kenneth Macklind's bedroom. He knew it was getting late but he had nowhere to go. He had his wife in his arms, and he could hear the kids playing/fighting in the living room. In Houston, Texas on this beautiful sunny morning…..life was good.

He laid there for a few minutes to see if he could fall back to sleep. When he realized that he couldn't, he meandered into the kitchen to put on a pot of coffee. He had morning breath, eight hour bed head, and a four day beard; but he was glad to be home.

"I'm starving, what's for breakfast?" he asked.

"Daddy, you're supposed to make breakfast," replied Christina.

"I'm supposed to make breakfast?" he grabbed her and gently tickled her ribs. The laughing drew the attention of the other kids. Before he knew it David had jumped on his back. He acted like he was too heavy and fell to the floor. Once on the floor another piled on, then another, then another…...until the pile-up had grown to a frenzied heap of giggling Macklinds.

This was it. This is what Kenneth had been missing. This is what was so essential to him that he left the most important piece of his life's work up in the air; after dragging his best friends into it.

"Okay you guys….. careful over there," shouted Barbara to no avail.

"Get over here and help me," laughed Kenneth from the bottom of the pile.

She cautiously approached the pile and began to attempt to remove children one at a time. But, Kenneth grabbed her by the ankle and it was too late. Barbara was now part of the wrestling match. It lasted a couple of minutes longer and then Kenneth began to work his way out from the bottom. He emerged with Barbara in his arms. He carried her out of the kitchen and set her on her feet. The laughing continued; it was his confirmation that he had done the right thing. He would leave the journal in God's hands. He knew this is where he was supposed to be.

Mike Rimmey

Chapter 14

Alden Harlock wasn't hard to find. William Wellshire sat at the bus station browsing the internet on his laptop, and his first search turned up nearly a hundred hits. But he was hard to see. William had tried to interview him in the past; he was more heavily guarded than the Queen. He took out his notebook and started jotting down everything he thought was interesting. He checked the tax records, marriage records, property records.....everything he could get through public searches. He was so busy writing and researching this Alden Harlock fellow that he missed his bus.

William was taking a bus to the airport so that he wouldn't have to pay to park his car. Now that he missed the bus it looked like he didn't have a choice. He was going to Northern Scotland to interview a farmer who had just won the lottery. He hated this type of empty news reporting but Ted had already demanded that he go, not to mention purchased the plane ticket.

William knew Ted had tossed him this useless task just to get him away for several days. Ted figured he couldn't keep up with his other story while he was out of town; that's how out of touch Ted was. William sat there poking away at his laptop for nearly two hours. He touched Rory's number on his phone, "Rory – Find anything out about this Alden Harlock?"

"No, but I should see Dr. Cranepool this afternoon. I'll see if I can get him to open up a bit."

"That would be great. It must be the same Alden Harlock that is the Curator of one of London's biggest museums. That might be a place to start."

"Museum….okay got it."

"And listen Rory……I couldn't find anything about this journal with the dragons. See if you can get more on that."

"Maybe there's a connection with the museum."

"Yeah maybe. Thanks Rory. Let me know when you get anything more."

"Will do William. See ya," said Rory as he hung up the phone.

William was seriously behind schedule for making his flight. He half-heartedly headed for Heathrow. The London traffic was worse than usual. He fought his way through, found a place to park and dragged his bag towards the main terminal. He checked his watch….flight departs in twelve minutes. "Probably began boarding ten minutes ago," he thought. He knew it was too late. "Aw screw it," he said.

He stopped right there on the sidewalk. He didn't want to turn around and go back to fighting traffic again. He didn't want to make the futile effort of trying to catch a plane he knew he was too late for either. He just happened to be standing in front of one of the airport pubs. "Why not, after a day like this I could use a drink," he thought. William walked up to the door and went in right under the sign that said "Downy Duck."

The place was quite happy. Commuters were killing each other on the freeways, travelers were rushing through customs complaining about waiting in yet another line; but at the Downy Duck, nobody cared.

There were several tables with people talking, but most of the customers were at the bar. It was a long bar; fourteen barstools wide, and only one currently vacant. William pulled it out, set his bag at the foot of it and climbed up.

"Good afternoon mate, what'll it be?" the bartender.

William smiled, "vodka martini."

"Coming right up," said the bartender as he immediately went to work on the martini. "Enjoy," he said as he presented it to him.

"Ahhh," William's sigh was audible.

"The bartender leaned in, "Is the drink that good or has your day been that bad?"

"The latter," William said. "But the martini is actually quite good."

"You know, you look familiar to me. Where do I know you from?" The bartender was squinting to help his memory.

"I don't know I get that a lot. Just one of those faces I guess," William replied.

"No he's right," said the guy in the barstool to his left. "I know you from somewhere too. I know…..you're on TV."

Now he was drawing attention. Everyone was getting a look to see if they could place him.

"Yeah, channel six news….right?" From a lady three bar stools down."

"Okay, Okay you got me. Channel six news. Come on its not like I'm a celebrity….it's just a job," William said.

"Alright you poor, dumb, cabbages, leave the man to his drink," exclaimed the bartender…..and with that most of them returned to their previous conversations, except the guy to his left.

"I don't watch much TV," said the guy to his left. "The news is mostly depressing and I don't have time for sitcoms."

"I know what you mean," said William. "It's mostly all crap."

They laughed and clinked their glasses together. "Hi, William Wellshire," said William as he stuck out his hand to shake.

"Nice to meet you William. I'm Benton, Benton Atwater."

"Well Benton what brings you here? I had no idea there was such a hang-out at the airport."

"I guess I'm like a postman that takes a walk on his day off. I'm a pilot. When I'm not in the air, I don't stray too far from the good old Downy Duck," Benton said as he lifted his glass again.

William laughed. He liked Benton. He sensed a down-to-earth honesty about him that made him feel at ease.

"How about you…..what brings the channel six newsman into this fine establishment?"

"Ahww, I was supposed to fly up to Aberdeen to interview that farmer who won the lottery. It was more like a reprimand for some interoffice mischief I'm currently right in the middle of. I guess I really just didn't want to go….so as luck would have it, I missed my flight. I'm sure my boss will be quite steamed."

Benton laughed. William laughed. The time disappeared as they sat at the bar of the Downy Duck; for William it was just what he needed. The vodka martinis were sliding down quite smoothly and Benton Atwater turned out to be a surprisingly interesting bloke. His tales of adventurous chartered flights with famous people had William on the edge of his seat. He told of the time he flew Paul McCartney to Japan for a court hearing; Paul was two days late and the Japanese Police were waiting for him at the airport. Also about the time he flew Roger Moore to Romania for the filming of a "James Bond" film. There didn't seem to be an end in sight of Benton's tales. William wasn't sure that any of them were true but he didn't care….it was fun.

"Alright, alright say that again," said William feeling the effects of the martinis. "You flew to Venezuela to pick up…..what?"

"Bitters."

"Bitters? Never heard of it?"

"It's an herbal flavored liquor," explained Benton. "I've never tasted the stuff but they made all different kinds of flavors. It's like forty-five percent alcohol. Back in the 1800's they were sold as medicine for everything from headaches to stomach aches."

"At forty-five percent, I bet that would cure a headache," William added.

"Yeah, the bottles I picked up in Venezuela were really old.....1872. The guy who bought them paid a three-quarters of a million pounds for just shy of six hundred bottles."

"You're kidding?"

"No. Beauty is in the eye of the beholder my friend. And to this guy, these bottles of bitters were absolutely priceless. It's the craziest thing I've ever seen," Benton said.

"Does this guy have money to burn?"

"I don't know much about him really. He lives in an old mansion....but, I've heard he inherited that. It's just old family money I guess."

"Probably never worked a day in his life," William guessed.

"Oh no, he works. Well, I don't know if I'd call it work but he holds a highly esteemed position running one of the museums downtown."

William perked up and got serious with his questioning, "Museum? What is this guy's name?"

"Whoa there pal. Let's not get too concerned about that. Let me tell you about the time I pulled the boots off of Roger Daltrey……"

"No seriously, what was the guy's name?"

"Look, Paul McCartney, Roger Moore…..I'm never going to see them again. This guy I still work for occasionally, and I'd like it to be more often. I don't want to screw it up mate."

"Alright look, I'm going to say a name. If it's not the same guy say so……Alden Harlock."

Benton's poker face wasn't working. He didn't have to say it. His reaction gave it away. He took a deep breath, took a long drink, and then said, "Now how do you know Alden Harlock?"

"I don't know him…..but I would like to. Can you set it up?"

"No." Benton motioned to the bartender for another drink.

William could sense that the situation was getting tense and he didn't want to lose his friendly connection with Benton. So he backed off a bit and hoped he could bring it up again later. "Alright, let's hear about Roger Daltrey and his boots," he said.

"No, No it's alright. It's not like I'm his best friend. What, do you want to interview him or something?"

"Yeah, something like that. Do you think he would meet me?" William asked.

"No, I don't. He is a very strange guy. He doesn't talk much and he doesn't go anywhere without his bodyguard."

William was really going for it now. He didn't know where it would lead but he knew he may never get a better chance than this. "Can you get me into the party?"

"How do you know about that?"

"Look Benton, I'm not a religious fellow. But, you have to admit; the odds of us sitting next to each other in a bar and hitting it off are astronomical. I must believe there is a reason for our meeting here tonight. Get me into that party. I want to get to the bottom of what's going on there."

Benton slowly shook his head with confidence. "There's no way I can get you in. I don't even know if I'm going. The only reason I considered going in the first place was to see about drumming up some more private charter business. But it's all too weird, you know….a little too dark and evil….it's creepy."

"What do you mean, what's creepy?" Now William felt like he was getting somewhere. He was getting Benton to open up. Just then two women walked in. Benton clammed up and William noticed. "What's wrong….who are they?"

"Oh crap, just some gal I met here last week. We ended up at my place and the next morning didn't go quite as she had hoped."

"Well here she comes…."

The woman walked over to them and began a conversation with Benton that William didn't feel he needed to hear. William got up and went to the bathroom, checked his messages, and by the time he got back…..they were both gone. "Wow, he's not that smooth of a talker…" William thought to himself. He reclaimed his seat at the bar and finished his drink. "Hey, what happened to Benton?" he asked the bartender.

"I didn't see anything," said the bartender, his standard response.

"Well I hope she doesn't kill him……I wasn't finished talking to him."

"Could you say that again ma'am?" Phil Balasky asked the young lady behind the counter at the Bristol Quarters, the hotel that their cab driver had recommended.

"Yes sir, it's one hundred and eighty-nine pounds per night."

Phil turned and looked at Ty, "That's over three hundred bucks a night."

Ty stepped up to the counter, "We'll take it."

The hotel was just across the street from the London Museum of Culture and History. They told the cab driver they wanted to stay close to the museum and asked him to show them an affordable place to stay in that area. They ended up at the Bristol Quarters. It didn't look like much from the outside, and the interior wasn't much different. But, it was a clean, comfortable room from which they could set up the headquarters for their investigation.

Ty slipped the bellhop a ten dollar bill as he unloaded their luggage into the room. As he shut the door behind him, they felt the sweet relief of completing the initial leg of the journey.

The room was very nice. There were two queen size beds, a sofa, a desk and two chairs, a refrigerator, a television, and free wireless internet. They had everything they needed. Ty flung open the curtains to see the view of the London nightlife. They had a view of the museum, but London streets are wide, with the lawn it was two hundred yards away.

Ty claimed the bed nearest to the window and jumped in to unwind. He fluffed up the pillows behind his head and took a moment to relax. Phil came out of the bathroom, "This place is great. But, one thing…..Ty, three hundred bucks a night…..I'm good for about three nights and then I run into trouble with the wife….."

"Phil, don't worry about it. I wanted to come; I knew what I was getting in to. I'll take care of the hotel bill."

"No I couldn't let you…"

"Yes you could…..and you will. I was coming here with or without you. If you hadn't come I would have dragged Matt along and then we probably would have ended up in a fight and in jail. If you look at it that way you're saving me money."

"Alright thank you Ty. So, what do we do first?"

"Well I'd say let's go see the museum… if it was still open."

"Are you hungry?"

They decided to stay in and order a late night snack from room service. Before the food arrived Ty unpacked his laptop; and they set up their command post. They had no idea where to start, but both of them couldn't wait to snoop around in that museum.

"Alright, first thing in the morning we hit the museum. What do we do ask the tour guide if there is anybody there with a silver ponytail?"

"Maybe the tour guide will have a silver ponytail," Phil said laughing. "In a situation like this Ty, you just have to go with your instincts, and keep your eyes open for God."

"What do you mean…..God's going to show us what to do, where to go?"

"Yeah, exactly…… Jesus never fails Ty. He will show us what we want or something better. I can promise you that. You just wait and see…..just watch."

"Alright, I'm watching. Let me know if I miss something," Ty said somewhat sarcastically.

"Oh, I forgot to ask you about the old lady on the plane. You said she was a prophet......what did you mean by that?"

Ty explained, "Yeah, she was just this nice old lady who sat next to me while she was waiting for her nephew to get her some coffee. So while we were waiting we were talking and somehow we got on the topic of my nonexistent girlfriend, and she told me I was going to find one on this trip."

"Find what.....a girlfriend?"

"That's what she said. But, she said it like.....real official. You know she proclaimed it; sounded like an evangelist from TV. Then she started talking about Holy Ghost power. That's when she lost me......but she was a nice old lady."

"I don't know Ty.....there might be a little more to it than that."

"What, you believe her."

"I'm just saying, she sounds like a mature, spirit-filled, believer. I believe that God uses people like that to speak into our lives. And I've learned to pay attention when someone like that has something specific to say about your future. Oh, and also....I love the Holy Ghost power part. You could use some of that power yourself."

Ty laughed it off; but on the inside he was starting to warm up to the idea of letting God be a part of his life. But for now he had heard enough. He was saved by the bell; room service was there with the food. They ate and did some searching on the internet. After an hour or so they both agreed they were ready to call it a day.

"You want a wakeup call?" Ty asked.

"No," Phil said. "Let's sleep as late as we can to try and get over the time difference."

"No Problem there."

"Hey!" yelled Matt Hampton as he walked through the door into his uncle Frank's hospital room. "Look at you sitting up and everything."

"Matt! Boy it's good to see you. This is nothing; I've been up walking all day. I'm ready to get out of this place."

"Yeah, I bet you are. What's the Doctor say about that?"

"Aw, he says another three or four days. I guarantee you I'll be out of here before that. I'll drive them all crazy. How is everything going with you?"

"It's going great. I just thought I'd stop by and hang out with you awhile. You got a DVD player on this thing?" Matt asked as he walked over to the TV.

"Yeah, most rooms don't but they brought one in here to give me something to do last night. I was complaining about being bored. They have a movie library at the nurse's station."

"I brought one of your favorites." Matt pulled out a DVD.

"Tombstone! Alright...... 'skin that smoke wagon and see what happens'...." said Frank, already quoting one of his favorite lines from the movie.

Matt put on the movie and they spent a peaceful, quiet evening together watching a movie that they'd both seen a hundred times. It's the little things.

The next morning showed up sooner than Phil or Ty realized. By the time they woke up it was past 10 a.m. The museum was open. Each got a quick shower; then they grabbed a pastry and a cup of coffee in the lobby as they headed across the street.

Neither of them knew what to expect as they approached the ticket window. They paid for the tickets and went in. It was a typical museum; terrazzo floors, soaring ceilings, tourists buzzing around in every direction following their own echoes. There were signs with arrows pointing to attractions and exhibits. Ty and Phil just stood there for a moment waiting for direction.

There were paintings, pottery, sculptures…..nothing that looked all that interesting. In the center there was a welded metal modern art display that looked something like a train wreck. They walked past it without stopping. Then Phil saw a sign with rather small print. It said…..Ancient Writings room……1st floor. "Oh, we have to check that out," he said.

They got on the elevator and went down to the 1st floor. The first floor hallway was quieter than the main level. There was a Japanese couple taking pictures by a wooden horse, a German family trying to find the elevator, and an older couple sitting on a bench; that was about it. Phil and Ty followed the arrow that pointed to the ancient writings room down the hall.

They entered the room. Phil remarked, "Boy, this just feels like a weird place." There was nobody else around.

"Walk like an Egyptian," Ty sang jokingly. "It all looks Egyptian….looks the same to me. What's BCE?" Ty asked.

"What?"

"BCE, see it's right here. It says this is Crete, from twelve hundred BCE."

Phil explained, "Oh that stands for Before Common Era. That's what academia calls it. It's the same as B.C., which stands for before Christ; but for people who don't believe in Christ."

"No kidding, I never heard that."

They moved through the room with some disappointment. There was very little that was biblically related and nothing that looked dangerous.

"Well, I don't see anything helpful here, what about you?" Ty asked.

Phil shrugged his shoulders, "me either," he said.

"Maybe we should just ask someone."

"Ask them what…..do you have any old journals that people would kill each other over?"

"No you know, just get in good with some of the help and get the behind the scenes tour."

"Ty, I think it would be best if we don't let anyone know why we are here, or what we are looking for. We don't know who we can trust so, let's assume we can trust no one."

Others were now entering the Ancient Writings room. It was two older couples who looked American…..obvious tourists. They passed Phil and Ty as they came in….. "Anything good to see in here?" The older man asked Phil.

Phil stopped, looked at the man and said, "No, I really don't think so, and I mean that literally."

Ty laughed, the old man and his wife just looked even more confused.

"Where to now?" Ty asked.

"Let's see if we can get some information on the museum staff. Maybe they have some informational brochures or something in the front lobby."

"What do we do if we see the guy with the ponytail? Tackle him, run and hide, ask him questions…?"

"I don't know. That's where the Holy Spirit takes over Ty, when that moment comes, it won't be me talking it will be Him."

They made their way back to the front lobby at the main entrance. Whatever it was they were looking for, they hadn't seen it yet. The museum was uncomfortably crowded. The acoustics inside were horrible; the marble floors and high ceilings made for an incredible echo. That, and the thousands of people talking, walking, running, laughing, yelling, etc., made it difficult to understand the person right next to you. They decided to go and have a seat in the museum café.

They managed to grab several different brochures on the museum and sat at a table in the café reading the brochures and having a cup of coffee. Just then Phil's phone rang.

He leaned way over in his seat to access his front pocket and dig out the phone; before he answered it he saw that it was Kenneth. "It's Kenneth, cat's out of the bag now," he said to Ty, and then he answered the phone. "Hello."

"Phil, please tell me you're not in London."

"Oh, hi Kenneth. How is everything with the family?"

"The family's fine Phil, where are you?"

"Well, my new friend Ty Hyvek and I are enjoying a cup of coffee at the café inside the London Museum of Culture and History. It's a lovely day here in London," Phil said trying to hold back a smile, and anticipating Kenneth's reaction.

"Phil, what are you doing? I really wish you hadn't done this. What's going on….tell me what you've found out so far."

"So how'd you figure out we were in London?"

"Well I called your house and talked to Lena, she tried not to tell me but…."

"We saw the pictures Kenneth. The pictures from Frank's trail cameras. The guy had a silver ponytail."

The silence lasted several moments. Kenneth didn't know if he should be scared or really angry. A million images were flashing through his mind……images of Peter, Frank, Ian; the whole thing seemed too weird to be true. Kenneth collected himself…..he had some things he needed to tell Phil. "That's gotta be the same ponytail from Peter's hospital room. This guy is very dangerous Phil. He got what he wanted, just let it go."

"Kenneth, we're just over here looking around. We're not going to cause any trouble. I can tell you there was a very strong leading on both of us to come here. I believe this trip is anointed."

Kenneth had known Phil far too long to discount his purpose if he felt led by God. He knew Phil would never joke about that.

Phil continued, "So far we haven't seen anything interesting. It's a pretty huge place. We've only been here an hour and a half."

"Alright, what can I do to help?"

"Stay available to us over the phone in case we come up with questions; and try to think of anything to send us in the right direction."

"Yeah, yeah, we should talk daily....at least once a day. Keep me up on what's going on, and don't talk to anyone else. Call me anytime.....day or night, I'll try and think of something else that might help."

"Okay, we'll stay in constant contact, and we'll just keep watching for God. By the way, how's Frank?"

"I'll call the hospital later......you know it's like five-thirty a.m. here. I'll talk to you guys later this afternoon."

"Alright buddy, we'll talk to you then."

Phil hung up. Ty leaned in and asked, "Is he freaking out?"

"Yeah, a little bit, but he's okay. Actually it is a good idea to keep him in the loop of what's going on here, both for safety reasons and because he's really the only guy who knows the whole Ian Burbrey-Peter Stroudlin story."

Ty asked, "Do you think we should try the police?"

"It seems like the right thing to do doesn't it. But, I agree with Kenneth on this one. The police are probably not going to help with this; in fact if we get the wrong one.....it could make it a lot worse. After the Houston incident and that diplomatic immunity nonsense, I say we stay away from the authorities."

 "Too bad Sharon Schaefer isn't here," Ty said.

"Who's Sharon Schaefer?"

"She's an investigative reporter back In St. Louis. She is one tough gal.....and easy on the eyes too. She is always investigating some corrupt politician or business, and coming to the aid of the independent little guy."

"Wow, that's it Ty."

"What Sharon Schaefer?"

"Yeah… I mean not Sharon Schaefer but, they must have a reporter like that here in London. Let's see if we can find one. I think it's worth a shot anyway."

"Let's look it up when we get back to the room. What do you say we finish this coffee and walk around some more?"

"Yeah, I want to see the dinosaurs."

Mike Rimmey

Chapter 15

A crowd was gathered in the break room at channel six headquarters. They were mostly pages and junior editors, but there were a few reporters joining in. It was past time for the afternoon break, but they were lingering and talking about the hot topic of the day. They were talking about how William Wellshire had missed his flight, and missed his interview with the lottery winning farmer from Aberdeen. The word around the office was that Ted was furious. Most of them agreed it was not his missing the interview that miffed Ted; it was simply another example of William's willful disobedience.

They got suddenly quiet when William came walking into the break room. He walked up to the vending machine and plunged his hand into his front pockets digging for change. He didn't see what was happening behind him but he could feel the tension in the room. Ted had followed William into the break room.

"Alright Mr. Wellshire, let's hear it…..what is it this time, your dog ate your report; your Grandmother died; no, I know…..you got a hot last minute tip on an even better story and made the decision on the fly not to carry out your assignment."

"Ted, I would prefer to discuss this in private," William said.

Ted turned around, kicked a chair out of his way and sped out of the room without saying another word. William knew he better follow.

"Ted," William called, trying to catch up. "Ted, wait up…" By the time he caught him they were both in Ted's office. William closed the door behind him.

"I don't know how I'm going to save your job," Ted said.

"Look, don't give me these dramatics. I'm the only one working on anything interesting around here, and you try and send me to Aberdeen…..that really sucked Ted. But, I did try to go….I missed the flight, honestly. Believe it or not, I don't really care."

The ball was back in Ted's court; and he knew William was right. He was his best reporter, and would get picked up by another station in a heartbeat if he let him go. He didn't want to let on that William was right.

Just then Ted's phone rang. He pushed the button to put it on speaker and yelled, "What."

It was his secretary. "We have two guests here in the front lobby that would like to speak to an investigative reporter. They say that the police won't help them and they would like help investigating a crime…..they won't say what it is."

Ted got a satisfied look on his face, "Alright Wellshire, here's you punishment…..go handle this. We can finish our discussion later."

William walked reluctantly up to the front lobby. He could see the guests sitting in the lobby from the hallway, he paused a moment to look. One man had long blonde hair and was wearing sunglasses, the other had on khaki cargo shorts, flip flops and a Hawaiian shirt. "Americans," he said. He walked into the lobby and stood at the door, "Hello, I'm William Wellshire, how may I help you?"

William escorted them down the hall to the conference room. "I don't have a private office, but we can talk in here," he said as he held the door open for them. "Now then, what's got the two of you so alarmed you're looking for help from good old channel six?"

Phil spoke first, "It's hard to explain.....I don't even know where to start. Someone, we think he's from London, tried to kill our friend, well several of our friends really. He broke into a home in Houston, Texas; in broad daylight, and was let go due to his diplomatic immunity."

William broke in... "Diplomatic immunity!" In all of Great Britain, outside the royal family, I could probably count the number of Brits with diplomatic immunity on one hand. It's very rare.....it's unheard of actually."

Ty jumped in, "Well it happened. Our friend's neighbor is a cop and he told him they couldn't even hold the guy. Then he went to Missouri and shot our other friend, stole some old journal. We think he works at one of the museums, and he has a long silvery-gray ponytail."

William sat there staring into space. This was way too hard to believe. "Alright, who put you up to this? Doug, Patrick Muldoon? Fun's over, thanks for stopping by. I'm sure we'll all have a big laugh over this...."

"Mr. Wellshire," Phil interrupted. "I can assure you this is not a joke. We don't think we can trust the police. We need help."

William looked over his shoulder, out the window to see if anybody was watching. "We need to talk. There's a sandwich shop at the corner of Tucker and Finch. It's just a few blocks north of here. Meet me there in fifteen minutes." William walked over to the door and said loudly, "Well, I really wish I could help you gentlemen, but we are so busy here. Thank you for coming. Good day."

They walked out quietly and walked down to the corner and hailed a cab. Phil and Ty arrived at the sandwich shop and chose a table outdoors on the sidewalk. The London traffic buzzed by; cars honked and sped past mere feet from the table. The sun had dropped low enough that they were shaded by the building. Neither of them had much to say, in fact they both felt a bit out of place. They ordered tea and sat waiting for William Wellshire to show up.

"Let's keep our eyes peeled for trouble," said Phil.

"It seemed like he knows this person.....if it's a friend of his we could be in trouble, if not maybe he can help," said Ty.

"Yeah but either way, we really need to be careful."

William was walking up the sidewalk. When he saw Phil and Ty at the table, he looked around to see if anyone had followed him. He walked up to their table and sat down. He leaned forward with both elbows on the table, resting his chin on his fist.

"Thank you gentlemen for agreeing to meet with me offsite; now, what's this all about?"

Phil and Ty looked at each other as Phil began, "Okay, first let me just say that we are not comfortable with this sort of thing…..I mean the guy we are talking about has already killed several people over this issue."

"And attempted another…" Ty added.

Phil continued, "I mean how do we know we're talking to the right person, or that you won't turn us over to this guy…..he seems to have everyone else in his back pocket."

"Well, you don't…..or I mean you can't…..know that you can trust me that is," William replied.

"Wrong answer," Ty said as he stood up to leave. "Let's get out of here Phil."

William stood up too, with a calming gesture, "No. No, No, don't go. I'm sorry, let me tell you about myself and let's try to set things at ease here."

"It's alright Ty, Let's hear what he has to say," said Phil.

Ty sat down, so did William. The early evening customers at the sandwich shop paid no attention to the scene.

"Now then, let's start over shall we. My name is William Wellshire. I am an investigative reporter for the channel six news. I cover police scandals, frivolous government spending, and government corruption…..that sort of thing. Needless to say, I have made a few enemies in this town. I have a few friends in key places, but for the most part…..the police department, fire department, the board of education, the Mayor's office, the Prime Minister's office….. even the Queen's office won't even talk to me. I do a daily segment on the six o'clock news and my ratings are tops. People.....I mean the real people in this city love this kind of stuff. That's the only thing I have going for me, the ratings.

Anyway, I can assure you I'm not in cahoots with the police or any government agency, and I would never knowingly put you in the path of danger or steer you in the wrong direction in any way.

The reason I got sent to meet you was sort of as a punishment. I was in my boss's office and he was losing the argument so he sent me out to the lobby to meet you. I was intent on sending you away as fast as I could, but when I heard what you had to say I almost fell over. I am currently working on a case that sounds quite similar......unbelievably similar in fact.

Now, why don't you tell me who you are, what is going on, and I'll see if I can help."

"I'm Phil Balasky, and this is Ty Hyvek. I am the Pastor of a small church in Knob Ridge, Missouri; and Ty here is a famous musician from St. Louis."

"St. Louis, is that the hometown of Tina Turner?" William asked.

"Yeah that's it," Ty said. "Same town."

So Phil and Ty took William through the story the best they could remember. They retraced the journal from Prague, then to London, then to Knob Ridge, and back to London. They listed the three deaths along the way that they were convinced were really murders. They told the story of

Frank Hampton being shot in his home the night the journal was stolen from a safe in his bedroom; and how they had seen the photos of the shooters on Frank's game trail cameras. Then they gave the description of the man they were after…..the man with the silver ponytail.

William listened intently and even took a few notes. He knew he would want to check out all of the names they had given him. If it all added up, he knew he was on to something big. After they had told all they knew to tell, William continued with his end of the story.

William took a long sip of his black tea, and then leaned forward. "Alright, now listen to this; you'll see why I almost fell over when you two came in with this today. Just last night, I was at the airport…..and I missed my flight. So I end up at a bar in the airport talking to this guy who is a private charter jet pilot for famous people and wealthy executives. Well, mostly I think he just sits in that bar and tells tales of charter jets, but I do think he occasionally lands a client. Anyway, after an hour and a half of chit chat, he tells this story about a client who he flew to Venezuela where he bought some expensive old liquor. The funny thing is I had spent that entire day researching the very same guy he was telling me about. The guy he flew to Venezuela is the curator of a museum. When I tried to question him further he just clammed up. Then you guys show up the very next day with more pieces of the same story. It's like the pieces of this story are just falling into my lap. It's like a miracle or something."

"No, it's not like a miracle…..it is a miracle," said Phil. "Let's work together. All we want is the journal."

"Well, as I said I have been researching some crime connected to the museum. My sources tell me about a journal.....written by some medieval knight who fought dragons....." Phil and Ty's reaction couldn't have been missed. "Oh, that's your journal, huh? My sources tell me its days are numbered. That's what I have been investigating."

"What do you mean?" Ty Asked.

"Well, I think that there is an elite group of academia, you know museum people, professors, and the like; who enjoy gathering together every now and then to delight themselves in the destruction of ancient artifacts. It's the weirdest thing I've ever come across. I think they usually focus on artifacts or relics that have some biblical significance. The guy with the ponytail, the guy from the museum.....I think he's the man of the hour. Anyway, I can explain all that later.....but, I am pretty sure this year's artifact in question is your knight's journal."

"So where is it....let's go get it back," said Ty.

"It's not going to be as simple as that I'm afraid," William said.

Phil asked, "So what do we do?"

William finished his tea and set his cup down on the table. "There is someone we should go talk to. Let's go to the airport."

The yard was mowed, the broken window was fixed, the house was clean, and the kids were finished with their school work; what a day. Kenneth sat on his back porch watching a squirrel scurrying about the yard. The birds were singing, the sun was shining, and the wife was happy; happy to have her husband home.

Kenneth's wife Barbara joined him at the patio table. "What ya thinking about?" she asked. "Sir Richard?"

"Well I didn't tell you this before but you may as well know…..Phil and Ty are in London. They're snooping around to see what they can find out."

Barbara flared, "You can't be serious…..you're not considering going…."

"No, I just found out….I didn't know they were going….I would have stopped them."

"What are they going to do…..I mean Phil is no James Bond, and you hardly know this Ty."

"You know Phil; he wouldn't have done something like this unless he was sure it was God's will."

"Well, what are you going to do? I don't want you getting involved. We just got this place put back together from that maniac, he got what he wanted, just let him keep it….Kenneth what if we had been home…..we'd all be dead right now."

"Barbara, settle down….. I'm not going to do anything. Phil is just trying to serve the Lord. He is certain this is his mission. And Ty has an incredibly strong loyalty to Frank Hampton….who I need to call by the way, and see how he's doing. Barbara, I trust Phil like my own brother, and above all I trust the Lord, who sent him over there."

"Please don't go…."

"Barbara, I give you my word…..I'm not going," Kenneth declared. "But, I was thinking of something I could do to help. Actually, I need your help as well. I want to call the nurse from Peter's room the night he was killed. She said if there was anything she could do to help she would. Maybe she could help Phil and Ty somehow."

"What do you mean I could help?"

"You know I mean just get on the phone with me," Kenneth said. It was their long standing policy that Kenneth, being a minister, and a public figure, did not associate privately with women. If he needed to be associated with a woman in any way….his wife was involved.

"Alright, let's give her a call," Barbara said.

"Her name is Jill Wright….I have her number stored in my phone." Kenneth dialed. The phone rang but there was no answer. He heard Jill's voice and after the beep, he left a message. "Hello Ms. Wright, this is Kenneth and Barbara Macklind from the United States……we were friends of Peter Stroudlin. I spoke with you briefly right after he passed away in your hospital. Anyway, we were hoping to talk to you again….if you could call we would appreciate it."

The squirrel was still bouncing around the backyard. Kenneth and Barbara were enjoying watching him. Barbara rested her head on Kenneth's shoulder. An acorn fell out of the pin oak and the squirrel rushed over to grab it. They laughed at him.

"Kenneth honestly, what could those two possibly do to help this situation over there?"

"I don't know. They were poking around the museum when I talked to them. Kind of like that squirrel, I guess. If you're in the right place at the right time an acorn might just fall out of the sky right in front of you."

Just then Kenneth's phone rang. It was Jill. "Hello."

"Yes, Hi, Mr. Macklind, this is Jill Wright. I'm sorry I missed your call."

"Hello Jill. I'm here with my wife Barbara. She will be on the phone with us."

"Hello Jill."

"Hello Barbara, what can I do for you?"

"Jill," Kenneth began. "Since I spoke with you last, there have been a few developments. Another friend of mine came very close to losing his life…..at the hand of a man with a silver ponytail."

"Oh my….." Jill said.

"Well it seems he was after something that at one time belonged to Peter Stroudlin. I brought it back with me and left it at a friend's house. It didn't take him long to track it down."

Barbara spoke up, "Jill, I know this sounds scary.....we don't want you to be uncomfortable...."

"No Barbara really, I'm not scared. I mean it's funny really......I would have been, terrified I mean naturally, but Peter made such an impact on me I really want to help in any way I can."

"Well Jill, we have two friends who are in London. I'm not sure what they can do....file a police report or issue a complaint or something, I don't know. They don't know their way around London; you're the only person we know....."

"Sure, I'd be glad to help.....you know show them around London or whatever....."

It was as if the weight was gradually being lifted from Kenneth's shoulders. Somehow, having Jill helping was comforting to him. She told Kenneth to have his friends call her anytime, even if it was just for directions, or to get her opinion on a restaurant. Kenneth could sense that she truly wanted to help, and with that, she was enlisted in the small but growing army against Alden Harlock.

William Wellshire, Phil and Ty took a corner table at the Downy Duck. William thought it would be a good spot from which to watch for Benton; since they last parted without saying good-bye, William wasn't sure if they had parted on good terms or not. They ordered roast beef sandwiches and crisps, and they spent the time continuing their conversation about this ready-or-not adventure that they were on.

"Funny how we have different names for things; I noticed you call these crisps," said Phil.

"Why what would you call them?" William said.

"We call them chips."

"Well now, there not really chips are they?" William countered. "They are slices of potatoes really, not chips. Calling them crisps refers to their texture…..I don't know where you get chips."

"Well you don't mind calling fries chips, I mean they sliced potatoes too, they aren't chips."

Ty was laughing in agreement with Phil.

William responded, "Let me set the record straight, fries and chips are two totally different things. Fries are actually just long, thin strands of crisps…..and by the way there is nothing French about them. But chips, real chips are different. They have substance, and style. The perfect chips will come wrapped in newspaper which soaks up just enough grease to allow them to be crunchy on the outside and wonderfully fluffy and starchy inside. They are a work of art, and the flavor has absolutely no comparison."

"Wow," Ty said. "I never spent that much time talking about side items."

The waitress arrived at the table with the food. William took the liberty of amending the order for all of them. "I'm sorry miss. I know the roast beef sandwiches come with crisps, but we simply must have chips with this meal. Would you please bring all three of us an order of chips?"

Phil smiled, "These chips have had a pretty big build-up."

"You won't be disappointed," William said.

""How long do you think we'll have to wait?" Ty said.

"He'll be here. From what I've heard, he's here pretty much every night. Let's just sit it out and watch. I'm quite sure this guy will be helpful; and I am pretty sure he knows the guy you're looking for."

"What are we gonna do, tell him his friend is a murderer, and ask him to help us catch him?"

"No, I don't think it is a friend of his…..it's just a business relationship. And, you don't want to catch him anyway; all you want is the book back, right?"

"Yeah, I guess so, but why would he want to help?"

"From what I could tell he's the type of guy who is up for anything that pays."

"Hey, we're slowly but surely draining our budget for this trip already," Ty said. "I'm not sure we can commit to paying off informants. How much are you talking about?"

"Well, look, times are tough guys; and to tell you the truth he's got to pay his bar tabs sooner or later. We might be able to get something useful for several hundred pounds. I can probably help you with that; the station allows me a small stash of cash for paying informants."

"Okay, now for the next question.....why would you want to help us?" Ty asked.

"It's a great story," William admitted. "This sounds like award winning journalism.....that and I love taking down villains. It makes me feel like a super hero."

"I would like to meet this guy, and talk to him first, to see just who we're dealing with. If he's Christian, I bet he'd be glad to help," Phil said.

Phil was a master at changing the subject. He could finish one topic in such a way that it led into another, and his other topic was always the same thing.....Jesus. He knew that by stating that this Benton fellow would help if he was a Christian would prod William to ask why. Over the years he had become an expert at taking the conversation from the natural to the spiritual. Phil waited briefly with a half smile on his face. The question came right on time.

"I assume you are referring to the content of the journal. So what is it about that journal that is religiously significant?"

Phil had a look on his face that said "Oh, I'm glad you asked." He leaned forward toward William and explained.

"You see William, the journal was written by a knight over a thousand years ago, who captured the details of his many adventures in this journal. Among the adventures he described were his battles with dragons. Most people think of dragons as mythical creatures, fairy tale stuff. But this was a real historical figure from the somewhat recent past who documented his encounters in great detail. Everything about the encounters are told and depicted in such a way that is obviously not fictional, but real occurrences. He even drew very detailed pictures of the dragons. These were real animals living in Europe only a thousand years ago. Now, here's the really wild part. The dragons he drew......they're dinosaurs."

William looked puzzled. "Dinosaurs?"

"Yeah, dinosaurs. You see the term dinosaur wasn't used until about a hundred and fifty years ago or so. Until that time they were called dragons."

"So you're saying that the journal demonstrates that dinosaurs didn't become extinct millions of years ago, and that Sir Richard was fighting them in medieval Europe?"

"What I'm saying is dinosaurs didn't go extinct millions of years ago, because there was no millions of years ago. I'm saying Sir Richard's journal is proof of a young earth, just like the Bible teaches. Dinosaurs didn't go extinct millions of years ago......they were just created about six thousand years ago; on day six when God created all of the animals. The journal is strong proof of that and apparently there are people who will do whatever it takes to keep this information from getting out there."

"Masons."

"What?" William's response surprised Phil.

"I bet it's got something to do with Masons; you know Freemasonry."

Ty said, "My uncle was a Mason. My Aunt hated it; he was always down at the lodge. It was a good excuse to get out of the house and drink beer with his buddies I guess, nobody knows what goes on inside those lodges."

William continues, "It's true they are a secret society, but I for one, know exactly what goes on inside those lodges."

Phil asked, "Care to expand on that?"

"It's all coming together," said William.

"What is?" Phil asked.

"Alright, I've been following corruption different churches and religious groups for a long time. It's sort of my thing. The Mormons…that's just a slam dunk; the Church of England …now you're talking about royals; the Southern Baptist Convention…don't get me started. But for several years now, I've been learning about the Masonic temple. I broke a big story a few years ago about how Masons help each other with favoritism in the business community, and got a rather large batch of death threats to go with it. Well, that just made me angry, and I've been watching and learning about them ever since. I'm pretty sure that the guy you're after is a high ranking Mason. I got a tip about this guy having some kind of party where they destroy a religious artifact. I don't know if they offer it up to some god, or Satan or what. But I have been close to getting this story for three years now and this time I'm really closing in on it. I think the artifact this year will be your journal, and I think it will be very soon. The party itself is probably not a sanctioned Masonic event, but I'm told there will be a lot of Masons there so, there is definitely interest. You would be amazed of some of the things I've heard, it really sounds a lot like witchcraft."

"I've heard the god of Freemasonry is really Lucifer, but I never really knew if I believed it, they do so many charitable acts," Phil said.

"Look, I'm not saying every Mason is evil, but at some point; at the higher levels, they become aware of a system that is very powerful and very evil. And the level we're talking about here is beyond your worst nightmare."

"Why would they do these things?" Phil asked.

"There is a group of the world's wealthiest, most powerful people who have tremendous influence in every government and are moving toward a new world order." William explained. "Their goals are to establish a one world government, one church, one monetary system; to cut the Earth's population by several billion; to control everything; you know..... rule the world. But I also think that sometimes they just want to have fun. That's what this party is...just a little fun."

Just then Benton strolled in. Phil and Ty were both still spinning from William's conspiracy theories. He didn't see them at first, and he took his usual stool at the bar. Several people stopped by to say hi, and then after he got his drink he spun around on the chair to take a look around the room. He saw several ladies he wanted to get to know, and then he saw them. William had his hand in the air motioning for

Benton to come and join them. Benton waved back and then got off his stool to make his way over to their table.

On his way he stopped at the ladies table. He talked with them for several minutes. They gave him a story about it being girl's night out while the husbands were playing poker. Once he realized he wasn't getting anywhere, he parted ways with the ladies and continued on to see William.

"Hey, channel six newsman, it's ummm....William, right?"

"Yes, William Wellshire. And Benton Atwater, I'd like you to meet my American friends, Ty Hyvek, and Phil Balasky."

"How do you do......How do you do." Benton shook hands with Phil and Ty.

"Benton, would you join us for a drink? I was just telling these gentlemen about meeting you last night; and about some of your adventurous tales."

"Alright, I'd be glad to join you, and most of those tales were true by the way. I was a bit juiced up last night, I don't remember you leaving."

"You left before I did. It looked like you found a lady friend."

"Oh, yeah, that's still working itself out. I am hoping not to run into her again tonight though." Benton turned toward Phil and Ty, "So, Americans ay; what brings you to this side of the pond?"

"Well," Phil said, "That's sort of a long story."

William jumped in, "Actually Benton, that is what we wanted to talk to you about. These gentlemen hail from the great State of Missouri. Haven't you recently been there?"

"Yeah, I flew a client home from there last week. Didn't get to see much though, didn't see it in the daylight."

"Well Ty here is from St. Louis, and Phil is from a little further out in a place called Knob Ridge," said William.

"That's right, it's a small town, not much to see compared to London," Phil said.

Benton's eyes were beginning to dart. He was connecting the dots and retracing the story in his mind that Alden and Adelph had told him. He knew they had been to Knob Ridge before he picked them up in St. Louis; and he knew that they shot a man. Benton was afraid to ask the next question but he knew he had to. "And what is it that you need to talk to me about?"

"Benton," William said. "I think the client who chartered your services last week shot their friend…" He pointed to Phil and Ty. "And then stole something out of his home. A journal. I also think this client of yours intends to destroy this journal soon. They would like to get it back before it gets destroyed. Any of this sound familiar?"

"Hey, what a client does is none of my concern. I just fly the plane wherever they pay me to go…"

William put his hands up stopping Benton's anxiety, "It's okay Benton, they don't hold you responsible, we were just hoping you would be willing to share any information you may have about what's going on."

Just then the waitress arrived with a tray of drinks. A Martini for William, iced tea for Phil, Ty had a beer, and Benton grabbed a tall whiskey on the rocks; which was empty before the others had even picked theirs up from the table. With the alcohol returning to Benton's system, he felt a little less nervous and began to open up.

Benton offered a warning, "If we are talking about the same guy…..you better be careful. Now, the guy I flew last week went to Houston Texas first. He slipped out of a small jam there and then drove to St. Louis where I picked him up. So, what about Houston, does that ring a bell?"

"Yeah," Phil said. "Kenneth's house…..he broke in and roughed the place up, looking for the journal. When he didn't find it, he drove to Knob Ridge."

Ty spoke up… "Did you see the journal?"

"Yeah I saw it, didn't look like much really….but that was the big prize; the journal of Sir Lancelot or something like that. He was pretty excited about it." Benton motioned to the waitress for another drink.

"This is unbelievable," Ty exclaimed. "That's him. We found it. Let's go get it."

Benton just smiled and rattled his empty whisky glass. He slowly shook his head and eventually responded. "You have no idea. You might as well just go back home before you try something as stupid as that."

"What about the party? Do you know anything about the party?" William asked.

"Yeah, I haven't decided if I'm going yet, but yeah, I know about it. It's on Halloween night."

"Can you get us in?" Ty asked.

"No way!" Benton said firmly.

"Alright let's think about this a minute," said William. "There's no way I could get in. I'm pretty recognizable from television and Masons hate me. What about you two….has he ever seen you? Would he recognize either of you?"

"Well he's seen my picture. He had a flyer from my church with my picture on it. And he knows I'm a friend of Kenneth Macklind, who's a famous speaker. He's never seen me in person though, as far as I know."

"No, you're out. If he had a flyer with your picture to hunt you down, we have to assume he'd recognize you. What about you Ty?"

"No he's never seen me."

William turned to Benton. "What about just Ty then. Can you think of any way to get him in?"

He repeated, "no way!"

"Benton, we really need your help on this, you're our only contact on the inside," said Phil.

Benton finished his drink and said, "Don't hold your breath…but, I'll see what I can do."

Mike Rimmey

Chapter 16

The arrangements were made. Benton agreed to call Olga and recommend Ty as the musical guest for the party. Everyone had phone calls to make. Benton called Olga; Phil called Kenneth; William called Rory; Phil called his wife; William called Ted notifying him in advance that he would be sick tomorrow (the martinis did the talking); and Ty called Frank.

He just wanted to check in and see how he was doing. Frank was so excited to hear from Ty. Everyone had been asking about him. He told Frank he just needed a vacation, and left it at that. He didn't want to upset Frank by telling him he was with Phil in London hunting down the journal and the murderer who stole it. Ty was relieved to hear that Frank was doing well; he was hoping to be going home in a few more days.

Phil and Ty went back to their hotel to relax. They both needed to kick off their shoes and unplug for a while. Phil took a nice hot shower and Ty lounged on the bed flipping through cable channels. He stopped on a station showing old Monty Python episodes. It was exactly what he needed. The ridiculousness made him laugh so hard the bed shook. With each belly wrenching laugh, the tension melted away.

By the time Phil was out of the shower, Monty Python was over, and Ty was asleep. He walked over to the TV and turned it off. He grabbed his Bible and sat in the chair by the desk. He searched the scriptures for wisdom and direction. The more he read, the more it stirred and strengthened his faith. He read the twenty-third Psalm. He meditated on each line. He read it over and over. He stood on the promise of God's word that He was with him. Phil knew that God would lead him, and prepare a table before him in the presence of his enemies. He was charged with confidence.

Then he turned towards the back of the book. He landed on the Gospel according to Mark, in chapter six, verse seven. It is the passage where Jesus called His disciples and sent them out two by two; and gave them power over unclean spirits. Phil began to feel that power rising in his spirit. His palms were burning as he raised them high in the air. Tears swelled in his eyes as he sensed the tangible presence of the Lord. He envisioned the room filled with angels and he knew that he knew that no dark power could stand against them.

In what seemed like an instant, two hours had passed. Phil flicked off the lights and drifted off to sleep with his mind full of Jesus.

Breakfast was served in the continental room, just off the front lobby of the Bristol Quarters Hotel. If one paid close attention, at least a dozen different languages could be heard among the guests clamoring for their free coffee and pastry. There were tourists from all over the world. London truly is a center for the international sightseer.

Ty stood in line behind a Chinese couple. They were having trouble deciphering the signs that were placed in front of the pastries. The Chinese man turned to Ty with a puzzled look on his face. Pointing to the pastry he asked Ty something about it in Chinese.

"It's apricot," Ty said.

Now the Chinese man was talking faster and looking even more puzzled. He was still pointing at the pastry.

"It's apricot!" Ty yelled. The increase in volume didn't help the Chinese man though. Ty picked up the last apricot pastry and left the Chinese man with one less choice to make.

He then went to the line for coffee. He stood patiently while an Indian couple filled their Styrofoam cups. He glanced back at their table and saw that Phil was talking to someone on his phone. He advanced in line and filled his cup with a robust African blend.

On his way back to the table, something caught his attention. Out of the corner of his eye, he noticed the color red. He turned his full attention to the most beautiful woman he had ever seen, wearing a bright red blouse. Her dark brown hair matched her eyes and brushed her shoulders. She was walking slowly, and looking intently around the room, as if she had lost someone.

"Please be looking for me..." he said. As soon as he said it, he couldn't believe that he had said it out loud.

She squared in front of him, looked him right in the eye and said, "Judging by your accent, I'd say you're right."

He wasn't sure what to do with that. It was not what he expected. "W…Would you like to join me for a cup of coffee?"

"No seriously…..I'm an acquaintance of Kenneth Macklind. I'm looking for Phil Balasky."

Ty's eyebrows raised. He stood there speechless; then realized this was another one of those moments that Phil had been pointing out; a moment where God was opening a door.

"Yeah," Ty finally said. "That's me….I mean that's not me, I'm Ty Hyvek. Phil is right over here…..follow me."

He brought her to their table and introduced her to Phil, and she joined them. They spent several minutes getting over the outlandish odds of her finding them in a city the size of London. Immediately, even though they had never met, Phil and Ty both felt they could trust her. They brought her in on their latest developments right away.

"So Jill, just to set the record straight, the ponytail man that you saw coming out of Peter's room that night…..his name is Alden Harlock. He is the Curator of the Museum across the street. We are certain that he killed Peter, as well as several others involved in this mess. He also tried to kill our good friend Frank Hampton."

"I know I spoke with Kenneth Macklind earlier. I just came by to see if there was anything I can do to help."

Ty couldn't take his eyes off of her. He watched the way she sipped her coffee, the way she blinked, the way she laughed….he felt like he was a high school boy with his first crush, but he tried not to let on. It was too late, Phil noticed.

"Well Ty here is going to be providing the musical entertainment at the big event. That's our in…..after that we're not sure. We are working on coming up with a better plan right now."

She wrote something on a napkin. "Here's my number, feel free to call if you can think of any way I can help. I'm actually on my way to work at the hospital now….I must be running."

Ty just stared. Phil said, "Thank you so much Jill, I'm sure we will be in touch."

Phil began laughing.

"What?" Ty barked.

With a smile, Phil said, "When's the last time you were out on a date, man? You were totally tongue-tied."

"Get out of here….What are you talking about?"

"Hey come on, I might be a married, middle-aged, ol' pastor, but I know infatuation when I see it."

Their room at the Bristol Quarters became the war room. Phil and Ty hosted a marathon strategy brainstorming session. William showed up about noon with a large paper flip chart and a handful of markers. They began diagramming scenarios. About one-thirty, there was a knock on the door. It was Rory. William had invited him to come by. He thought Rory would be great if they needed to do any sneaking around; plus Rory had the floor plans of the Grand Olympian hotel from the county courthouse history files. Just after that, Benton arrived, sober and steady.

Around five-thirty, they ordered sandwiches from room service. They had no choice but to stick to it and come up with a workable plan, Halloween was tomorrow. Here is what they had so far: Guests were set to begin arriving at seven-thirty. Benton was to arrive early, and Ty shortly after him. They would arrive separately though, so it wouldn't look like they were together. Ty would begin setting up his equipment and sound system and run through a sound check. With his many trips in and out, Ty was to find a clear moment when he could slip Rory in, who would be hiding in the bushes, without anyone seeing. Once inside Rory would get in the dumbwaiter and wait for the journal. At some point Ty would pass the journal to Rory in the dumbwaiter, and he would get down to the lower level and sneak out the back door.

It sounded simple…..too simple. Ty was not confident. "This is the stupidest plan I've ever heard. I've seen dozens of movies like this…..you know, '*Ocean's Eleven*'; '*Heist*'; now they had plans."

Phil responded, "That's in the movies…..that's fiction. This is the real thing Ty, it's never like the movies."

Benton agreed with Ty, "Actually I think he's right. This is right up there with the most ridiculous plans I've ever heard. So Rory's in the dumbwaiter, so what! You haven't even addressed how Ty is going to get the journal out of its beautifully lit glass dome......this is the focal point of the party you know......everyone will be watching. These people would be glad to kill you. That would actually add to the fun and excitement of the party."

"Maybe we need a diversion," Rory said. "Like an explosion or a fire or something."

"Yeah, that'd be great, let's just set the bloody place on fire," William joked.

"Actually, I like that plan better," said Ty. Let's set the hotel on fire, and watch them run out like cockroaches."

"And then what, stand outside and let the journal burn..... isn't that Harlock's plan anyway?" Phil said.

Frustration was setting in. They had no plan, and it was less than twenty-four hours until go-time. It seemed hopeless. The risk seemed too great.

Ty grabbed his black leather jacket, "I'm out. This ain't worth getting killed over."

With that he slammed the door behind him. No one else spoke; no one knew what to say. Without Ty, it looked like they were sunk.

Ty walked down the sidewalk. He just needed to think. "Why am I doing this," he wondered. Everyone else had a good reason. Phil just wanted an adventurous, mission for the Lord; William wanted an inside scoop on that story; Benton and Rory were in it for the money; but, Ty was not sure why he was there.

Was it revenge? In many ways Frank Hampton had been like a Father to him. The idea that someone thought so little of him, that they would shoot him just to get a book out of his living room infuriated Ty. Though Ty admitted to himself, this didn't feel like revenge. What was it?

He walked three blocks and then stopped at a small park. He sat on a concrete park bench and watched people walking their dogs. "What's in it for me?" Ty thought to himself. He was searching for a reason to go back to the room and finish planning this seemingly certain fiasco. "Alright, let's say I get the journal back......how does that help Frank?" Now he was talking out loud. "I'm supposed to walk into a killer's private party and steal his most prized possession right out from under his nose.....on the very night he's planning a big party, where the journal is the main focus of the entire evening?"

A lady passed closely while walking her dachshund, she looked in Ty's direction with a puzzled look on her face. Then he realized he had said that out loud. "I must sound like a nut," he thought.

He got up and started walking again. As he walked he realized that he felt very out of place……walking around a park, halfway around the world from home, with no idea why he was there or what he was doing.

He just kept walking; he had no idea where he was going. The street lights were on, and the breeze had turned into wind. He put his hands in his pockets to warm up and he felt a piece of paper that felt like it didn't belong there. It was Jill's phone number.

"Hi Jill, this is Ty, we met this morning…."

"Yes, I remember, you were the only Ty I met all day."

"Listen, I was just taking a walk and thought maybe I'd stop in somewhere for a drink, and I was just wondering if you would like to join me."

"Oh, I'm sorry I don't drink," Jill said.

"Oh, umm, aahh…"

"But, I would love to join you, if it means helping you stay out of trouble," Jill laughed. "Are you near your hotel?"

"Yeah, I'm a couple of blocks south of there; I've been walking around this park. I'm like the only one here without a dog."

"I know that park….I can be there in about twenty minutes."

"Oh Jill, that would be great. I'll be sitting on the corner feeding pigeons or something."

"Wow," Ty thought. He hadn't expected this. He sat and waited, and suddenly found himself nervous instead of frustrated. He wasn't even thinking about the journal, or the party, or the killer with the ponytail anymore......he was thinking about her.

She circled the park twice, and found a place to park. He still hadn't seen her when she came walking up. "Hello there, Mr. Hyvek," Jill said with a warm and tender voice.

"Hey, that was quick." Ty got up and went to meet her. He stopped and hesitated, she extended her hand first. "It's nice to see you again," Ty said.

They began by walking; just walking and talking. The conversation flowed effortlessly. They walked around the park; an hour passed in what seemed like only minutes. They discovered enough about each other's past to move beyond the casual acquaintance phase, they were now working on building a friendship.

"Are you cold?" Ty asked. "Is there a place where we can move the conversation inside?"

"Ty, this is London. There are ten thousand places to move our conversation inside," she replied. "But I'm not cold, it's such a lovely evening, let's stay outside and keep walking." Jill was prepared for a cool autumn evening; she even wore a wool scarf around her neck.

"Okay with me," said Ty. And they continued their walk. They laughed, and joked, and several times they stopped to look into each other's eyes when there was something important to say. All the walking didn't bother Ty at all; he felt like he was floating on air. He knew he was interested in her from the meeting at breakfast, but without even realizing what had happened she had consumed his evening and his every thought. Now several hours had gone by and neither of them had even broached the subject of the matter looming at hand. At the first break in the conversation, at just the right moment, Jill kicked it off.

"Tell me Ty, how well did you know Peter Stroudlin?"

"I didn't know him at all. I never even met him. I'm not even sure who he was. I have heard the story several times but to be honest, I didn't catch all the details."

"Well I only knew him for several days and he changed my life. He taught me about things I should have learned when I was a kid…..if I'd been paying attention. He read the Bible to me, and…..when I should have been taking care of him, he was taking care of me. I've been a Christian all my life, but Peter helped renew a fire in my heart for the Lord."

"Wow, you're starting to sound like Kenneth. I mean Phil is a Pastor, but so far he's pretty much left me alone with my own religious views. But, Kenneth, he's kind of pushy."

"Ty, I only knew Peter for a very brief period of time, but in that time…..in those several nights in that hospital; he became part of my life; like a father……he cared for me, I could see that in his eyes. That's why I'm here; because that journal was very special to Peter…..it was worth his life. That's why I'm here, how about you?"

"I'm here because I am a friend of Frank Hampton's. He is the one who got shot in Missouri; when this creep came to get the journal. I guess that's why I'm here, out of loyalty to Frank."

"So Frank asked you to come here and get the journal back for him?"

"No, he doesn't even know I'm here. He's still recovering in the hospital in St. Louis. It's just that I needed to do something. I couldn't just sit there and let somebody do something like this. Nobody just waltzes into my town and steps on my toes like that."

"So you're doing this for yourself?"

Her directness almost knocked Ty over. No one had ever talked to him like this. There was something very different about her….and Ty liked it.

"No I'm not doing this for myself. I want to get this journal back, and help put this guy in his place, and set things right. What's right is right."

She pondered that for a dozen or so steps. She stopped in front of a park bench and sat down. Ty stood in front of her. She looked at him and said, "Ty, you have wonderful intentions, but if you are doing them for the wrong reasons, then….. what's right is wrong."

He sat down next to her, showing his confusion. "I don't understand."

"Ty you said…. 'you can't let somebody do something like this'. Is that because nobody gets away with wronging the

mighty Ty Hyvek? And you are going to set things right?
Ty, this is a spiritual issue, and I can tell you one thing.
You are not wise enough, nor are you strong enough to do
this. You have been on your own so long; your life has
always been all about you. Unless you have His wisdom,
and His strength, you'll never have enough; and most
importantly, you have to learn to put the needs of others
before your own."

"Look, I'm just trying to do the right thing….." Ty
responded, although he knew she was right. He had known
for a long time now that there was more to life, but his
years of going solo had left selfish and stubborn imprints.
"What is the right thing?" He asked shyly.

"Ty I have a Bible verse for you…..Colossians, chapter
three, verse seventeen. Look it up. And consider what it is
that God wants you to do."

Ty's blank stare said it all. He had no words. He couldn't
argue, he couldn't question, he couldn't agree.

Jill stood up and took several steps toward her parked car.
"It was wonderful getting to know you this evening Ty; I
hope we can see each other again soon. You've got a lot to
think about tonight. Remember Colossians, three,
seventeen." And with that Jill walked off into the cool,
foggy, London night.

Mike Rimmey

Chapter 17

The night had fallen. The wind was getting angry and starting to bite. Ty zipped up his jacket and began walking back to the Bristol Quarters. By the time he got back to the hotel it was almost eleven. In the lobby of the hotel a sixty-something gentleman was playing the piano and had drawn an audience. Ty stopped to listen and just caught the end of an old Burt Bacharach song. The small gathering loved it and wanted to hear more.

"I'm sorry mates," the man said. He shrugged his shoulders and threw up his hands as he stood up from the piano. "I'm out of material."

He was hit with moans urging him to play more. Without missing a beat Ty jumped onto the bench and proceeded to bang out Elton John's "Crocodile Rock". The entire lobby was rocking and singing along. Ty was right in the middle of his element. This is what he understood…..entertaining people with music. He was no virtuoso on the piano but, he could knock out the songs good enough for a hotel lobby. As each song ended, the crowd cheered and yelled out requests; and Ty kept playing.

It was Ty's way of escaping the inevitable angst that was awaiting him. Instead of sitting alone and worrying, he had surrounded himself with smiling faces, and he had joined them. Happiness had spread through the air like a wildfire. The hotel manager came out from behind the counter to join in with the fun. He hadn't seen anything like this in quite a while.

People were coming up to the manager and asking him, "who is this guy?" He didn't know. What he did know was that he was witnessing a true entertainer. He played Billy Joel, Neil Diamond, Ronnie Milsap, Stevie Wonder, Mickey Gilley.....every genre with Hyvek style. The Lobby of the Bristol Quarters hadn't seen this much fun in years. The requests were too many; Ty looked around at the audience and he noticed a familiar face sitting at the end of the fireplace. It was Phil.

A smile overtook Ty's face, and he pointed to his friend. "You, at the end......what do you want to hear?"

Phil stood up and asked, "Do you know Amazing Grace?"

Ty looked down at his hands. He drew a blank. He could vaguely hear the song in his head but he couldn't come up with it. He couldn't come up with a key, a melody....he had nothing.

"I'm afraid you stumped me," Ty replied.

It was like the air had been let out of the balloon. Once he was stumped the people lost interest and dispersed. The manager approached Ty about playing again tomorrow night. Ty explained that he was only in town for a short time and he didn't know what tomorrow had in store. He hung around the lobby for a few more minutes talking to people and waiting for the crowd to dissipate.

Ty was severely bummed out. He had never been asked to play a church song before; and he certainly never desired to. But somehow, he had never wanted to play a song so much. Amazing Grace was now etched in his mental song list in the must learn category.

As the room cleared, Ty saw Phil getting up from the fireplace. They both moved toward the hallway that led to their room.

"That was fun," Phil said.

"How long were you sitting there?" Ty asked as they walked toward the room.

"I don't know….. Billy Joel."

"I needed that. To me that's normal. I just needed a little normal."

"Yeah I know what you mean," Phil said.

"Did you guys get anywhere after I left?"

"No, it got worse. It was a bad idea. Those guys aren't working together," Phil said as he unlocked the door to the room. He held the door for Ty. "There was no direction. Everybody wanted their own thing."

"So, we have no plan?"

"Not yet……there's still plenty of time for that."

Ty lay on the bed turning through the cable channels. "Nothing." He reached down to the nightstand between the beds. He pulled open the drawer and grabbed the hotel Bible. Phil saw him pick it up but didn't say anything.

Ty looked at it. He opened the front cover and read through the credits and publishers information. He thumbed through slowly looking to see if anything looked familiar. He looked at the back cover; and then he thumbed through it again.

"Hey Phil, is this thing any good? I mean is this the right kind of Bible?"

"Yeah it's good. That's a King James Bible; believe me that's the one you want."

Ty opened it again. He saw the first book; Genesis. He read the first line…. 'In the beginning, God created the heaven and the earth.' He kept reading and then he thumbed through to the book of Joshua. He read the first line…… 'Now after the death of Moses, the servant of the Lord, it came to pass, that the Lord spake unto Joshua the son of Nun, Moses' minister, saying….' "Hmmm, Moses, I've heard of him" Ty thought to himself.

"Hey Phil, where's Colesians?" Ty asked.

"Colesians? Do you mean Colossians?"

"Yeah I guess so, where is it?"

"It's way in the back. Here let me see…"

Ty handed him the Bible. Phil flipped to Paul's letter to the Colossians and handed it back. "What are you looking for?" Phil asked.

"Well, I saw Jill earlier tonight...."

"Oh, I knew it. I knew you wouldn't be able to stay away from her. I was just telling Lena about you two...."

"Hey....." Ty interrupted. "Will you just let me finish? We talked for a long time and got to know each other. It was great. Then we got into this situation and she accused me of being selfish and told me to look up Colossians, three, seventeen."

"Ahh... 'And whatsoever ye do in word or deed, do all in the name of the Lord Jesus, giving thanks to God and the Father by him.' That's a good one."

"What?"

"Go ahead read it."

He read it. 'And whatsoever ye do in word or deed, do all in the name of the Lord Jesus, giving thanks to God and the Father by him.' He read it again. He just wasn't getting it. Phil watched his eyes darting about the page and that he wasn't getting it.

"Hey Phil, what is this supposed to mean. Am I selfish?"

"Ty, it means that whatever you do.....I mean whatever you set out to accomplish in this world; you'd better be doing it for the right reasons. Whatever it is, do it for Him…..and give Him the credit."

Ty was shaking his head. "Why, why Him…..I don't even know who Him is."

Phil turned and reached for his bag on the floor on the side of his bed. He couldn't reach it so he got up. He unzipped the bag and pulled out a DVD. "Here, why don't you watch this."

"A movie? You want me to watch a movie…..What is this suppose to prove all your points?"

"Have you ever seen it?"

Ty looked at the movie box. "What is this, Mel Gibson's movie?"

"Yeah," Phil said, *'The Passion of the Christ.'* You watch this movie, and just keep in mind that everything Jesus goes through in this movie…..He went through for you.   He died for you Ty."

Phil laid back down and yawned. "I've seen it many times, so don't mind me if I drift off to sleep. Feel free to wake me up if you have any questions." He turned over and closed his eyes with a smile on his face.

Ty held off for about five minutes and then his curiosity got the better of him. He put in the movie. He watched it. The movie had succeeded in changing his view of Jesus, but that wasn't enough. Not for Ty Hyvek. "Hey Phil," he said softly. No answer. Phil was out. Ty had picked up the

Bible and was going to ask Phil what the best place to start reading was. "Aww forget it I'll figure it out," he said.

To Ty it didn't make sense to start reading a book anywhere but the beginning. So that's where he started......Genesis. The room was quiet except for Phil's snoring, and by the light of forty watt bulb he read, and read, and read. He couldn't put it down. It was all new to him, like another world he'd never even heard of. Yet somehow, he knew it was true. He believed as he read, and he read as he believed. He learned all about Adam and Eve, and Noah, and Abraham, Isaac, Jacob, the twelve sons, and Moses, and Joshua. He kept going, he kept learning. He couldn't get enough.

The hours rolled by. Night turned into morning. The sun had taken away the need for the forty watt bulb. It was seven fifty-three. Phil stretched and squinted to see the clock. He noticed that it was morning. He sat up. Slowly he got out of bed and went to the counter near the bathroom to put on a pot of complementary coffee. He went into the bathroom and then came out to wash his hands. He splashed some water on his face. It was then that he noticed Ty lounging back in the chair by the window. He was reading.

"Ty you're up early." Phil walked toward Ty. "What's this....the Bible? Oh Halleluiah. God's Word is awesome. What part are you reading?"

"Acts."

"Acts huh. Well, I would have had you start with the Gospel of John, but....it's all good," said Phil.

"Oh I read that too."

"You did? How long have you been reading?"

"All night."

Phil raised his eyebrows in astonishment.

"I just started at the beginning....I couldn't put it down. I skipped most of the Old Testament after Exodus. But, I read all four gospels and now I'm in Acts."

"Ty that's incredible. Did get any sleep?"

"Oh I haven't slept. I'm just not sleepy. I do have some questions about some of this stuff though. Wanna go get some breakfast?"

At breakfast Ty bombarded Phil with questions. Phil handled them one by one and helped to set Ty on the right track. Then he had one more question. "In the front of the Gospel of John, what is the Word?" Ty asked.

Phil responded, "Ty, the Word is Jesus Christ. He is the Word of God. Through Him all things were made."

"Yeah, it said that the Word was in the beginning with God....."

Oh, I think I see what you're getting at," Phil said. "You see, Jesus Christ existed before He was born in that manger. In Genesis, three, eight, when the Lord was walking in the garden in the cool of the day…..that was Jesus. When He spoke to Moses from the burning bush….that was Jesus. You see His earthly existence began in the manger in Bethlehem, but He has always existed. He is eternal. He is God. As the Word of God, the Son of God, the Lamb of God…..Jesus Christ is God."

Ty fell to his knees. He closed his eyes tightly and tears streamed from them. He bowed his head and said "my God."

Phil put his arm around him and said, "Ty He loves you. He has such an awesome plan for your life, and He wants you on his team. Are you ready now?"

"I'm ready." Ty said.

Mike Rimmey

Chapter 18

The Grand Olympian Hotel was the tallest building on the block. It was built in 1790, and has proudly stood as East London's prim and proper luxury hotel ever since. Everything about the hotel was grand. Though most of the East End neighborhood had seen better days, the Grand Olympian continually struggled to maintain its regal status.

It was four o'clock. A plain, dirty, white delivery van pulled onto the parking lot of the Grand Olympian Hotel. It secured a spot on the lot with a clear view of both the front door and the side delivery door. Behind the wheel was Rory, and in the makeshift surveillance post, was William Wellshire.

Rory jumped into the back with William. "Anyone see us?" He asked. The windows were heavily tinted so no one could see inside.

"No, we blend right in here. This is perfect we're in position two hours early. Let's just take our time and make sure we're ready."

"Do you think the Americans will show?"

William replied, "If they do great…...If they don't, that's great too. I'm getting this story either way."

William and Rory settled in and prepared themselves for what was probably going to be a stressful evening. At 5:20, a catering crew arrived and unloaded dozens of large stainless steel trays of food. "It looks like they're going to be eating well," Rory said.

Then at 6:40 a black Mercedes pulled right up to the front door. Three people got out. The driver was a huge man; he opened the back door for the two other passengers. William grabbed his binoculars. Out stepped a small woman, and a man. The woman was pulling a black roller bag, and the man was on the phone; he was wearing a black suit with a red shirt, and no tie. His hair was pulled back into a ponytail.

"That's him," William exclaimed.

Rory sprung to the edge of his seat. "Look at the size of his driver."

"Don't worry about him, he's most likely even dumber than he looks. Check out the case the woman is pulling behind her......that's probably the journal."

"It's very diligent of them to take such caution with it, so it's in good shape when they destroy it," said Rory.

"Alright Rory my man, guests should be arriving in another hour, let's make sure our communicators are working."

They each had a small microphone wired to the lapel of their jackets, and a small earphone in one ear. It was a crude two-way radio system that William found in a drawer at the station. He knew it probably hadn't been used in years, but he knew he had to be able to communicate with Rory once he got inside.

They each turned their units on and then Rory got out of the van and walked up toward the building. Standing on the curb just in front of the main entrance Rory tested the radio, "Can you hear me now?" he said.

"Yeah I hear you loud and clear. How far do you think this is…..about forty or fifty meters?"

"Yeah, about fifty I'd say. I'll take a walk around and see if I can see anything. What do you want me to look for?"

"Anything you can use Rory…..that's why I brought you to this party, you're the expert at this sort of thing.

Rory walked around the corner and towards the back of the hotel. He was out of William's line of sight and the radio was still working fine. He nosed around the back lot for a while, and noted all of the points of entry. He didn't think it would be a problem to get in.

"Hey Rory," William said into Rory's ear.

"Yeah."

"Come on back to the van. Some more cars have pulled up to the front. I want to get into position."

Rory got back into the van and just as he did, a taxi pulled up to the front of the hotel. Two men got out. William was anxiously on point through his binoculars trying to see who it was. Then he got a clear shot. It was Phil and Ty.

"What in the world are they doing?"

"Is that who I think it is?" Rory said.

"Yeah, I don't believe this." William opened the side door of the van and stood on the running board. He gave a loud, alerting whistle. When they turned to look he waved. "Get over here you idiots," he said although they were too far to hear him.

Phil and Ty both turned to look at the whistle but they weren't sure who it was. After another whistle and more "get over here" waving, they figured they better go see who it was.

Somewhat nervously they approached the van. They walked up to the side door where William had been waving. The door slid open.

"Get in, get in," William said. "What are you doing?" he asked.

Phil answered, "We're getting the journal back."

"I'm surprised…..I didn't think you'd show up."

Phil just shrugged his shoulders.

"What were you going to do just walk right in and say 'we're here!'? You must have something better than that."

"Actually," Phil said. "We don't. I mean, I know one thing…..we're getting that journal, but we don't have all the details yet. But, we know this is where the journal is, so we figured let's start by showing up. What about you guys, what have you got?"

"Aren't you supposed to be playing music?" William said to Ty.

"I'm not in a very entertaining mood right now," said Ty.

Rory looked at William as if he was asking for permission to tell them. William gave him the nod. Rory said, "Well mates, this party is by invitation only…..but you will need a password to get in. I intercepted the password at the University yesterday. I'm going in with a two way radio wired under my coat. I will be getting names and the inside scoop on what's going on for Mr. Wellshire here. If you get in…..don't acknowledge me, don't even look at me. You just go about your business and I'll go about mine."

"Okay by me," Ty said. "You gonna tell us what it is, or what?"

"Tubalcain."

"Tubalcain? That's a password?" Ty questioned.

"That probably refers to Tubalcain, a descendant of Cain from the Bible in Genesis chapter four. He was a forger of iron, and a craftsman of some sort," explained Phil.

"It's a Masonic password," William said. "Just don't shake hands if you can avoid it. They have secret handshakes and if you mess it up you'll stand out like a sore thumb."

"Will everyone in there be a Mason?"

William replied, "No. We're not sure how extensive the guest list is; that is my main reason for being here. Hey!" William shouted. "There's Benton."

Guests were arriving one after another. Benton Atwater had just arrived alone.

"Well it's been great sitting around and talking with you gentlemen, but Tubalcain it is….I'm going in," Ty said.

He walked up to the main entrance and held the door for another couple who was coming in close behind him. "Hi, how ya doing?" Ty said. He got a quick, "fine thanks," in return. In the entrance hall people were mingling, champagne was flowing, and they were lining up to get into the ballroom.

The entry to the grand ballroom was through a double door pass-through. There was a man at the first door allowing people to enter, one at a time into a small, dim, four foot by four foot room; where they would give the password to Adelph, and then be allowed to enter into the celebration. Ty got in line. He saw Benton Atwater go through a dozen or so people ahead of him. He kept inching forward. Now he was next. The man at the first door opened it for him. "Right this way sir," he said.

Ty stepped forward. "Jesus help me," he whispered under his breath. That very moment he felt it. His spirit stirred with confidence and strength. He walked into the pass-through, looked Adelph right in the eye and said, "Tubalcain!"

"Good evening sir, and what is your name?"

"Name's Tyler." Said Ty, but he didn't like the way Adelph was questioning him. It felt like he was suspicious of him.

"Yes, Mr. Tyler, and who are you with?"

Without thinking, Ty smoothly and confidently said, "I'm afraid I'm by myself. I do hope to catch up to associates of mine from Dr. Cranepool's group." It was the perfect response; Adelph didn't know Dr. Cranepool, but he had seen his name on the "A" guest list. It validated Ty's attendance. It was not a lie, he heard the name from Rory, and he did hope to catch up to him.

With that, Adelph opened the door, "Enjoy yourself, Mr. Tyler. It's going to be a wonderful evening."

"Oh, I'm sure of that," Ty said as he entered the grand ballroom.

He was struck by the elegance of the room. The ceiling was thirty feet high and the floor was covered with bright red carpet. There were elegantly set tables, but no one was sitting. The room was beautifully lit. The hundreds of chandeliers were glowing just like candles. There was music, but no band. Classical strings were piped in through the house system. The walls were lined with huge Roman pillars, and there was a balcony overlooking the dance floor.

It was more crowded than he had imagined. Ty was pretty good at judging crowds, and he was thinking two to three hundred people. They were talking, and drinking, and laughing; they were having a good time…..a very polite, high class kind of good time.

As he entered the room he went to the right and ended up walking along the stage. He noticed a nice heritage-cherry sunburst Gibson Les Paul guitar in a stand on the side of the stage. A waitress with a tray of drinks walked past and offered Ty his choice of wine or champagne. He stopped her, "When does the band start?" he asked.

"Oh there is no band tonight," she said.

"Well I just noticed the guitar there next to the stage and I assumed there was."

""Do you play?" she asked.

"Yeah, that's a beautiful guitar," he said while admiring it."

"Well honey, if this party gets any more boring, I'll see about getting you up there to entertain us," she winked.

He grabbed a glass of red wine, and continued walking. "Okay, here goes…" he thought, and put on a big smile as he approached an older gentleman who also appeared alone.

"Hi," Ty said. He opened his hands and tilted his head, "wonderful evening."

The man looked glad to have someone to talk to. "Why yes," he said with an aristocratic English accent. "I am so delighted to be here. I am reminded of the first time I enjoyed this grand hotel in 1968. Have you ever been here….I detect you are an American."

"No, I've never been here, but it reminds me of the Fox theatre in St. Louis. I saw the Allman Brothers there in 1988."

The gentleman looked puzzled. Ty was just having a little fun with him. But then he saw her. Through the crowd, as if in slow motion, he saw her. He didn't even hear the gentleman's question. "I'm sorry, I have to see her," Ty said to him. The man looked quite offended and turned away. Ty began slowly walking in her direction. It was Jill.

She hadn't seen him yet. She was waiting for a coke at the bar, by herself. He continued towards her. He had never felt this before, it was at this very moment that he was absolutely positive that he was in love with her. She looked so beautiful. The light danced off of her brown hair with a shimmer. She was wearing a gorgeous black evening gown that was made for her figure.

They were still fifty feet apart when she looked his way; and then…..their eyes met. She smiled. He smiled. He fought his way through the crowd without taking his eyes off her. She felt it too.

"Hey, I heard you had quite a night after I left," she said and gave him a tight hug.

Ty hugged her back and held on even tighter.

"Ty, I'm so happy for you. Phil just told me what happened. You're saved. If nothing else comes from this it was worth it…you found Jesus!" she said and then suddenly became aware of her surroundings. "Although, perhaps we should talk about that later."

"So you saw Phil?"

"Yes, I saw him in that ridiculous van they have staking out the parking lot."

Ty laughed, "I know, William thinks he's Maxwell Smart."

"So, have you seen it…..there it is," she pointed to the journal. It was perched on a wooden book stand; it was closed, but in full view for all to see on a table in the front of the ballroom. Red velvet rope guarded it with a ten foot perimeter.

"Hmmm," Ty raised his eyebrows. "I thought it would be more heavily guarded."

"No, it's right there in the open…..doesn't mean it can just be picked up, this isn't a bookstore."

"Let's go have a look," Ty said. He extended his right arm and she took it.

She held on to him through the crowd. There were several small groups gathered around the red velvet rope. They were checking it out, laughing and sneering at it. "The worst part is…..…" they could over hear a man talking to a small group of onlookers. "The idiot creationists would have a field day with this journal. They would be forcing the idea that "dragons were really dinosaurs and demanding biblical timelines."

On the other side of them, they overheard a man say…..… "No telling what they would have done with this. The truth in the wrong hands is a very dangerous thing."

It was then that Ty realized that the opposition was in two camps. There were the intellectual elitists who simply didn't believe in God, or a biblical creation and laughed at it condescendingly; and then there were Satan's evil helpers who knew the truth, but would do anything to distort or destroy it. He didn't know which was worse, but he figured the majority of the crowd was the latter.

Ty and Jill stood there at the red velvet chains. They were only ten feet away from the goal, and seeing it only made Ty aware of the limited time.

"Doesn't look like much does it?" said Benton Atwater. Ty hadn't noticed him; he had been standing there for a minute or two.

"It doesn't really matter what it looks like," Ty said.

Benton leaned in close so no one else could hear, "Why don't you get out of here and just go home. You're a nice guy Ty; I don't want to see you do something stupid," and then he calmly walked away.

Benton had only gone a few steps when someone called his name. "Benton, come over here, I would like you to meet my friend Dr. Gates." Benton turned and walked in that direction. He shook hands with several men in the group without letting the smile slip off his face. Then Ty saw the man that had called him over; he was a handsome gentleman, who wore a black velvet jacket with a red shirt buttoned all the way up. He had whitish silvery hair that was pulled back and no facial hair.

"That's him."

Jill was looking too, "Yeah, I see him. The man with the silver ponytail; that's the man from Peter Stroudlin's room the night he was killed."

"Yeah," Ty said. "That's the guy that tried to kill Frank."

"Rory, can you hear me?"

Phil and William were perched in the surveillance van in the parking lot. Rory had gone in the side entrance, disguised as a waiter, twenty minutes ago and they hadn't heard from him yet. They were wishing they had planted a camera on him so they could see what was going on.

"Yes, loud and clear. I'm in…..having a lovely glass of champagne."

Phil took the mic, "Rory do you see Ty, is he okay?"

"Yeah I see him, he found his lady friend," Phil shook his head and smiled at William. "They are right in front of the journal looking at it."

"Do you see Harlock?" William asked.

"Yeah, he's here….the man of the hour. Guess who else is here? You're going to love this…."

"Who, who do you see?" William yelled.

"Can't blurt out names right now," Rory said. "I'm going to walk around and mingle. I'll try to get some pictures and strike up some interesting conversations for you."

"Okay Rory, thanks."

Rory walked around looking to see if he recognized anyone. He saw Dr. Cranepool walking his way and knew he had to steer clear of him. He ducked and did an about face. He stood behind one of the columns for a moment until Dr. Cranepool had passed. He stepped back out into the scene, cool as a cucumber.

For the evening, Rory was pretending to be a professor from the University of York. He knew how Universities operate and York was a bit less known. He felt confident that he could pull it off.

Rory moved around the room and drummed up several conversations that William enjoyed hearing. He generated a decent guest list and kept William involved in the evening. Then he could feel the buzz of the crowd. Something was happening, he could sense a stir, and people were getting quiet.

"Hey William, are you listening?"

"Yeah, I'm here."

"Good, I think this is the moment you've been waiting for."

Alden Harlock took the podium. Rory got close to the loudspeakers so William could get it clearly.

"I would like to thank you all for coming tonight. I do hope everyone is having a good time."

The crowd cheered. Alden delivered a short speech in which he announced that the climax of the evening will occur at midnight when the journal of Sir Richard the Elder of Landolte would be burned.

"At least now we have a timeline," Phil said.

Rory made his way over to the area of the ball room where he last saw Ty and Jill. He found them, they were seated and talking.

"Hey, you two enjoying yourselves?" Rory asked.

"Yes and no," Ty said.

"Well according to our hero's speech you have less than ninety minutes to get your prize."

"Got any ideas?" asked Ty.

"Yeah, but I could really use a very loud thirty second distraction," said Rory.

Ty was interested, "what do you mean?"

"You give me thirty seconds with the entire crowd looking the other way and some cover noise; and I'll get it. But it's got to be precisely timed," predicted Rory.

"Alright.....when?"

"What's you distraction?"

"There's an old Les Paul on the side of the stage. I'll turn the amp up to eleven and wail for a couple of minutes.....no big deal."

"That just might do it. Jill here will watch me. When I get into position, she will let you know and then I'll just wait for the guitar."

"What's your plan?" Ty asked.

"Don't worry mate. It would take too long to explain; you just get the guitar and draw a lot of attention."

Ty knew he could handle his part of the scheme, but he wondered about Rory. He didn't even know the guy. But, somehow he felt confident with Jill by his side.

"Hey there…." Ty called. It was the waitress that he met earlier in the evening. "Remember when you joked that if things got too boring you'd let me get up and play that guitar…..I think we're there."

"Honey, I couldn't agree more. Go for it."

"Well could you help me….I want to surprise everyone," he said.

"Yeah, come on……This is just a part time job that I don't like anyway. Why not."

She led him backstage. Jill stayed and watched Rory from a distance. In a blink of an eye, he vanished under the table. She approached the table to be sure she really saw what she thought she just saw. She did. He peaked out at her and winked with a thumb up. Rory was in position.

Ty was backstage; he gathered the cords and plugged everything in. He knew this had to be spontaneous; no sound check tonight. He strapped on the guitar and powered up the amps. He smiled when he heard the buzz of wattage surging through the speakers of the house sound system. He turned the amp up good and loud and stepped on a distortion pedal. He peaked through a seam in the curtain. He could see Jill off to the side. He poked his head through and managed to get her attention. She gave him the thumbs up. He smiled.

Ty stepped out onto the stage with Les Paul shouldered proudly. He stood there a few seconds and watched; nobody had even noticed him standing there yet. He took a deep breath and blasted into a searing lick that immediately turned every head in the place. The waitress was standing off to the side and threw on the lights. Ty was in the spotlight; this was his domain.

He walked as he played. It was loud enough to cause a great deal of confusion. Some liked his playing and were happy to see something unexpected happen.....but not Alden Harlock. He looked for Adelph; he wanted to know who this person was and what was going on.

The guitar solo continued; it screamed; it scolded. Benton was laughing. Jill was amazed. Phil and William were on the edge of their seats and Rory was hard at work.

As soon as Rory had heard the guitar, he fired up the saw. It was a high-tech cordless circular saw that looked like something out of Mission Impossible. He borrowed it from a friend at the University. It spun the super sharp slitting blade at an ultra high speed; and it was relatively silent. The saw wasn't noticeable over Ty's guitar solo.

Once Rory cut the hole in the floor, he popped up, grabbed the journal and then in a flash he disappeared under the table. He and the journal dropped through the hole in the floor to the room below. Rory never missed a beat; he rolled onto his feet and ran down a dark hall, up the stairs and out the staff entryway on the side. He was yelling "Roll, roll, roll, let's go…..I got it. The side door….the side door."

William flew into the front seat and started the van. He peeled out leaving a puff of black smoke and screeched to a stop in front of the side door where Rory was anxiously waiting for him. The side doors of the van flew open, and Phil extended his hand to help Rory in. William stomped on the accelerator again; Rory was mostly into the van; his legs were still hanging out. Phil secured the journal and then grabbed Rory by the shirt as they hung on around a sharp corner. Finally, Rory got his body in the van and the side doors slammed.

"Ty, Ty……What about Ty and Jill?" Phil was yelling. He pulled out his phone and texted Ty; "we got it….get out of there."

William was several blocks away and still pushing it. Rory was reclining in the captain's chair, "Wow….that was a smooth operation."

Phil was trying to get through to William, "Let's swing around and pick up Ty and Jill."

"Doesn't sound like a good idea. Let's get a few kilometers between us and Harlock first."

Jill did the wise thing; just as Ty was wrapping up the guitar solo, she went to him. She knew they were going to have to get out of there fast, and she wanted to be with him. Ty struck one last chord, and set the guitar in the stand. Always the polite entertainer, he took a bow. He was met with a strange mixture of applause and blank stares.

On his way off stage, he grabbed Jill's hand, and they ran together through the kitchen. Ty saw Phil's message and pumped his hand into the air, "Yes!"

Ty's waitress friend saw them running through and said, "Leaving so soon…?"

Ty said, "Listen, thank you for all your help, but we need one more favor. Get us some cover and get us out of here."

"Honey, they're not going to be that angry over a little guitar playing, I mean it was a little on the loud side but…."

"No, you don't understand there is a lot more to the story."

She looked at Ty and saw that he was serious. She saw the urgency in Jill's eyes.

"Please!" Jill pleaded.

"Oh, things are getting crazy out there…." They heard another waitress declare.

"Can you hide us?" Jill asked.

"Alright follow me," she said. She led them through the pantry into the busiest part of the kitchen. "Get in here," she said.

Ty and Jill climbed into a huge stainless steel cart. After they got in and ducked down, a large dessert tray was placed on top of the cart. They were now invisible. "You just rest easy; we'll cover for you," the waitress said.

It was so dark Ty and Jill could barely see each other. Light streamed in where there was a thin gap between the cart and the tray.

"They got it," Ty whispered.

"How do you know?" Jill asked.

"I got a text from Phil; it said 'we got it…..get out of there.' I hope they're not waiting for us."

"Reply to his message," she said. "Let him know we are okay and to get the journal safe."

Ty held his phone up to the thin band of light. He thumbed out a message to Phil. As he finished sending the message there was a commotion in the kitchen. "Where is he?" came from a loud rough voice.

Someone answered, "Who?"

"That guitar player…..He ran back this way where is he?"

Ty's waitress friend stepped up to Adelph. "He ran through that way. He had a girl with him. I think they went out the side door."

In anger, something had gotten thrown. There was steel crashing throughout the kitchen. Then there was silence.

"She's just like Rahab," Ty whispered.

"Thank God," Jill said.

By the time Ty had finished his guitar solo, many had already noticed the journal was missing; including Alden Harlock. The anger he felt when he saw that empty table came from deep within. It ripped through his system like a tsunami; it consumed him. He ran to the table, yelling obscenities and banging his head; he lifted the tablecloth to find Rory's hole underneath. He slammed the table, cursing it.

In light of the situation, and the host's raging fit; many of the guests began heading for the door. Adelph came back from the kitchen. "Some of the kitchen staff say they saw him and a girl run out the side door. And, I just heard that a white delivery van peeled out of the parking lot."

Alden threw a chair, then sat down and closed his eyes. He cupped his hands and planted his face in them. He was still breathing heavy.

Now there was a steady stream of people leaving the Grand Olympian and bailing on Alden's party. It was just too uncomfortable.

Dr. Cranepool walked by the table and stopped to speak with Alden and Adelph, "If I hadn't just seen that with my own eyes, I would not have believed it. A heist, right in front of our very noses," he said.

Adelph responded, "Ahh Dr. Cranepool, I was looking for you earlier. I wanted to ask you about some of your associates from the University that were here tonight."

"Oh?"

"Well actually, one in particular. The guy who was playing guitar; he said he was with you. He knew the password; he was an American."

Dr. Cranepool was upset, "No, no, no, no, no......he most certainly was not with me. I have never seen him before in all my life. And, I have no associates here from the University, and, certainly not an American."

"It's alright Dr. Cranepool. Obviously someone did some homework on this evening's festivities and caught us off guard. Please, try and enjoy what's left of the evening," Alden said.

Dr. Cranepool walked on. Adelph turned to Alden awaiting instructions. "This party's over. But the night isn't."

Ty and Jill were hunched down in the steel dessert cart for twenty minutes. "I can't feel my right leg," Ty said.

Jill said, "This seems so completely crazy and stupid, yet I am sure we've done the right thing. Don't you think we can get out of here now?"

"Well I can't sit like this anymore." Ty popped up and took a look around.

"Whoa, down, down....," came a screaming whisper from their waitress friend. I don't know what you guys did but they're still looking for you. Here put these on and then follow me; I'm leaving." She tossed them both a white jacket, just like the staff was wearing.

Ty and Jill put on the white waiter's jackets and followed her out to the parking lot and into her car. She drove them back to the hotel where they got out. "God Bless you....I can't thank you enough..." Ty said as she drove away.

They went into the lobby where Ty was recognized from his piano sing along from the night before. "Hey, how about a song..." cried someone from the bar.

"Maybe later…" Ty replied. He and Jill were hoping to see Phil in the room. They walked down the hall to the room. They opened the door and there he was.

"We did it!" Phil was yelling before they even got in the room. He was jumping and pumping his fist in the air. He ran to Ty and picked him up in a big bear hug. Ty laughed.

"Man, I have to admit, that was easier than I ever could have imagined," Ty said. "That Rory, what a character, he's really something else."

"Oh, he was great…...and don't worry he's getting paid nicely. But what about you….you just pick up a guitar and start wailing; that was brilliant."

"That was God. There's no reason it should have been there; and with an amp too. That was just a miracle."

"Are you kidding?" Jill asked. "The whole night was a miracle. You just walked in there with absolutely no plan and walked out with the journal."

The three continued celebrating for ten or fifteen minutes; until they realized it was time for the next stage of the quest. They had to get the journal back home.

"I say we just go straight to the airport and get back home right now," Phil said.

"It's after midnight, we missed the last flight out by several hours," Ty replied.

"Well then, first thing in the morning we get to the airport. Hey, let's call Kenneth." Phil said.

He dialed; it rang in Houston, Texas. "Hello," said Kenneth Macklind.

"Kenneth, it's Phil. We got it."

"You got it? You got the journal?"

"Yeah. We'll tell you the story when we get home....Ty was unbelievable."

"Phil, you know I can't wait to hear it, but please.....be careful. This just doesn't seem over yet for some reason."

"We will. We'll be on the first flight out of here in the morning."

"What an awesome day. I have some other good news for you guys. I just got off the phone with Frank; they let him come home today."

"Hey!" Yelled Phil. "Praise God!"

"What, what?" Ty wanted to know what was so exciting.

"Frank came home today."

Ty smiled and tears welled up in his eyes. Then his chin wrinkled and he lost a tear. It rolled down his face. Jill grabbed his arm to comfort him.

"You guys this is all so awesome. You have to surprise Frank tomorrow with the story. He knows something is going on, but I don't think he knows you guys went to London. He will love this. Thank you guys."

"That sounds great Kenneth, we'll call you when we hit the ground tomorrow. Where do you want to keep the journal?"

"Oh, I don't know maybe we should just get a safe deposit box or something."

"Well think about it. We'll talk tomorrow."

Phil put away his phone, "Well He truly is a God of second chances."

"Amen," said Jill. "Okay, you guys look like you have everything under control. I must be going."

Ty walked out with her. Though he was excited about the journal, he was more excited about her.

"Jill...I ...."Ty tried to put words together, with little success.

She turned towards him, "I know. This is difficult. I had hoped to see you again."

"Jill, come with me to the United States. Let me show you around, and spend some more time with you. We're just getting to know each other."

She said nothing. She just looked at him. Her eyes were fixed on his, and suddenly he realized he'd been talking too much. He took her in his arms and kissed her. It was a long, soft, passionate kiss.

"Wow," Ty said.

She just smiled. She was considering his offer of going with him; but, that also seemed a little sudden. She needed some time to think about it.

"Ty, I have many things to consider, I think I should get home tonight and try to get some rest."

They had walked through the lobby and out onto the sidewalk. She waved down a cab and was about to get in when all hell broke loose. It was disorienting. There was glass shattering, people screaming, and the rapid fire 9mm pop of Adelph's Uzi. It turned out several of Alden's out of town party-goers were also staying at the Bristol Quarters. They recognized Ty from his ripping guitar performance and called Adelph right away.

Adelph wasn't in the mood for asking questions. He just wanted them dead. Ty and Jill scrambled, along with a dozen or so bystanders. They ducked back into the hotel with 115 grain chunks of lead whistling through the lobby. It was absolute panic. There was glass everywhere. In the midst of the chaos, Ty and Jill scattered like everyone else. In the confusion Adelph didn't see which way they went.

Adelph walked through the front window, crunching glass under his feet. The lobby was completely vacant. He walked over and pulled up the guest list on the computer behind the front desk, but he didn't know the name of the guys he was looking for. He began to narrow it down, half of the names on the list were either Indian, or Muslim, or Asian. He jotted down the possible room numbers and went to check.

He kicked in doors, he overturned drawers, he dumped out luggage. He had temporarily given up on looking for the people; he was looking for the journal. He came to Phil and Ty's room. He didn't know it was their room, at this point he was kicking in doors quite indiscriminately. The room was empty.

"Ty...... Ty...." Phil was quietly calling for his friend. He had the journal clutched tightly under his arm, but he had no idea what had happened to Ty and Jill. He could only hope and pray for the best.

Phil scampered out ran across the street. He was desperately looking for Ty; but he knew he had to get out of there. A cab stopped right in front of him.

"You waiting for a ride....?" The cabbie yelled.

Phil stalled, "Yeah, just wait a minute, I'm waiting for someone."

He could see Adelph stomping through the lobby of the Bristol Quarters. He was standing right in front of the museum holding the journal, but he didn't want to leave without Ty.

Now it was starting to rain. He didn't want the delicate, old, book to get wet. He could hear Adelph yelling. It was the most surreal moment of his life. He knew he had to go; but he heard a voice say, "wait."

He turned to see who said it; there was nobody there. He didn't feel right about the cab…. "Go ahead, looks like we're not going to make it."

Just as the cab pulled away, another car screeched to a halt. "Get in, hurry!" It was Benton Atwater. Phil jumped in and they sped away for the airport.

"I have to admit you crazy Yanks did it," Benton said. "Now, a mutual friend of ours, Mr. Wellshire, has asked me to give you a ride, so to speak."

"What do you mean?"

"Well when we heard the bullets start to fly at the Bristol Quarters, William knew this was bigger than he had ever imagined. He is busy writing the story of his lifetime, and he asked me to fly you boys home, so that's exactly what we're going to do. We're going to get in a private jet and get you back to America without looking back. William said he will be in touch for a follow up story in a week or so."

"But wait, what about Ty and Jill. I mean I don't even know if they made it out of the lobby."

"There's no time to look back now, mate. Harlock owns the police around here….no use even trying that route. Your best bet is to just get out of here."

They rushed to the airport. Benton took care of the necessary paper work and procedures for an international flight, and was given a flight number and the go ahead. They boarded the plane and prepared for immediate take-off. As Benton sat on the runway, he was about to punch it when air traffic control came on the radio, "Flight 2119.....hold please."

"Copy that control tower....what's the problem?" Benton asked.

"Customs has requested more information about your passenger. Please hold your position.....they're on their way."

Benton knew this wasn't right. It wasn't customs.....somehow Alden had tracked him down. This was bad! Now Benton was on the side of Alden Harlock's opposition; not a comfortable place to be.

"What's wrong?" Phil asked from his seat .

"I don't know, something about customs. We're not going to wait around to find out." The acceleration threw Phil back into his seat. The plane was in the air in seven seconds.

"Flight 2119, you are violating direct federal orders to hold your position. Return to the ground immediately."

Benton didn't answer. He just kept flying. He stayed low until he got out over the ocean. The control tower finally stopped yelling at him. Benton had violated at least a dozen regulations as well as broken several international laws; he knew he wouldn't be flying airplanes in England again. And yet, somehow he was okay with that. He felt an unexplained peace about what he was doing. He thought maybe it was breaking the ties to Alden Harlock.

They flew through the night, Phil slept very little. He talked with Benton to keep him awake. "Will they be waiting for us when we land?" Phil asked.

"Yeah probably, they will know there is a rogue plane coming in. I mean you can't just take off without clearance. Especially leaving the country and going international without clearance from customs. I'm surprised they didn't shoot us down. Unless I can think of something...."

And then it hit him..... He thought of his friend in Reykjavik, Iceland. It was several hours out of the way to the North, but not that bad considering the alternative.

Benton met Jon Pall Bjornsson in 1989. They were both pilots waiting out a layover in a Denmark Tavern. Jon Pall was the first guy in two hours to walk into the place that spoke English. They hit it off and became lifelong friends.

Over the years they had helped each other through various tough spots. Two years ago Jon Pall happened to be in London hiding from his ex-wife.... He took refuge at Benton's place for a week until the air cleared. Benton was sure that Jon Pall still owed him for that.

He made the call and Jon Pall met him at the airport. Jon Pall pulled a few strings, fabricated a tall tale, and managed to get Benton another plane and a new identity. But, there was a slight problem. St. Louis, Missouri is 3256 miles from Reykjavik. The plane that Jon Pall had secured for him was much smaller, and only carried enough fuel for about three thousand miles. The distance was possible only if the winds were just right; and they would literally be landing with nothing but fumes in the gas tank.

Benton made the decision to go for it. They really had no choice. Benton knew he had left Jon Pall in a sticky situation; and that somehow Jon Pall would have to answer for the British aircraft now sitting on his runway. But, he would make it up to Jon Pall later, if he made it out of this mess.

"Why did you get involved in this Benton? Surely William isn't paying you enough to take this kind of a risk." Phil asked as they flew toward Missouri.

"You're right about that. I mean business has been very slow this year, so I can really use the paycheck, but there ain't enough money in the world for this kind of job."

"So why do it?"

"I don't know."

Phil just stared at him, he raised his eyebrows as if to say, 'What do you mean?'

"Aww; it's a very strange story; but okay….don't laugh. Yesterday morning, I was walking down to the bakery to get something to eat and a cup of coffee. And this guy stopped me on the sidewalk…..A big guy. I mean this guy made Adelph look like a little kid. He must have been eight feet tall. Anyway, he stopped me and said, 'Help the Americans.'

"What…… you're kidding."

"I ain't kidding. I looked him right in the eye and said, 'What Americans?' And he said, 'The Americans with the journal. The Lord has called on you to see that they get home safely.'

"What did you say?"

"I thought he was a nut, so I just kept walking. I got about half a block down the sidewalk, and I turned around to look, and he was just standing there watching me. I thought it was kind of creepy, but here's the weird thing. You know it was a pretty dark, and cloudy day yesterday; well when I turned around and looked back at him....." Benton stopped.

"What?" Phil begged. "C'mon, what."

"He was glowing. I mean it wasn't like sunshine or even a light bulb, but there was a definite faint glow to him. I don't know; it's hard to explain."

"Then what happened?"

"I kept walking, sat down in the bakery and had a nice hot cup of coffee. You know, I woke up a little, shook the cobwebs out of my brain and figured it was just last night's gin playing tricks on me."

Phil leaned in to hear more.

"So then when I got to the Grand Olympian last night, I went through the line to get in like everybody else. I went through the little pass-through to chat with Adelph, and he was in there. He was standing off to the side with a great big smile on his face. The thing is....Adelph didn't see him.....or couldn't see him, I don't know. This sounds so crazy."

"Not at all, what did he tell you?"

"He said……. 'You can do this Benton. The power of God has come upon you.' And then he just vanished."

"Did you see him again?"

"No, that was enough. I mean it was like all of a sudden I knew……I mean I just knew, the evil that fills Alden Harlock. I just knew. And I wanted nothing to do with it ever again. I couldn't even look at him. The second I saw Ty on stage with his guitar is when I left. I went and got my car. I didn't know what was going to happen, but I knew it was happening."

Phil was intrigued by the story. He asked, "Benton, do you have a Christian background? This is one of the most awesome supernatural experiences I've ever heard. Do you even know what happened to you last night?"

"I was raised by my Aunt. She drug me to church every Sunday morning and every Wednesday night. I gave my heart to Jesus Christ when I was eleven years old. Since then I guess I've back-slidden a bit……or I guess you could say back-avalanched. But, yeah, I think I was visited by an angel last night. I guess that is pretty awesome."

"Pretty awesome? It's completely awesome. Hallelujah brother. Glad to have you back on the team. Now let's get this journal home."

Rain poured down on London like the whole town needed a shower. Ty was in the back alley behind the Bristol Quarters hotel. He hadn't heard any gun shots for several minutes now. The only thing he could think about was Jill. Somehow in the chaos, he had lost her.

He sat up and checked his ankle. It was throbbing with pain and he could see blood. He pulled back the cuff of his jeans and revealed an inch long piece of glass that was half-way into his ankle. He pulled it out and had to hold some pressure on it for a minute until the blood stopped spurting.

He could hear whimpering. He crawled over to his left, and looked behind the trash dumpster. It was a hotel worker, a porter. She had been shot in the leg, but was so stricken with fear that she couldn't move.

"Ty crawled up close to her and said, "You're going to be okay. We'll get you to the hospital right away." She couldn't speak, just too terrorized.

Then he heard more voices from the next dumpster over. "Hold still, hold still it's going to be okay..." someone said in the darkness.

Ty got up and went to check on them. He limped through an ankle deep puddle, and the cold water brought new pain to his already throbbing laceration. It was dark, and the rain was coming down so hard that it was difficult to see. He could make out several people on the ground, and one standing. He moved closer.

"Hey, about time you got here, I could use some help."

It was Jill. A seasoned registered nurse, and a natural born leader; she had five wounded people resting in the alley, and was administering first aid.

Ty smiled as he watched her. She was doing the best she could with no real medical equipment. "These five are doing fine, nothing too serious here. But, there's a guy over there on the side of the building who didn't make it." It was then the nurse's tough exterior melted away and revealed the scared, tender heart of a young woman who had just had a close call with death. She broke down in the middle of the alley.

Ty hobbled to her and held her. There wasn't much he could have said that would be helpful. He simply said, "Jesus help us."

Jill quickly regained her composure. "He is helping us, and there is no time for standing around sobbing. This guy needs a bandage on that arm….." She pointed to the man sitting on the ground holding his right shoulder and wincing in pain. He too, had been hit by one of Adelph's random shots.

Jill had done an amazing job of assessing the injuries and treating everyone. They all felt better to know they had been seen by a nurse, even if she couldn't do much for the injuries at the moment.

Jill looked at Ty and said, "Do you think he's done shooting?"

"Yeah," Ty said. "I think he's moved on by now. I just hope Phil made it out okay."

The siren and flashing lights arrived just before the ambulances, and several police cars. The police jumped out of the car and came over to see what was going on.

Ty leaned in to Jill, "Let me handle this….remember we don't know who we can trust around here."

"Here……we have injured people over here…." Ty yelled.

The paramedics rushed out with some equipment. Jill announced herself as a nurse and alerted them to the most critical cases first.

Ty was questioned by the police, and he gave his version of the story. Actually it wasn't the entire version; he left out the parts about the journal, and the party. He just told them that a really big guy showed up and opened fire on the place. They took everyone's name and contact information for the report and ensuing investigation.

The ambulances loaded up Adelph's victims, and got them off to the Emergency Room. The police called in detectives to lead the crime scene investigation, and then waited inside the Bristol Quarters. And suddenly, Ty and Jill found themselves alone.

It had finally stopped raining. Ty and Jill hesitantly walked around to the front of the building, carefully watching for any sign of evil.

"Jill, wait right here…..I just want to grab my bag out of the room and then we can get out of here."

"No way. You're not leaving me out here by myself," Jill said.

So they went together. The door was wide open and splintered wood from the frame lay on the floor. It had been kicked in. Ty peaked in the room. It had been searched. Everything was thrown around, the tables had been overturned, the bed's mattresses tossed aside. Ty saw his luggage had been opened and emptied. He didn't even want the stuff. He took Jill by the hand and said, "forget it……let's just get out of here."

Jill's car was still at the Grand Olympian; and there was no way either of them wanted to go back there any time soon, so they took a cab to Jill's apartment. She rented one side of a duplex in west London.

"Wow, this is really a nice place you have here," Ty said as he walked into her apartment.

"Thanks, the old couple who live on the other side own the place. They are friends of the family…..they give me a break on the rent or I probably couldn't afford this neighborhood."

"Well, I like it. It's homey," Ty lounged back on her sofa.

They sat and talked and calmed each other down. They felt safe together in the apartment. Jill attended to Ty's cut ankle. She thought he should probably get a dozen stitches, but neither of them wanted to go spend the night at the hospital. Besides, she got the bleeding to stop and cleaned it up nicely. Ty sat on the sofa with his ankle elevated on some pillows, and Jill sat next to him with his arm around her. They watched some TV, and talked. Jill rested her head on Ty's shoulder and got so comfortable she fell asleep.

At that moment, Ty knew that he never wanted to be without her. He rested his cheek on her head and then he fell asleep also.

<u>Chapter 19</u>

The blue in the sky was deep and liquid against huge patches of gray, and the sun was fading in and out behind the clouds. The white oak and hickory trees had given up most of their leaves now; it was a cool, breezy day in early November in Missouri.

"Hey, this place doesn't look so bad," said Frank Hampton as he walked in the front door of his house upon returning from his hospital stay.

"I stopped by last week and picked up a bit, I thought you'd be home sooner," said Matt, his nephew. But what he really meant was, he didn't want Frank to come home to a bloody crime scene. Matt had taken good care of the place; and of his uncle too.

Frank walked in, his left arm in a sling, and looked in the fridge. You know, I have no desire for this beer, you want it?"

"No, keep it here for visitors if you don't want it."

"You know what I really want. They wouldn't bring me anything but water in that blasted hospital, what I really want is a Dr. Pepper."

"….. And a couple of hamburgers; right?"

"Yeah, now you're talking. Let's fire up the grill; it's a gorgeous day. Why don't you run into town and get some hamburger and some Dr. Pepper. I'll stay here and sit for a while."

Before Matt could get out the door a car pulled up in gravel drive honking the horn like crazy.

"Hey, it's Phil," Matt yelled. Frank practically jumped out of his chair to see what was going on. The car skidded to a stop and Phil and another man got out. Phil reached into the backseat for something. He pulled it out and turned around holding it high in the air over his head.

"Well Shhhhhut my mouth," Frank said in amazement. He recognized the item Phil held up in the air. It was the journal.

Phil ran up onto the front porch where they stood and handed the journal to Frank. "Here you go Frank, weren't you supposed to be keeping this for Kenneth until he gets the museum up and running?"

"How in the world….?" Frank said with astonishment in his eyes.

"I told you I was overdue for a missions trip," Phil said. "Oh, we couldn't have done it without this guy. This is one of my new friends here…….this is Benton Atwater."

Benton shook hands with Frank and Matt. "I've heard so much about both of you."

"Well, it's good to see you home and on your feet. How are you feeling?" asked Phil.

"I'm feeling fine, but didn't you say we? Where's Ty?" asked Frank. Matt was thinking the same thing.

Phil shoulders sagged. "I don't know."

"You don't know?"

"Well, it was a pretty wild scene, we got separated…my old cell phone quit working… Benton has tried calling several times he hasn't answered."

Phil went on to tell the story. He told about how they met William Wellshire, and Benton, and Jill, and Rory. He told them about one miracle after another leading the way. Benton told them about the Angel, and about the way they defected out of the United Kingdom. Phil told them about Ty meeting Jill, and how they hit it off; and he told of how Ty met Jesus Christ. Frank and Matt were both in awe.

He told them about the party in the fancy English hotel and about Ty's guitar solo, and about Rory's quick carpentry work on the floor under the table; and then about Adelph shooting up the Bristol Quarters. Just as he was winding up, Lena walked in. The two ran to each other and hugged. She had already heard much of the story over the phone.

Lena loosened her grip on Phil and looked around at the others, "Where's Ty?" she asked.

Frank answered her, "That's what we'd all like to know."

Everyone in Knob Ridge, Missouri knew each other; and there were very few secrets. The group at the diner included: Frank, Matt, Phil and Lena, and the stranger in town......Benton Atwater. They were trying to enjoy a dinner together and discuss some of the lingering issues; but they were suffering frequent interruptions from nosy neighbors wanting to know who the English fellow was.

They managed to have a conversation. They all wanted to know if Ty was safe; they wanted to know what Kenneth was going to do with the journal, they discussed where to keep it until Kenneth came to reclaim possession; and then Lena brought up a point nobody had thought of yet.....what if Alden Harlock showed up again? That hit everyone differently. Nobody knew what to say.

The next day after a good night's sleep in his own bed, Frank got up, had a cup of coffee, read his Bible for a little while, and then grabbed his fishing pole and headed down to the lake. He thought it would be a good idea to get out of the house for awhile and let Matt sleep late.

The lake was cold and choppy. The clouds were thick and the wind was steady. The fish weren't biting. Frank pulled his hood up and sat down on the dam overlooking the beautiful valley. He prayed as he sat there. He prayed a lot in the hospital, but this was different. He was home now and just having a good long talk with God.

He prayed that Ty would be okay. He prayed for Kenneth to have success with the new museum. But most of all, it was just a prayer of thanksgiving. He thanked God for the wonderful life He had given him, and he thanked Him for another chance. Frank realized how much he had to be thankful for.

He prayed for a good long time. He sat on the dam and watched deer walking in the valley. The wind was blowing so steadily that he didn't even hear Matt walk up behind him.

"You're not going to catch anything that way," Matt said.

Frank smiled, "I'm giving the fish a break."

"You should start thinking about hunting and put away the fishing poles for the winter. Deer season opens next Saturday."

"I know, I'll probably just watch.....I gotta get my cameras going again."

"Well, you might want to think about shooting something for the freezer, Lord knows there's nothing in that place to eat."

Frank laughed, "Hey, I've been away for a while. Give me a break." Frank stood up. "Tell you what.....why don't you run into town and get some hamburger meat, and I'll fire up the grill."

Matt agreed and after a hot shower, he drove into town to the market. Frank lit the grill and then went into the kitchen to begin the preparation for his famous hamburgers. While he was in the kitchen the phone rang.

"Hello," Frank answered.

"Hey Frank, How are you feeling?" said Kenneth Macklind.

"Kenneth, I'm great. We're still praying for Ty though. What's happening?"

"I know Ty is fine. I'm sure we'll hear from him soon. Did you hear? I found a perfect site for a museum. Now I just have to pull together some investors, and I can take the journal off your hands. I'll be glad to see it on display at the new museum."

Frank would be glad to be handing off the journal, but until then he was on guard duty. He returned to the kitchen to get ready for the burgers and he glanced out the window to check on the fire. There was a car in the driveway that he didn't recognize.

Matt's trip to the Knob Ridge Market was successful. He picked up three pounds of extra lean ground chuck, a twelve pack of Dr. Pepper, some chips, buns, pickles, a couple onions and a few other things.

He was starting to enjoy the quiet life of living in small town USA. He waved at people and they waved back. Of course the 1956 Green and white Chevy Nomad wagon was a very recognizable car; people knew him as Frank's nephew.

As he came around the corner, he slowed so he wouldn't miss Frank's driveway. Just before he turned in, he saw the car parked in front of Frank's house. He didn't recognize the black Mercedes, but somehow he knew it meant trouble.

Instead of pulling into the driveway, he passed it and pulled in behind the lake. He drove around the dam to get a clear view of the house. He couldn't see anything; still he knew something was wrong.

He got out and ran down the hill and quietly approached the house. There were a million thoughts racing through his mind; most of them were violent. He tip toes through some knee high grass and got on the air conditioning unit that allowed him to see in the side window.

He was right. There was a big guy with a gun in the dining room just calmly standing there. It was Adelph. He wasn't pointing the gun at anything; he was just holding it down at his side. He was talking with someone else, but Matt couldn't see who it was. He also couldn't see Frank.

But Frank could see him.....or actually not him but his car. Something caught Frank's attention out the window. It was down by the lake; Frank could see the Nomad wagon parked on the dam. Confidence was returning to Frank.....now that he knew he wasn't alone.

Matt sunk down below the window so he wouldn't be seen. What to do.....Matt searched his brain for a plan.

There are times when a crucial decision must be made on the spur of the moment; without time to weigh all of the options and calculate the risks. This was that moment for Matt Hampton. He did not have his cell phone with him…..calling the police was out. This was the guy who shot Frank before; he couldn't let that happen again.

Matt headed for the back door. On the back porch was an old tire iron that Frank used for poking the coals in his barbecue pit. Matt picked it up and stood at the back door. He could still see Adelph. He tried the door knob, it was open. Matt slowly turned the knob, and lifted up on the door as he pulled it ajar. Adelph was beginning to wander; he now stood in the kitchen only ten feet from the back door.

Matt flung open the door and charged him. Adelph spun around and fired the gun. The shot whizzed harmlessly past Matt's left ear and out the kitchen window. With everything he had, Matt struck Adelph on the wrist with the tire iron. He dropped the gun and fell to his knees in pain. Adelph's radius was badly broken, but it wasn't enough to stop him.

Matt went for the throat. He wrapped his arm around his neck and flexed his bicep cutting off Adelph's air supply. As he tightened his grip he continually slammed Adelph's head into the wall. Adelph started to stand up. Matt banged his head into the wall a few more times and Adelph fell to one knee.

This left Frank and Alden alone together in the living room…..and Alden didn't have a gun. Frank's leather-neck, United States Marine Corps training was no match for Alden Harlock. He simply walked over to Alden and punched him right in the nose. Alden fell backwards into the couch and didn't get up. Frank went to check on the action in the kitchen.

Matt had Adelph's bloody head wrapped up tight. Adelph's arms went limp. Matt dropped his hold and let Adelph fall to the floor.

"That's the S.O.B. that shot me….. man he's a big one. You okay?" Frank said to Matt.

Matt was out of breath but otherwise not harmed. "Yeah, I'm, okay…..how about you?"

"Yeah I hit Mr. pony-tail; he's out on the couch."

Frank reached for the phone to call 911. Matt bent over and picked up Adelph's 9mm. "Don't touch that," Frank yelled. "That's evidence."

"Too late," said Matt as he noticed movement out of the corner of his eye. Adelph had rolled over and pulled another gun from his pants. He had it pointed at Frank when the shot was fired.

The bullet struck Adelph square in the chest. He collapsed back to the floor, this time for good.

Matt and Frank looked at each other as if to make sure there was only one shot fired; there was.

Frank was still holding the phone and again he was about to dial 911 when he looked in the living room. Frank dropped the phone, "He's gone." Frank yelled, as he ran into the living room.

The couch where Alden got punched out was now empty. Frank looked out the door; there was no sign of him.

"What happened?" Matt asked.

"I punched him in the face and he fell out on the couch. I thought he was out cold, I guess he came to."

"Either that or he was faking."

The Mercedes was still there; and it dawned on Frank that he probably didn't have the keys. "Keep an eye on the front," Frank said as he went back into the kitchen. He checked Adelph's pockets and found the keys to the Mercedes. "Look here," Frank said as he came back into the living room jangling the keys. "Big Bird had the keys. Pony-tail man is out there on foot."

Chapter 20

Alden Harlock wasn't cut out for this kind of stuff. He was alone, running through the woods, in Central Missouri, in November. It was cold, windy, and starting to rain. For the first time ever, things were going wrong for him…..terribly wrong.

He searched every pocket twice, but couldn't find his cell phone. Adelph had the keys to the car, and the guns. All Alden had was cold, wet feet; a headache; and a very sore left cheekbone, where Frank's fist had connected.

He had never been in this situation before, and he didn't know what to do. He never expected these people to fight back. He was pretty sure that Adelph was dead. That's when he made the split second decision to run. He didn't want to be left alone with them. He had always relied on Adelph to handle the rough stuff.

Alden had several hundred dollars in his wallet; he was hoping that would get him back to civilization, where he could make the arrangements to get out of this mess.

He was afraid to stay on the road. He thought the folks with the journal would be looking for him. He found a dry creek bed that ran parallel to the road and he followed it; cursing as he went. He had never felt so alone.

Alden stumbled along the creek for several miles. His black, Armani pants were wet up to the knees and fraying around the cuff. In addition to the bruised cheekbone, he now had a gash on his eyebrow from a tree branch that he didn't see coming. He needed a heavier coat, his thin blazer was soaked through and providing very little protection from the elements.   And now, it was beginning to get dark.

In his desperation, he let himself agree with a weak plot. He had yet to cross paths with another human being; but he had decided he would simply offer the first person he came across money to drive him to the nearest town with a rental car. It wasn't a plan he was proud of, but it would have to do.

He wasn't sure if it was the cold, or the fear, but he was certain that he had never been so lost.

<u>Chapter 21</u>

When police sirens howl in Knob Ridge, Missouri, the chain of phone calls that immediately emanate is staggering. Within minutes of the police swarming at Frank's place, Phil Balasky got a call. It was one of the ladies from church, telling him about the sirens and flashing lights all over Frank Hampton's property. Phil felt as if he had just taken a blow to the chest. He knew what had happened.

"What is it?" His wife Lena asked, she could tell it was bad news.

"It's Frank!" he shouted as he grabbed his denim jacket.

"Wait, I'll come with you," she said.

They hurried over there as fast as they could. They couldn't turn into the driveway, because of the "police line-do not cross" tape. There were three State patrol cars, two County Sherriff cars, and both of the local Knob Ridge police.

The local officer recognized Phil and Lena sitting in their car waiting at the end of the driveway. He walked over to them, "Hey Phil…..can't let you in here right now," he said. "There's a big investigation getting started here."

"Wait," Phil shouted as the policeman turned to walk back to the action. "Is Frank alright?"

He walked back to the car and bent down to speak into Phil's window. "Yeah Pastor….. Frank's okay; and his nephew is okay too. There's been a shooting though…..big guy got killed. Evidently there's another guy that took off running on foot. We're about to start a search mission."

Phil took Lena's hand as the police officer walked away. "Thank God, they're okay. This is almost over."

"What do you mean? She asked.

"I can just tell….this is almost over," he said. "I know that God has been directing this whole ordeal every step of the way. A lot of good is going to come out of all this."

He drove home.

"What should we do?" Lena asked.

Phil answered, "Pray."

They went inside, sat down, joined hands, and agreed in prayer. "Heavenly Father," Phil said. "We come together in the name of Jesus Christ. Thank you that You protected Frank and Matt. Please let us hear the same report from Ty soon. Lord, we are so thankful for this opportunity to work for You. I feel that there is still more that I can do. Direct us; lead us Lord into this moment….."

Before Phil could finish the prayer, something caught his eye. It was a dark figure at the corner of the field in Phil's back yard. Through the kitchen window, Phil and Lena watched a man stumbling along woods edge.

"Oh my God…." Phil said. He went for the binoculars in the kitchen junk drawer. He could see a man dressed in black, walking with his arms folded…..obviously wet and cold. "Lena, that's him."

Phil grabbed an old wool sweater and charged out the back door. Lena just watched, and covered him with prayer.

Phil walked slowly and calmly towards him. The man in black stopped as Phil approached. Still twenty yards away; Phil said, "Hi there…..I can see you are lost and cold; I brought you a sweater."

Alden stood still; he wasn't sure what to make of this yet. His shivers did the thinking for him, "Yes, thank you," he said as he walked up to Phil and accepted the sweater.

"So what happened?" Phil said; still not letting on that he knew who he was.

"Well, suffice it to say…..I ran into a little trouble and now I find myself without a car and just trying to get to the nearest airport. Can you help me?"

"Nearest airport, hmmm," Phil said. "Nearest major airport is in St. Louis; that's a two hour drive."

"I can pay you for your trouble; I just really want to get out of here…"

Phil led them to the side of his garage where they had held bon-fires for church outings. There was an old fire pit and some wood covered with a tarp. He made a careful pile and then doused it with lighter fluid. "Some people think it's cheating to start a fire with lighter fluid," Phil said. "I say it's just resourceful."

"Oh that feels good," said Alden. The moment the warmth of the fire reached him he felt grateful. "Thank you so much."

"For what…"

"The sweater….the fire."

Phil pulled a couple of lawn chairs over to the fire. They sat and warned themselves. The rain had stopped and for Alden the slow process of drying was just beginning.

"You're welcome," Phil said, sitting in a lawn chair next to him. "I wish I could invite you in the house Alden, but I just can't do that."

Alden closed his eyes but didn't say anything. He was calmly contemplating his next move. He took a deep breath and without opening his eyes, he said, "News travels fast in small towns, huh."

"Yeah, it does," Phil said. He turned toward Alden, "Hi, we haven't actually met…..I'm Phil Balasky."

"Should I know you?" Alden asked.

"Yeah, I guess you should. I'm a friend of Kenneth Macklind. You came into my church just before you shot Frank and stole the journal. Myself and another friend have been half way around the world trying to track it down and stop you from destroying it….and; I might add, that was a successful mission."

"I'll get it back," Alden declared. "I always get what I want."

Phil just shrugged his shoulders as if to say "Whatever."

Alden got a puzzled look on his face and said, "Why are you being so nice to me?"

Phil responded, "Matthew 5:44."

"What?"

"It says… 'But I say unto you, love your enemies, bless them that curse you, do good to them that hate you, and pray for them which despitefully use you, and persecute you….' Those are the words of Jesus Christ," Phil explained. He stretched out his hand over Alden, "Alden Harlock; I release you to the knowledge of Jesus Christ as Lord and Savior. I bless you in the name of Jesus Christ the Righteous to fulfill His desire for your life. And in Jesus' name I break every curse and stronghold binding you to darkness. I bless you to walk in the light, in Jesus' name…..Amen."

That very moment, Alden felt a change in his heart. He felt warmth, and it wasn't from the fire. He felt relief from a heaviness that he had carried as long as he could remember. He wasn't sure what had just happened, but there was no denying it…...it happened.

Phil saw it happen. He saw the light bulb come on as the curse was broken. In a moment, forty years of hate-clouded mystery was turned to something else…..something lovely.

To the physical eye, it was just two men sitting in lawn chairs around a camp-fire. But, the spiritual scene was much different. It was a fierce battle, mighty angels on each side clashing in a colossal confrontation. It was the power of Phil's blessing that swayed the battle. The dark side was wiped out; with a word they were annihilated.

Without the presence of evil in the immediate vicinity, Alden was able to feel the difference. There was a palpable change in the air. Alden Harlock was feeling the presence of God.

Phil drew on the many years of experience he had in ministering to lost people, his God given wisdom, and the Holy Spirit, to say just the right things. He threw another log on the fire and they talked.

Lena too, was following God's direction and helping in any way that she could. She had been watching from the kitchen window for half an hour and she could tell something had happened. When she saw Phil throw another log on, she figured they would be there a while and brought out some hot tea.

"I thought you would enjoy something hot to drink out here. Everything okay?" she asked.

Phil looked at her with a caring smile and shook his head yes; but it was Alden who spoke up, "Yes, thank you Mrs. Balasky. I do believe everything is okay," he said.

She smiled and turned back towards the house, "Let me know if you need anything else…."

"Thanks honey," Phil said.

Lena hurried back into the house because she could hear the phone ringing. "Hello."

"Hi Lena, is Phil there?" said Frank Hampton.

"Oh yeah he's here alright Frank….he's outside drinking hot tea around a campfire."

"Campfire? Didn't you guys hear what happened over here?"

"Yes Frank, we heard. Are you and Matt alright?"

"Yeah, we're alright. They finally finished up with all the questioning and evidence gathering. I think we are in the clear. It was a clear case of self-defense."

"I'm just glad you two are okay."

"I didn't know Phil was a big campfire guy…..what's he doing out there."

"Oh, he's not alone Frank. Guess who he's sitting with having tea around the fire."

"You're kidding!"

"Maybe you better come and see for yourself."

"We'll be right there."

Frank slammed the phone down and quick-stepped to the closet for his jacket. Matt was just coming in from the back room. He stood there for a moment to try and figure out what was going on.

"Frank, settle down…..what's wrong?"

"I'm okay Matt. You're not going to believe this. I think I know where the pony-tail man turned up…..He's over at Phil's."

"What….are Phil and Lena alright?"

"Yeah, they're alright. They're sitting around a bon fire chewing the fat," Frank said as he threw on his denim jacket.

"Hang on, I gotta see this, I'm coming with you."

CHAPTER 22

Thirty-six thousand feet above the Atlantic Ocean, Ty Hyvek watched the sunshine bouncing off the clouds. He noticed colors that could never be painted. He realized that he was floating through the ultimate masterpiece.

It is a long flight overseas from London back to the States. There was plenty of time to think. He thought about London, and that he was actually going to miss it. He thought about William Wellshire and Rory, and the parts they played in the most incredible week of his life. He thought about Phil and hoped that he made it home okay; and he thought about Frank.

He prayed for Frank. He wasn't worried though; somehow, he knew Frank was okay. He thought about Matt and how everyone at Gildersleeves; and how most of them were just as lost as he was; or used to be.

The flight attendant came by offering drinks. "Anything to drink sir?" She whispered as not to wake the woman in the seat next to him. But it was too late, she woke up. Jill had been sleeping for an hour or so with her head on Ty's shoulder. "I'll have a coke," Jill said sleepily.

Jill turned and looked at Ty with a smile and a twinkle in her eye. "I can't wait to see your place, St. Louis I mean. What's it like?"

He meant to answer her question, but when he looked into her eyes he saw a little glimpse of forever. For a moment, he was speechless. Ty Hyvek was in love, and he wasn't scared.

One year later:

White and silver balloons filled the high, coffered ceiling of the main lobby. White rose petals marked the path to the beautifully ornate rose covered archway where the main event would soon take place. The string quartet saturated the space with music. The North American Museum of World History was nearly complete.

The guests were seated, and waiting. In the front row in his best brown suit was Frank Hampton. He sat next to Lena Balasky. Just behind them were the Macklinds...all eight of them; Kenneth, Barbara, and their six well behaved, home-schooled children. Behind them, filling several rows was most of the crew from Gildersleeves, and a sampling of friends and family. Also in attendance was Benton Atwater, who had chosen to sit on the groom's side due to the fact that he now considered himself an 'American'. This far away from the Downy Duck, Benton was forced to go stag.

Across the aisle sat the friends and family of the bride, who all happened to be from England. William Wellshire was there with a date, alongside Rory, his wife, his daughter, and son-in-law...whom he still hadn't warmed up to. The Wright family and friends filled the first five rows of chairs. All of the British guests had been flown in three days earlier, to allow time to adjust to the time difference. The airfare, hotel, rental cars...everything, had been paid for so that nobody would be unable to attend the big event. The tickets were included with the invitations.

The minister stood at the marble pulpit, anticipating the moment. As the clock struck two, he stepped up to the microphone and addressed the guests.

"Good afternoon everyone," said Phil Balasky. "Please rise."

They all rose to their feet. The quartet began a light, wonderful piece, and Matt Hampton stepped out from the right hand side of the archway. Right behind him was Ty Hyvek…the groom. They took their places near the podium and looked down the aisle of rose petals.

The quartet transitioned into a sweet and airy arrangement of the Bridal Chorus, and everyone turned to watch the moment they had all been waiting for. Holding her father's arm, Jill walked down the aisle in a gorgeous, flowing, long white gown. At the end of the aisle, her father met Phil and joined her with Ty.

Frank swallowed hard, and tried to fight back the tear, but it had already escaped. With a smile on his face and a tear streaming down his cheek, he watched the son he'd never had on the biggest day of his life.

Phil joined the couple in holy matrimony. In the presence of their closest friends and family, and in the name of Jesus Christ, he proclaimed the two had become one. Matt held in his hand two rings, Phil took them and passed hers to Ty, and his to Jill. Then they placed rings on each other's fingers and kissed. It was official.

Immediately following the service was the reception. A beautiful banquet had been prepared. Everyone ate, drank and shared a wonderful afternoon. After dinner, the Macklinds got a chance to mingle, they found Frank and Phil and Lena.

"I don't think I've ever seen a more beautiful wedding," Lena said.

"I know, ours was close, but I have to admit this was amazing," Barbara responded.

As the women continued their conversation, the men drifted off into their own.

"How ya doing Frank?" Kenneth asked.

"I'm doing great, now that I'm here. It took me a while to get on board with this…you know under the circumstances. The whole idea was a little weird," said Frank.

"I know what you mean. When Barbara and I first got the invitation, our first thought was 'no way', but after talking to Phil, there was no way we would have missed it."

Phil smiled, "We all played a part in this; isn't it awesome to be in the right place at the right time? And just wait until after the ceremony at the unveiling…"

"Ladies and Gentlemen," the Maître d' drew everyone's attention for an announcement. "The best man wishes to say a few words." He bowed and motioned for Matt to take the microphone.

"It is wonderful to see a couple so much in love and so perfect for each other," Matt said. "Me, I'm single by choice. Not my choice…that's been the choice of all the women I've dated." He paused for a hearty round of laughter. "But I can honestly say, when Ty pulled me aside one night several months ago, and told me he was going to ask Jill to marry him….. I had mixed emotions. First of all, I was nervous and a little embarrassed for Ty, because I thought it was only a fifty-fifty shot that she would say yes….." again he paused for laughter. "But most of all, I was truly happy for both of them. I know they will be truly happy together. May the Lord continually pour the richest of blessings on your life." Matt lifted his glass, "To lifelong friends and then some…."

The cheer was overwhelming. Love and laughter filled the museum. Matt walked over and shook Ty's hand; Jill jumped up and gave him a big hug. When Jill was done, Frank's arm flung around Matt's neck, "Very well said Matt," Frank said.

They danced and laughed for another two hours. Kenneth temporarily lost his seven year old son; he was found safe and sound sneaking a peak at the dinosaur fossils. The wedding was so lovely they had almost forgotten they were in a museum. And then the music stopped. The Maître d' announced another speaker. Everyone turned to see.

"Good afternoon," said Kenneth Macklind. "This museum is the result of a very long string of miracles. There is no other way to describe it." Kenneth turned to clear his throat. "First of all, thank you all for coming. Officially, the grand opening will be tomorrow, but I thank God for a wonderful and memorable beginning to this place. Ty and Jill, it is my pleasure, and a sincere honor to call you both friends. Thank you for agreeing to share your special day here with us," Kenneth looked out at his wife Barbara, who was smiling widely.

"This museum is unique. As you all know, we have decided to call it 'The North American Museum of World History'. It will be dedicated to true history; that is what makes it unique. Here, we will display exhibits that depict the history of the world as it really happened; as is told in the Bible. The V-shaped building consists of two wings. They will be named after two of my heroes. They were two strong men of God, without whom it would not have been possible. To the East, the Ian Burbrey wing will be dedicated to archeological artifacts that support the accuracy of the Bible." Kenneth paused for a heartfelt applause. "And, to the West, the Peter Stroudlin wing will be dedicated to exhibits that clearly and unequivocally support a biblical creation." The applause erupted even louder.

The thought of Peter brought a tear to Jill's eye. Ty held her tightly.

Kenneth continued, "And right in the center; the focal point of the museum. Now, as you all know, a year ago there was quite a stir over a journal that was kept by a knight who had quite a story to tell. This journal's historical significance is beyond precious, and worthy of this central display. The work to create a fitting display has taken more than seven months and the grand opening of the display for the entire world to see will be tomorrow.

Frank Hampton smiled, "I can't wait to see that…"

"But now for this very special audience," said Kenneth. "I am delighted to give you the first showing of the exhibit." Kenneth motioned for assistants on each side to pull the curtain to the side, unveiling the exhibit. "There it is everyone; the quest for this book has changed many lives. I give you the journal of Sir Richard the Elder of Landolte."

They were amazed at the exhibit. The journal was on a wooden book case under a glass dome. A beam of white light beamed down from above. A huge painting of Sir Richard the elder of Landolte stood behind the journal; and a ten foot tall panel to the right of it held the words that told Sir Richard's story. Each page of the journal was boldly on display. Kenneth had his photographs enlarged onto four foot panels which stood at the left side of the exhibit.

While the journal was the central focus of the exhibit, it was not alone. It was surrounded by fantastically realistic recreations of dinosaurs. There were knights on horseback jousting the fierce Allosaurus. Also, there was archeological evidence displaying the relative 'young' age of dinosaurs. To the right of the journal, was a Tyrannosaurus bone that contained perfectly preserved soft tissue, including red blood cells. To the left was a display explaining the presence of Carbon $_{14}$ in dinosaur fossils, and how even the slightest trace of Carbon $_{14}$ would be gone in only several hundred thousand years. Yet every dinosaur fossil has measurable amounts of the substance, indicating a much younger fossil than the popular theory.

Sir Richard's journal exhibit was breathtaking.

Kenneth continued, "Each and every one of you here today has had a part in this. And the story just keeps getting better and better. Truly, we serve a God who overflows our cups with blessings." There was more applause and a half a dozen Amens.

"Yes, there is more to the story; and here to tell us about it… Pastor Phil Balasky."

Phil stepped up to the podium and pulled an envelope from his lapel pocket. "Thank you. As Kenneth said, this story just keeps getting better. I think what I have to tell you will come as a very pleasant surprise." Phil paused to make sure he had everyone's attention.

"Many of you have been asking about the production of this wonderful ceremony; the costs of flying in overseas guests; and the secretive nature of these provisions." Phil continued, "I apologize for the mystery, the donor asked that his name be withheld until the day of the wedding and he also asked me to read this letter." Phil held up the envelope for all to see.

"Ladies and gentlemen," Phil was now proceeding with the announcement. "This wonderful ceremony, including luxury provisions for each guest; and the entire wedding ceremony have been provided by Mr. Alden Harlock." The gasps were audible. Their reactions varied from surprise to shock.

"And that's not all…Kenneth, would you come back up here for one moment please," Phil paused to allow Kenneth time to approach the podium. "Before I read Mr. Harlock's letter, I want Kenneth to say a few words about the museum."

"Thank you Phil," Kenneth said. "As I told you before, this museum is the result of a very long chain of miracles.

What I haven't told you….actually we haven't told anyone yet… is that Alden Harlock played a very important role in one of those miracles. Ten months ago, Phil was contacted by Mr. Harlock and the three of us sat down and had a very important meeting."

Kenneth continued, "At the end of that meeting, he made it clear that he wanted to help us make this museum a reality. One week later, I got a call from Mr. Harlock that almost knocked me over. Alden Harlock donated thirty-three million dollars to our museum project. It was his funding that allowed this to happen….Phil."

With that Phil stepped back up to the microphone, "Now, we all know who Alden Harlock is…let's hear what he has to say." Phil opened the envelope that contained the letter, and began reading.

Alden Harlock writes: 'First of all congratulations to Ty and Jill on their wedding day; and also to Kenneth Macklind and Phil Balasky for enduring to the point of opening the museum. Thank you all for coming. I wanted my involvement to remain undisclosed until now for fear that some of you would not attend. I hope everyone has had a wonderful time.

I would like to begin by explaining myself. Without going into the gruesome details, I know that you know who I am; and what I've done. Thank you for this opportunity to be heard and to apologize.'

Eyes were peeled, and mouths were wide open. They couldn't believe what they were witnessing.

Phil kept reading, 'I am sorry. I am heartily sorry; for everything I have done to each and every one of you. I know that in some way I have negatively impacted each of your lives. I am writing this letter from my cell in Wandsworth Prison near London, England. I do not know if I will ever be free of these walls, but there is one thing I do know... it does not matter. I have never been so free. Thank you for allowing me to make restitution, in some small way, by contributing to both the museum efforts and to this happy occasion.'

The crowd was dead silent. 'And now I want you to know how it happened. When I was down; when you had a chance to kick me; you blessed me. You showed me kindness; you gave; and you showed me the light. I was cold...you gave me a sweater and a warm fire. I was hungry...you gave me food. I was thirsty...you gave me a drink. I was looking at you, but I saw Jesus Christ. First in Pastor Phil, and then in each of you...thank you.'

The letter continued, 'I gave most of my life to the darkness, I know now that I was under many curses; it was Phil's blessing that broke them. I want you all to know, that I have truly repented and given my life to Jesus Christ."

Now applause erupted, along with a few woo-hoos. Smiles were creeping onto their faces. People were looking at each other in approval.

'I know that I am forgiven by God's grace; I truly wish to be forgiven by each of you. Even if I never leave my current location to say it in person, I want each of you to know how sorry I am – and that in a very short time I will see each of you in Heaven. I was very lost, and now I am indeed saved. And yet, it wasn't me, it was as if I'd been given a break from myself. I remember one moment in particular; that night in Phil's back yard sitting by the fire. I remember looking down on myself. I was high in the air; higher that the trees and I was looking down. I could see Phil and myself sitting there by the fire; only Phil was lit up…almost glowing and I was shrouded with darkness. At that moment I began to know the difference between true and false.' In the letter, Alden explained what he went through on that fateful night.

Frank listened intently; he remembered that night as if it were yesterday. There were so many times he sat and wondered what had happened.

The letter continued, 'I know it sounds crazy, but I truly believe that I had an out-of-body experience that night. The Lord allowed me to see myself as I was…spiritually. It scared me. I knew I needed him, and somehow I knew I had him….it was just that fast. I repented on the spot; well, from my vantage point thirty feet in the air that is. And when I came back into my body… I was different. I could feel it; and I've never looked back, not once. The academic circle of friends with whom I was formerly engaged, think I have lost my mind. Some news has apparently already leaked out. I received my first death threat months ago.'

Somehow Frank was amused by that, he smiled.

Alden's letter continued, 'But, many will love it; and most importantly, many will be brought closer to the knowledge of Jesus Christ though it. It is the least that I can do; and I am forever grateful to each and every one of you for the part you played in this journey toward my salvation.'

Everyone seemed to believe Alden's sincerity. After all, the museum was boldly displaying a major exhibit on biblical creation. That is, everyone except William Wellshire.

"Hey Phil, I've seen enough; take care," William said as he headed for the entrance.

"Wait… William, what do you mean? What's the matter?" Phil chased.

"I've studied this guy and guys like him for long enough to know better. I don't know his angle yet, but he's got one…and it's crooked."

"People can change William," Phil said. But William didn't look back. He just kept walking.

Alden Harlock had changed. It turned out that the very thing he needed was the exact opposite of what he had spent his entire life pursuing. He needed Jesus.

"Wow, a happy ending," Matt said to Ty. "I don't think I've ever actually seen one."

Ty turned to Matt with his arm around his new wife and looked him square in the eye with a wide grin, "This is just the beginning Matt, just the beginning."

Frank walked over to the group and tapped Ty on the shoulder. He turned around and saw Frank holding a guitar.

"We just happened to have a guitar…I think you know what to do with it. I mean…son, it's such a special day…would you sing us a song?" Frank asked.

Rory said with a smile, "Oh yeah, you're the guitar player…"

Everyone laughed.

Ty sat down. "A year ago, I was asked to play this song, but I couldn't. I mean this song… you have to feel it, you have to live it. My life has changed so much in a year. I have been given pleasure I don't deserve." Ty strummed a chord to check the tuning. "I love you guys, but I dedicate this one to my wife…"

With a tear in his eye and a lump in his throat he sang '*Amazing Grace*'. It was a beautiful rendition and everyone joined in. Tears of happiness streamed down every cheek in the room. Frank Hampton thanked God for this day. He even thanked God for Alden Harlock.

The end

The Dragon Journal

Mike Rimmey

ABOUT THE AUTHOR

Mike Rimmey is an author/singer/songwriter from St. Louis, Missouri. In 2006 Mike was nominated for "New Artist of the Year" at the Inspirational Country Music Awards in Nashville, TN. He has had four #1 singles, two songwriting awards, major market radio airplay, and performances at the Grand Ole Opry and the Whitehouse. This national attention quickly garnered Mike "Male Vocalist" nomination at the 2008 ICM Awards and several national television appearances.

In addition to Mike's musical accomplishments, he is also a dynamic speaker on the topic of Creation Science. With a B.S. degree in Biology, and as a former evolutionist; Mike loves to share with secular and church audiences alike, the many historic and scientific evidences of the miracle of creation.

Mike Rimmey has appeared on the following major Christian Television Networks:

TBN
NRB
TLN
Daystar
Cornerstone
Worship Network
Gospel Music Television
TCT

Watch Mike Rimmey on youtube

www.sonicbids.com/mikerimmey
www.mikerimmey.com